FLAMES OF LOVE

A FRIENDS-WITH-BENEFITS FIREMAN ROMANCE

FIREFIGHTERS OF LONG VALLEY ROMANCE
BOOK ONE

ERIN WRIGHT

Thanks, Charles the Firefighter, for putting up with my endless newbie questions. You rock.

*Oh, and **thank you** for serving your fellow Idahoans. This world is better because of people like you.*

CHAPTER 1

JAXSON

JANUARY, 2018

J AXSON ANDERSON PUSHED the plate-glass door open, the overhead bell tinkling, announcing his entrance. The warmth, the yeast and sugar smell…it rushed over him, surrounding him, and he almost stopped dead in his tracks, wanting to do nothing but breathe it all in. He hadn't been in an honest-to-God bakery in ages, and had forgotten how damn delicious they smelled.

Before he could make a real ass out of himself by literally drooling just from the smell alone, though, a head popped up from behind the front counter. A cute brunette, her hair in a braid flopped over her shoulder, shot him a smile. "Welcome to the Muffin Man," she called out, pushing some stray tendrils out of her face with the back of her hand. "You been in here before?"

He'd hardly been in the town of Sawyer more than a couple of hours. "Nope, first time here," he said as he walked closer to the front display case, and the adorable brunette behind it. She looked a little younger than him, with wide, innocent eyes that made her appear even younger as she peered up at him.

She was this tiny little thing that he was sure he could tuck under his arm and run with down the football field. Between her tiny stature and her wide eyes, she gave off the impression that she was twelve.

Except…he gulped. Those curves. No 12-year-old girl had *those* curves.

"Well then, an extra welcome!" she said, sending him another dizzying smile. "I'm glad you stopped by. Are you a… tourist?" She looked a little puzzled at that idea, giving him a quick up-and-down glance.

No, he probably didn't look a damn thing like a tourist. Most fire chiefs didn't.

"Just new in town," he told her. "What is good he–*Sugar*?!" he said. He was staring straight at her delectable chest.

Which was probably not his best move. He knew he was being rude, but hey, *she* was the one who'd pinned her name tag on it. "Your name is *Sugar*?!"

She rolled her eyes at him, which now that he was close enough, he could see they were a deep brown color. Like the color of the chocolate cake sitting in the display case between them. "Don't bother making a joke," she told him pertly. "I've heard every one of them that is funny, and a whole lot that aren't. I promise you, you won't be original."

He leaned on the clear glass goodies counter, content for a moment to ignore the copious amounts of sugar underneath his arms, and instead focus on the Sugar in front of him. "So… basically, your parents hated you."

"Pretty much!" she said cheerfully, shooting him a laughing grin. Right then, a guy came through the swinging doors from the back, and Jaxson nodded towards him.

"Is his name Flour?" he asked dryly.

"No, but I like how you think!" Sugar looked over at her co-worker and laughed. "Gage, he thinks you ought to change your name to Flour!"

Gage looked up from off-loading a batch of muffins into a

side display case. "Hey, my parents didn't hate *me*," he drawled in a deep voice, proving that he'd overheard their discussion. "Don't drag me into this."

"I think I'm gonna start calling you Muffin," Sugar mused, shooting her co-worker a grin. "Or maybe Baby Cakes."

Gage rolled his eyes. "That's just what this town needs to hear," he grumbled and disappeared into the back, carrying his empty tray with him.

"Woke up on the wrong side of the bed," Sugar said in way of explanation, complete with a shrug, as she turned back to Jaxson. "So, what can I get for you? Coffee? Donuts? A… *muffin*, perhaps?" Her voice was a little *too* innocent.

Jaxson's eyes shot up to hers. Was she teasing?

Her eyes were glinting with mischief. She was.

"I was thinking that I might be in the mood for some baby cakes," he said, his tone as innocent as hers. She burst out laughing.

"I think I like you," she said, shooting him a wide grin after she caught her breath.

"You'd like me even more if I had some coffee and a donut in me," he informed her. "I'm a lot more fun to be around when I'm awake."

"Even *more* fun?" she echoed, wrinkling her nose as she turned to grab a to-go cup. "Damn. I'm not sure if I can handle that much fun. Maybe I shouldn't get your coffee after all."

"Never come between a man and his coffee," he intoned, only three-quarters joking.

More like half, really.

"Fair enough," she said, filling the cup from the dispenser. Tendrils of steam encircled her hand and then melted away. "So what brings you to Sawyer, if you're not a tourist?"

She turned back around, deftly grabbing a lid and pushing it into place even as she was sliding the cup across the counter to him.

Yeah, she had some experience serving up coffee. He

wondered for a moment how long she'd worked at the Muffin Man.

"I'm the new fire chief in town," he said, pulling the already warm cup towards him to sip at the life-giving liquid inside. He was staring down at the display case as he said it, contemplating which donut was the most deserving of being eaten, but even out of the corner of his eye, he could tell she'd stiffened up. His eyes shot up and caught her look. She was staring at him, mouth open. "What's wrong?" he asked, confused. He looked behind him, thinking maybe someone had snuck up behind him who she didn't care for, but no one was there.

He looked back at Sugar and she was smiling again, although it didn't appear nearly as natural as it had before.

"Nothing," she said. She cleared her throat. "What kind of donut did you want?"

"Maple bar, please."

She nodded, slipping the long, golden donut into a brown paper bag.

"Hold on," he said, another sip of coffee helping his brain begin to actually do something useful, "why don't you make that a dozen donuts? I'm meeting with the guys down at the station for the first time this morning – holding a little get-together, you know? I should probably bring donuts with me. Help break the ice."

She mumbled something under her breath that sounded suspiciously like, "You're gonna need more than donuts," but when he shot her a questioning look, she just smiled back innocently.

"Do you care which kind?" she asked.

"Variety," he said, shrugging.

She got to work, sliding some bear claws, a cake donut, some more maple bars, and a couple of sugar donuts into a cardboard box stamped "Muffin Man" on top. She rang him up quickly and after he slid his card into the machine, entering his PIN, she pushed the box across the counter to him.

"Good luck today," she said, sending him an overly brilliant smile. She followed it up by mumbling something else under her breath, and this time, he only caught the word "need."

"What?" he asked, irritated.

"Nothing! Enjoy your donuts, sir."

"Jaxson."

"What?"

"I figured I knew your name; you should know mine. Jaxson. Plus, I'm too damn young to be called sir."

"Enjoy your donuts...Jaxson."

He slid the box onto his arm and, balancing his coffee cup in his other hand, made his way back towards the door. If every damn person in Sawyer was gonna take up mumbling underneath their breath while they were talking to him, he was gonna be stark-raving mad within the week.

CHAPTER 2

SUGAR

"DID I HEAR HIM RIGHT?" Gage asked as soon as the front door closed behind the newest resident of Long Valley. Sugar stared after him, the sight of his ass in his tight Wranglers not something she was gonna be able to forget for a long time.

Maybe never.

"Hear what?" she asked absentmindedly. She hadn't seen a man that hot since—

"Is he the new fire chief in town?" Gage asked, a note of impatience creeping in.

She jerked her head back towards her boss. "Oh. Sorry. Yeah, he's the new guy." She wrinkled her nose.

Gage walked up and stood next to her at the front counter, staring out into the early morning, sparkling frost covering every barren tree branch and frozen metal bench in sight. "Do you think he has any idea what he's in for?" Gage asked rhetorically, wiping his hands on his apron.

Sugar answered him anyway. "No clue," she said with a shrug, and then nibbled on her lower lip. "Well, he probably wouldn't have taken the job if he'd known, so I'm gonna say no, he has no idea."

"People don't tend to take on new jobs where they're the most hated guy in town, before they even start," Gage said dryly.

"Not usually."

"Think you should've warned him?"

"Nope. He'll figure it out on his own soon enough. Plus, this way, he might come back here and let me dry his tears with a jam-filled donut or two." Sugar winked at Gage and he just rolled his eyes and laughed and sighed. All at the same time.

It was a talent, truly.

"If he wanted to ask you out, you'd just turn him down anyway," he said matter-of-factly. "Poor guy doesn't have a chance in hell."

Sugar opened up her mouth to protest, and then closed it again with a snap. She *hated* it when her boss was right. Or anyone was right, when she wasn't also. "Being wrong" was on Sugar's Top Ten List of Shit She Hated, right along with throwing up, discussing politics, or eating oysters.

She shuddered.

"You know why I can't date," she said tartly. "Hot, sexy firefighter he may be, but that still doesn't mean I'm gonna do it."

"So you have a thing for sexy firefighters now, huh?" Gage drawled, raising one eyebrow as he looked at her.

She sighed. She knew where Gage was going with this, and it broke her heart. Her best friend, Emma, had told her a long time ago that Gage was in love with her. Emma was probably right, considering she was Gage's younger sister. The chances were pretty damn high that she knew what the hell she was talking about.

But still...*Gage*?

Objectively, Sugar could tell her boss was cute. Maybe even handsome. You know, when she closed one eye and squinted real hard, she could *totally* tell that her boss was attractive.

For the 517th time, she wondered why she couldn't just fall for him. A lot of her problems would be solved if she could dredge up something more than friendship for the guy standing next to her.

Speaking of closing one eye and squinting real hard at her boss…She reached up to wipe the streak of flour off his nose that she'd just noticed, but he dodged out of reach. "Hey!" he protested.

"You had flour on your nose," she informed him. "You look like a chimney sweep, except in your case, the soot is all white."

Huh. That was probably it. She'd seen him with flour on his nose one too many times to think he was sexy. Otherwise, she'd probably be all over him.

Yeah, that was *totally* it. She felt better already. She hated not understanding her own mind at times. Mysteries were fun to read, not to live.

"Personal boundaries. They're a thing!" Gage called out as he headed into the kitchen again, through the swinging doors. Sugar rolled her eyes and looked back out through the front door again, and the large picture windows showing the streets of Sawyer beginning to wake up to another day.

"Good luck, Fireman Jaxson," Sugar said softly to the empty bakery. "You're gonna need all the help you can get."

CHAPTER 3

JAXSON

J AXSON PULLED UP to the fire station, his stomach a jumble of nerves. The city council had told him that he ought to start off with a sort of staff meeting to meet everyone, even though the term "staff" was taking it a bit far. He was the only firefighter who was on payroll, the rest of them only getting paid when they were called out to a fire.

For a town the size of Sawyer, it was pert near impossible to fund even a full-time fire chief, and anything beyond that was *completely* out of the question. To be honest, Jaxson had been surprised that the position they'd advertised for was full-time. Maybe they had deeper pockets in the City of Sawyer than he'd realized. A lot of fancy vacation homes with high property taxes to foot the bill? Perhaps.

However they were doing it, it wasn't really any of his business. He was hired on to do the job, and that's what he would do. Before this, he'd worked for the Boise Fire Department, which had almost two dozen stations around the city and just under 300 firefighters on payroll, so working in a town this size was gonna be…real different.

He looked around at the other vehicles in the parking lot –

all of which were trucks – spotting a few hunting rifles in back windows and mud flaps the size of Texas.

Real different.

He swung out of his SUV – a late-model Ford Explorer – and grabbed the box of donuts. He'd only intended to get a cup of joe when he'd gone into the bakery, since he had yet to locate his coffee maker in the boxes stacked in his tiny living room, but hell, donuts had become a better idea the more he thought about it. Who wouldn't appreciate a few sugary carbs to start off their morning?

He walked into the fire station, donuts in one hand, coffee in the other, smile firmly plastered on his face. No reason for nerves. He was the new fire chief of the Sawyer Fire Department, dammit. Every guy in the building was his subordinate. He was going to be just fine.

The quiet chatter among the men died out as soon as he came walking in, every eye on him. "Hi!" he said, a little too loudly, his voice echoing in the cavernous space. He gulped. He sounded way too eager. "I'm Jaxson Anderson," he said a little quieter, spotting a table and working his way over to it to set down the donuts. He needed to shake hands, and he couldn't do it while juggling donuts and coffee like a damn circus clown.

Hands free, he turned back to his crew.

Who were all still just staring at him.

Graveyards were louder than this group.

He felt an overwhelming desire to flip a U and head back towards the door, to his SUV, and out of this town. His spidey senses were causing the hairs on the back of his neck to stand straight up. There was something *real* wrong going on here but damned if he knew what it was.

And if he didn't know what it was, he was pretty damn sure he didn't want to have to fix it.

One of the guys, a tall, dark-haired man who looked about

Jaxson's age, cleared his throat and stepped forward. "Hi Jaxson, I'm Dear, but everyone just calls me Moose."

Jaxson stared at him for a moment, his hand automatically going out to shake Dear's even as he tried to process what the man had said. "'Dear'? As in 'Dear, would you fetch me some coffee?'"

Dear shook his head, laughing a little. "No, Deere as in John Deere. My dad owns the John Deere dealership in town. Said our family owes everything to the brand, so he ought to name me after it."

"And then the nickname Moose…" Jaxson felt a smile creep over his face as he put it together, and he laughed. "I just met a girl named Sugar and a guy named Moose. Let me guess, your name is Couch," he said, jerking his head towards one of the men in the group gathering around him.

The man's mouth dropped open. "How did you know?" he whispered, his eyes wide. Jaxson's heart stuttered to a stop – *no damn way!* – when "Couch" burst out laughing, the men around him laughing too and slapping him on the back. "Just kidding, sir," he said around gasps. "I'm Levi. No animal or food name for me, not even as a nickname."

"No one calls you 'Jeans' for shits and giggles?" Jaxson asked, a smile tugging at his lips.

Levi grinned. "Apparently, all of my friends just aren't creative enough."

"Well, aren't y'all just boring," Jaxson drawled, grinning and sticking his hand out to shake Levi's.

"As white bread," Levi confirmed with a firm shake.

Jaxson felt a little weight lift off his shoulders. He didn't know what he'd been worried about. Whatever was causing him to panic before was obviously wrong. He would get along just—

"I'm James," a man said as he pushed his way out of the small crowd to stand in front of it. The chuckles and cheeriness disappeared from the room and everyone just froze, eyes bouncing between James and Jaxson.

"Hi James, nice to meet you," Jaxson said with a forced smile, putting his hand out to shake. This was it. Whatever was going on here with James, it wasn't pretty. Jaxson could feel it from the tension in the air – James was out for blood.

The older man grasped Jaxson's hand in a vice grip and he began squeezing. Hard.

A dick-measuring contest, eh? Instead of squeezing back and dropping James to his knees like he really, really wanted to, Jaxson just jerked his arm back, forcing James to let go or be pulled up tight against Jaxson's chest. He was *pretty* sure James would choose letting go, but he still let out a small sigh of relief when James actually did, ever so reluctantly.

"How long have you worked here, James?" Jaxson asked. A non-confrontational topic was best; a good way to head off… whatever this was.

"I don't. I'm a *volunteer*. You're the only one who *works* here." The sneer in his voice was almost palpable as he spat the words out.

Jaxson's spine stiffened. This James guy needed to take it down a notch, and pronto. Jaxson wasn't used to having people sneer at him, and he wasn't about to start letting it happen now.

Outwardly, he concentrated on projecting an aura of calm. He couldn't let James know he was getting under his skin. James would only needle harder if he got a rise out of him. All bullies operated the same way – they liked the reactions.

Jaxson wouldn't give him the satisfaction of one.

"You're right," he said evenly, keeping his gaze firmly locked on James'. He had a scruffy, longer gray-white beard and a significant potbelly. In the right costume, James would make a perfect Santa. Well, in the right costume *and* with a personality change. "So how long have you been a *volunteer* here?"

"Twenty-two years. I was Chief Horvath's right-hand man for pert near all of it."

Oh.

It all snapped into place. Chief Horvath had retired, which was why the city had an open position for Jaxson to apply for, but instead of hiring the previous chief's right-hand man, the city had chosen an outsider.

Oh Lordy. I'm in for it now.

"Then you'll have plenty of knowledge you can share with me to help me learn the ropes," Jaxson said calmly, trying not to let his worry show. He'd inadvertently walked into a personnel fight between the City of Sawyer and James the Right-Hand Man.

It wasn't Jaxson's fault, but it was about to become his problem.

James let out a bitter laugh. "If you think I'm gonna help you learn the job that was rightfully mine and stolen from me after years of hard work and dedication, you're an even bigger dumbass than I thought you were. Robert, let's go. We have deliveries to make. *Some* people have to work for a living." He spun on his thick work boot heel and headed for the door, a skinny older man following right behind him. The door slammed shut behind them, the sound ricocheting off the rafters.

Well, at least he didn't mumble his thoughts to me…

CHAPTER 4

JAXSON

J AXSON SAT AT HIS DESK, staring at the mountains of paperwork in front of him. Somehow, when he'd been a kid and had daydreamed about fighting fires and wrestling with fire hoses, he'd skipped right past all of the paperwork that he'd have to fill out as a firefighter.

Correction: As a fire *chief*. As a regular ol' firefighter in Boise, he'd been pretty paperwork-free. He wasn't entirely onboard with this new way of life quite yet, honestly. Too bad he really had no choice in the matter.

He looked at the ticking, utilitarian clock on the wall. 7:17 a.m. He'd had the dumbass idea of showing up to work early so he could wrestle the stacks of paperwork that littered every available spot in the cramped office to the ground and win a round, dammit. He'd forced himself to start in on the dusty stacks of papers yesterday afternoon, until Moose had stopped by and casually mentioned that Chief Horvath had quit filing paperwork months before his retirement party, because he'd thought that the new chief would "need the practice."

Pissed, Jaxson had lost all desire to continue the paper-sorting project after *that* announcement.

Now, Jaxson groaned in frustration as he looked around the

dirty, small office. Chief Horvath was like every other red-blooded male out there – he hated paperwork, and so he'd chosen to use his upcoming retirement as an excuse to ditch his duties off onto someone else. Full stop. Jaxson was just the lucky soul who happened to be that "someone."

Jaxson pulled a file folder off the top of a precarious stack that had "Grant" scrawled across the tab in what Jaxson was starting to recognize as Horvath's distinctive handwriting. He flipped it open and began scanning through it. Apparently, the firetruck in the bay was a fairly new addition for the fire department. He scanned down the specs, his mouth twisting in disappointment as he read. The size of the tank seemed awfully small, as did the length of the hose. It didn't even have a ladder on it. The department had bought brand-spanking-new – which was unusual for a small fire department to do, to say the least – and it looked like a whole lot of the money was spent on flash rather than substance.

He'd been told that the department owned another fire truck, but that it was down at the John Deere dealership, getting some repairs done to help limp it along. He was curious what kind of shape it was in. From what he could gather, it was quite old, but if the water tank was large, it might actually be more helpful in the case of a fire than the shiny new toy currently parked in the bay.

Hopefully, Moose would be able to bring it back to the bay soon so he could do a full inspec—

His black, handheld radio sitting on the counter squawked, startling Jaxson half out of his chair. "Fire down at the old Horvath mill," said an older man, urgency clear in his voice. "Calling all EMTs and fire personnel to respond. Repeat, fire down at the old Horvath mill."

Jaxson froze, half-in, half-out of his chair, staring at the radio. *Horvath Mill? As in Chief Horvath?* He shook his head, trying to clear it. Today was his third day on the job, and he'd only had the one get-together with the other firefighters that first morning. He barely even knew where the damn keys were at for the damn firetruck. This was *not* going to go well.

He'd been called out on countless runs as a firefighter in Boise. He knew just what to do there. There was structure and rules and a process in place. Here, he was the only full-time employee. Was he supposed to wait for the other firefighters to show up before he answered the call? Was he supposed to drive over right away and they'd meet him over there?

His mind raced through the possibilities. All of the other firefighters had full-time jobs. For all he knew, it could be an hour before they were able to get away and come to the station. If he sat there and waited and twiddled his thumbs...

He jumped to his feet, the chair shooting out behind him and crashing into a decrepit filing cabinet, sending a cloud of dust into the air. Apparently, Chief Horvath didn't just ignore filing. Jaxson choked and coughed as he grabbed the phone off his desk and quickly dialed the city dispatch phone number that someone had conveniently taped to the wall above the phone. He heard a weird beeping noise, and then...nothing.

Oh. Dammit. He was probably supposed to dial 9 first. He slammed the phone into the receiver and picked it up again, this time dialing 9 and then the number.

"Sawyer City Dispatch," an older male barked. It sounded like the same guy on the radio. Good. Jaxson could ask questions without broadcasting them to the whole city.

"This is Chief Anderson. Where is the Horvath Mill?"

"Main Street," the man snorted, his disdain clear. He obviously thought he was dealing with an idiot. "Down by the high school. Big brick building. You can't miss it. Especially with *flames* shooting out of it."

Click.

The dispatcher had hung up.

Jaxson bit down hard on his cheek until he tasted blood. He wanted to call dispatch back and inform the man that just because he hadn't lived in the same tiny, one-horse town all his life didn't mean that he deserved to be treated like an idiot, and street addresses were a thing, and...

But he stopped himself.

He couldn't do it.

Well, he *could*. But he wouldn't. Antagonizing the grumpy dispatcher further would only exacerbate the problem.

He looked through his interior office window out into the bay, the small red gleaming truck sitting there, waiting for him to drive it to the rescue.

He felt that familiar adrenaline rush through him at the thought. *This* was why he'd become a firefighter. Not to fill out grant applications or file paperwork, for God's sake, but to put out fires. To help people. Maybe it meant he had a hero complex. He didn't know, and didn't care.

All he knew was that it made him feel damn good. It was time to get to work.

As he was shrugging on his turnout gear, the bulk and weight of it as comforting as it was oppressive, the side door to the bay opened and in walked a younger kid – maybe 18 or 19? – who hadn't said much at the meet-and-greet the other morning. Dixon? David? No, it was Dylan. Jaxson raised his hand in greeting, and the kid waved back, a grin breaking out over his face.

"I was on my way out to Luke's place when my radio went off," the kid said as he hurried over to where the turnout gear was stored. "I've never been called out to a real fire before! Oh, and my boss says he'll be here shortly."

"Who's your boss again?" Jaxson asked as he slid his feet into his boots.

"Luke Nash. He's a volunteer, too. He couldn't come the other morning. I don't know if you've met him yet or not. His foreman is Ol' Willie. Ol' Willie is my uncle. Luke hired me 'cause Ol' Willie is getting old and needed help on the farm. Ol' Willie used to be a volunteer here too, but isn't anymore.

His back is getting bad. His hip is gonna need surgery soon, too."

Jaxson's head spun. The kid talked a million miles a minute. Keeping up with his story and who was related to what was probably going to require a flow chart.

And no adrenaline rushing through his veins.

Jaxson settled for nodding his head abruptly. "Do you guys normally meet up here and then head over to the fire? Or do you drive separately to a fire and just meet up over there?"

Dylan shrugged. "This is my first fire," he reminded Jaxson. *Right.* He'd just said that. If Jaxson's heart wasn't racing so much, he would've caught that.

"Well, you're here and I'm here. I say we get over there and put this fire out. Do you know where the mill is?"

"Of course," Dylan said, shooting him a confused glance. "Down on Main Street. You can't miss it."

Jaxson nodded again, ignoring that last comment. If people in this tiny-ass town were going to continue to insist on treating him like an idiot because he didn't know every nook and cranny of a town he'd just barely moved to, he was gonna have to spend his off-hours driving around town, trying to memorize every block of it.

The sooner the better.

He was an outsider, and it seemed like every soul in town was not about to let him forget that.

"Ready?" he asked Dylan, who nodded, helmet and mask tucked under his arm. "Then let's go."

Jaxson grimaced as he glanced up at the utilitarian clock ticking away on the wall as he headed for the gleaming row of keys. He'd have to focus damn hard on decreasing response times. Even if there were no full-time firefighters on staff other than him, and certainly no firefighters living at the firehouse 24 hours at a time, they still needed to be able to get out the door at a reasonable speed. This messing around shit wasn't gonna work.

He snagged the keyring with the creative label of "New truck" and heaved himself up into the cab of the fire engine to start it. The diesel engine came to life, settling down into a dull roar after a few seconds. He hit the garage door opener, and the overhead bay door slowly began to rise, revealing a white, frozen wonderland outside. Dylan jumped up into the passenger seat, yanking the door shut behind him.

With a nod to Dylan, Jaxson shifted into first gear and pulled forward. At least the crew here was in the habit of backing into the bay when parking the truck, so he wasn't forced to back out of the bay when rushing to get to a fire.

Some good habits were in place. That was a start.

He hit the siren switch, the lights and siren flaring to life. *This.* This was what he lived for.

CHAPTER 5

SUGAR

S UGAR LISTENED TO the excited chatter of the customers, all comparing notes on the Event of the Year. Someone had set the old Horvath mill on fire, and that "somebody" appeared to be the mayor's son. Sugar rolled her eyes as she listened to the gossip swirling around the little bakery.

"Angus was probably out smokin' with his buddies," Mr. Stultz said firmly, with a nod of his head, as if agreeing with himself.

Sugar wiped down the counter and then the coffee dispenser as she listened. All of the customers seemed to be highly caffeinated and sugared up, and weren't in need of her services, at least for the moment. They were all too busy trying to one-up each other with "insider knowledge."

"What's the mayor gonna say about that?" Mrs. Hoffmeister asked, taking a swig of her coffee. "Do you think he's actually gonna rein in his son for once?"

"Not damn likely," Mr. Stultz grumbled. "I think it's more likely that a unicorn appears in town square tomorrow, or the Shop 'N Go starts charging decent prices for their groceries, than it is that the mayor actually puts a check on his son."

Murmurs of agreement drifted up at that one. Sugar had to say he was right. It was well-known that the mayor let his son get away with murder, turning a blind eye to it all. Angus wasn't above taking advantage of that fact, not one little bit.

"Well, *I* think the new chief set the building on fire," said Spittin' Fred. A few of the customers within range covered the tops of their cups with their hands to protect them from the spray. "He wanted to prove to everyone that we actually need to pay more in taxes for his worthless ass to sit down at the station. Probably realized that if he don't put out a fire real soon, we might realize that we can fire him. I betcha—"

"The building is starting to go!" Peter Cowell yelled, busting in through the front door of the bakery. "Shit's flyin' everywhere!"

The stampede of customers for the front door almost caused a natural disaster of its own, but Sugar found herself right in there with them. It wasn't often that a building caught on fire, especially not an old historical building like the Horvath Mill.

She stood on the sidewalk with the rest of the gawkers, shivering in the cold wintry air. The sky was a leaden gray – dark and oppressive – and the wind whipped along Main Street, biting and needling her bare skin.

And also whipping the flames higher. They were shooting out of the windows of the mill, reaching into the sky, brilliant red and orange against the grays. Despite Peter's warning, it didn't look like the building was in any danger of collapsing, although at this rate, it might get there soon.

She looked around for the new fire chief. Why wasn't he spraying the building? She didn't know much about firefighting, but it seemed like spraying the fire with water was a pretty good place to start.

The murmurs around her grew louder as people began to ask each other the same thing. Sugar finally spotted him. He was just standing there, watching the fire burn, as the new fire truck idled beside him. A few firefighters milled around, talking to each other, but no one seemed to be much focused on actually fighting the fire.

Sugar spun around and headed back inside. Her thin t-shirt and jeans were fine for standing behind the counter in the bakery; not so fine for standing out in the street in the first week of January. The angry shouts of the crowd swelled up behind her.

Chief Anderson's head was gonna be on a platter by the end of the day, and with that, he'd head back to wherever he came from.

Sugar allowed herself only a small sigh of regret. He was never going to be anything more than eye-candy for her anyway; although she had to admit, if only to herself, that he was damn fine eye-candy.

CHAPTER 6

JAXSON

J AXSON COULD FEEL his back teeth grinding together. He was pretty sure he'd have nothing but powder in his mouth if he kept this up.

But it was either that or *really* lose his shit.

He watched the building in front of him closely, since there wasn't much else he *could* do. The flames were starting to die down, now that all of the easily flammable guts had been burnt out, so there wasn't much for him to do except watch it burn and keep embers floating on the wind from starting fire to neighboring buildings.

Of course, he wouldn't have to conserve every drop of water in the tank on the truck if the damn fire hydrants worked. He felt the anger begin to rise in him again. Who'd heard of letting fire hydrants fall into disrepair for years on end? It was enough to make him wanna—

"Hey, mister!" he heard an angry voice shout in his left ear as someone tapped on his shoulder. He spun around to confront an older man in blue-and-white overalls with a stained and dirtied Carhartt's jacket over top. He had a big wad of chew in his lower lip that he spit and then glared up at Jaxson.

"Ain't you the new fire chief?" the older man demanded. He barreled on, not giving Jaxson a chance to respond. "Last time I checked, flames came from fires. Ya oughta use this here fire truck to put it out!" His voice rose in pitch as he got angrier, his cheeks starting to flame red from anger or the cold, Jaxson couldn't tell.

"Sir," Jaxson said, trying to keep his voice an even keel and realizing that he was probably failing miserably, "the fire hydrant for this area is apparently in disrepair and has been for a while." *A lot longer than I've been fire chief!* He managed to keep that thought to himself, although just barely. "The tank on this truck is on the small side. If I use all of the water in it to try to contain this fire and then the building next door catches, I'm out of luck. I need to save the water in case—"

"Sounds like a real good excuse to just stand around and do *nothin'.*" The man spat a black glob into the snow. "Damn lazy city folk. My taxes go up and my buildings burn down. Every last one of those damn city councilmen are gonna be run out of office for this one!"

Another older gentleman came up and put his arm around the shoulders of the man standing in front of Jaxson, cutting off whatever else he was about to say. "C'mon, Stultz, let's go. We can talk to the city council about this later."

"Damn right I'm gonna talk to the council 'bout this!" Mr. Stultz practically growled, but he let his friend lead him away.

Jaxson turned back to the fire, trying to keep his face blank, even as anger and worry roiled in his guts. He hadn't even been on the job for a week, and people were already talking about calling for his resignation.

He couldn't be fired from this job. He just *couldn't.* He had too damn much riding on it. He wasn't going to let Kendra win. He wasn't going to lose his kids. This job didn't just give him a paycheck – it gave him a way to get his kids back. They'd have to pry it out of his cold, dead hands.

Once the fire died down, leaving just a shell of blackened

bricks behind, Jaxson began winding the hose back up on the truck. The snow on every rooftop in town certainly helped in keeping the fire contained. If it'd been the middle of August when this fire had started…Jaxson shuddered to think about it.

He drove back to the firehouse, no sirens or lights flashing this time, his spirits equally as depressed and quiet. This was *not* how he'd envisioned his career would start out in the Sawyer Fire Department. Dylan was sitting in the passenger seat of the firetruck and in stark contrast to the excited babble on the way to the fire, Dylan was stone-cold quiet now. Jaxson snuck a look at the kid out of the corner of his eye, but Dylan was looking out of the passenger-side window. Was he hiding his face from Jaxson? Was he that angry or disappointed or whatever in his new chief?

Jaxson carefully backed into the open bay, hitting the garage door fob once he was squared away, the grinding gears of the closing of the overhead door the only sound in the dead silence of the fire station.

Jaxson was climbing out of the truck wearily when James started in on him. "What the hell was that?" the man shouted, his bushy mustache bouncing with every word. "We go to a fire so we can watch the building burn? If I just wanted to stand around and watch shit burn to the ground, I coulda skipped a whole lot of training hours!"

Jaxson advanced on the older man, his patience gone. Snapped. Disappeared along with the flames of the mill fire.

"Are you screwing with me right now? Whose brilliant idea was it to leave fire hydrants scattered around this podunk town that don't damn work?!"

"Podunk town? You're the one who applied for this job! If you don't like it, you can just take your ass back to Boise, and don't let the door hit ya where the good Lord split ya!"

"I would like this job just fine if I had working equipment," Jaxson ground out.

"I could've told you that the fire hydrant on that street

corner didn't work, if you'd bothered to ask! But noooooo… you have to run on down to the damn mill without me or anyone else who knows anything, so you could play *hero!*"

"I took the crew who was here and ready to go," Jaxson growled. "Not my fault that you weren't! Dylan managed to make it here on time. What's your excuse?"

"Not all of us get to sit around at the firehouse all day, shuffling papers around. Some of us actually do something with ourselves for our paychecks. Speaking of which, there's a whole lotta people right now who'd probably like their propane so they don't freeze their asses off tonight. I still have to do deliveries for Frank's. C'mon, Robert. Let's get some *real* work done."

The smaller man trailed behind James, the door slamming shut behind them. Jaxson turned to the rest of the crew. "Anyone want to tell me why on God's green earth you have fire hydrants that don't work?"

A man about Jaxson's age with dark brown hair stepped forward. "That fire hydrant hasn't worked for a while. Chief Horvath always said that the city just didn't care too much about getting 'em fixed, so…" He trailed off, shrugging.

"And you are?" Jaxson asked. He hadn't met this guy at the meet-and-greet earlier in the week, he was pretty sure, although faces were starting to blend together on him.

"Luke Nash." He shook Jaxson's hand. "My worker Dylan rode over with you."

"Well, Luke, do you or anyone else know why the hell the tank on this truck is so damn small?" Jaxson jerked his thumb at the fire engine.

A couple of the men shrugged, and then Moose spoke up. "The truck at the dealership has a much bigger tank. We use that one when we have to pump off the truck, and this one when we can access a fire hydrant."

"A fire hydrant that actually works?" Jaxson asked dryly.

"Yeah, one of those." Moose shot Jaxson an apologetic smile.

"When is the tanker due back from the dealership?"

"Tomorrow afternoon, probably."

"Well, let's hope that nothing burns down between today and tomorrow afternoon, then. Thanks for your help, everyone. I'm guessing that you have paperwork that you have to fill out to get paid for this fire?" At the nods of the men, Jaxson jerked his head. "Better get to it. Oh, does anyone have the time or inclination to drive with me 'round town? I'd like a map of all of the hydrants, and I want someone who knows whether they're in working order or not, so it needs to be someone who's pretty damn familiar with them."

Levi spoke up. "I'd normally tell ya to talk to James, but since that's not gonna do you much good, I'd be happy to go with. I'll tell you all I know."

"Much 'ppreciated," Jaxson said. "Thanks, everyone."

The men began to drift away, and Levi came up. "When do you want to do this?" he asked, leaning against the wall.

"Well, what does your work schedule look like? Where do you work, by the way?"

"The John Deere dealership," Levi said.

"Hold on, I thought Moose worked there," Jaxson said, confused. He could feel the tension begin to build between his shoulder blades. Too many men, and all of their stories were starting to get mixed up on him.

"He does. His dad owns it. Moose's my best friend. I work as a TIG welder for his dad, Mr. Garrett."

"TIG welder, eh?" Jaxson looked at Levi with new respect. Welding aluminum was damn hard work, and paid real well. Levi probably made as much as Jaxson did.

"Yeah, Mr. Garrett sent me to welding school on his dime. Said it was an investment so he could hire a reliable welder when I graduated." Levi shrugged, a slight tingeing of red blossoming on his cheeks. "I've been working there ever since."

"You got a vacation day you can put in for tomorrow? I'd like to get started on this as quickly as possible."

"Sure do. January ain't the time most farmers are wanting me out there fixing their tractors anyway, so it's real slow right now. Might as well do something productive. I can only rearrange my tool bench so many times."

Jaxson chuckled, the first time he'd wanted to even smile all day. "I'll save you from boredom. In fact, meet me at the Muffin Man tomorrow morning at 8:30, and I'll buy you some coffee and donuts before we head out."

"Deal." Levi shook his hand and then headed out of the bay, the echo of his footsteps fading away, leaving Jaxson alone.

And very, very worried.

CHAPTER 7

SUGAR

S UGAR DID A QUICK WIPE DOWN of a table, dumping trash
into the garbage can by the door and then heading back
to the kitchen with the tray. It'd been a busy morning,
what with every Sawyerite in the area wanting to come in and
give their personal opinion on the job Chief Anderson was (or
was not, as the case may be) doing. Sugar wondered if Betty's
Diner was as busy as the Muffin Man had been. Somehow, she
was gonna guess yes, although of course she hadn't had a
chance to make it over there herself.

"…stupid." The front door swung open, letting the last
word drift in on the breeze, as Robert, James, and Mr. Stultz
came walking in. Sugar barely repressed a groan. This was
gonna be a whole lot of no fun whatsoever. No more
judgmental men existed on planet Earth than these three,
Sugar was sure. If she sneezed right then, she was sure they'd
tell her that she'd done it wrong.

"Now we have a fire chief who won't hook a hose up to a
fire hydrant or a tanker," Mr. Stultz railed. He slammed his
oversized coffee mug down on the counter with a jerk of his
head towards Sugar. She obediently picked it up to do a refill
on it while he continued on. "I can't believe I'm paying more to

this damn city in taxes so we can have a worthless fire chief who stands around and *watches* buildings burn down."

"I told him that, I did," James told him, and then turned to her. "A bear claw and coffee. Black." He turned back to his shadow and his sycophant.

Just what a man like James needed – two men egging him on and telling him he was right. Even if he *was* right, James wasn't the kind of guy who should be told that. Absolutely no good could come of it.

As Sugar began filling up two coffee cups and grabbing two bear claws – since Robert would eat exactly what James did – James began railing on the new chief. "He told me that I could help him learn the ropes because I know so much shit. I told him I wouldn't teach him anything. Didn't I, Robert?"

"He did," Robert said, nodding seriously. "Everyone heard 'im."

Sugar carried a tray over to the table the men had settled in at, and offloaded the coffee and donuts onto the table inconspicuously. No one even bothered looking up.

"He needs a lot more training than *I* could give him," James announced. "I can't believe that damn council picked him over me, and all because of some stupid-ass training levels. Why, I've worked in this fire department since *Chief Anderson*," he sneered the name, "was in diapers, and the city thinks a few hours of training means he's more qualified than I am? Idiots, the lot of 'em."

Sugar slipped into the back and leaned against the cool cinderblock wall, closing her eyes in frustration. No matter how right James was, he was also a dick. There was only so much James Lasley time that Sugar could handle before her right eyeball started twitching.

"Still dissing on the new chief?" Gage asked quietly, somewhere to her right. She nodded, keeping her eyes closed.

"It's their new favorite past time. I imagine it's gonna be for quite some time." She heard the jingle of the doorbell over the front door and fading away of footsteps. *Good.* She was surprised they'd left so quickly, but damn happy. This would give her some time to relax before the next person came in to badmouth Jaxson.

She opened up her eyes as she pushed away from the wall, swinging around and heading back out front. She should probably do a sweep up of the dining area before another rush came in. She—

She stopped abruptly. Jaxson froze, his hand hovering over the small dinner bell that sat on the counter for customers to ring in case she was in the back.

"Oh!" she yelped. "I didn't hear you come in!"

Levi was standing next to Jaxson, his cowboy hat off, quiet as usual. Levi didn't say much, except to other guys, at least that Sugar could tell. Even though they'd graduated from high school together, Sugar wasn't sure if they'd ever exchanged more than a hundred words in the twenty years of knowing each other.

"We came in when the...other guys were leaving," Levi finally offered up, when Jaxson didn't say anything.

"Oh," Sugar repeated weakly. *I bet* that *was awkward as hell. I wonder if they even bothered to stop badmouthing him long enough to say hello.*

She decided to keep that thought to herself.

"Levi here is going to show me 'round town and we're gonna inspect fire hydrants," Jaxson said with an easy smile. Sugar felt her insides flutter, like freakin' butterflies had taken up residence in her stomach.

She smiled back faintly. She couldn't let her nerves show. He didn't need to know that he affected her because any minute now, she was going to get her nerves under control and he wasn't going to affect her anymore.

Any minute now.

She scrambled for something to say, when Jaxson's words

finally registered. "Inspect fire hydrants?" she asked, confused. "Why would you need to do that?"

"So that next time someone sets fire to a historical landmark in town, I can actually use the fire hydrant and put the damn fire out," Jaxson growled, his easy smile disappearing.

"Hold on, you couldn't use the fire hydrant yesterday?" Sugar was openly staring at him now, which was probably rude, but dammit all, she was totally and thoroughly confused at this point.

"Of course not; otherwise, I would have. But, it was broken. Apparently, it's been out of repair for *years* now. As it was, I had to conserve the water in the tank on the truck in case the sparks set something else on fire. I sure as hell didn't have enough in that tank to put out the mill fire *and* another fire, if it came to that."

"*Ohhhh…*"

She knew she was repeating herself. She knew she sounded like an idiot. But things were finally making sense. Pieces were clicking into place as she stared at him, her mind whirling.

James knew this. He had to have known this. He was at the fire yesterday. And yet, he came in here and was badmouthing Jaxson to Robert and Mr. Stultz and probably anyone else within a ten-mile radius. He's an asshat, but this is low, even for him.

There were words being spoken, and then Sugar shook her head. "Sorry, what?" she asked blankly.

"I asked if you're okay. You look…off." Jaxson was staring at her intently. She wanted to laugh and brush him off, but she couldn't.

"You need to watch out for James," she said impulsively, and then gulped. Why was she sticking her nose in where it didn't belong? Jaxson was a big boy. He could take care of himself.

Jaxson's face shut down, a guarded, quiet look settling over him. "In here talking shit 'bout me?" he asked, his voice hard.

She nodded, the tension in her stomach growing. She tried

real hard to stay out of city politics; it was safer that way. But she couldn't stay on the sidelines this time. She could warn him once and *then* get out of the middle of it. He could take care of himself after that. "He…may not have mentioned that the hydrant was broken."

"Left that part off, huh? Anyone else bother to bring up that fact?" He was practically growling at this point.

Sugar just shook her head. "No. I'll be honest – I didn't know that. No one does. Everyone just thought that you were…"

"Standing around and watching buildings burn to the ground because it's *fun*?" he cut in.

She nodded, her face flushed, eyes glued to the ground. She hadn't helped spread those rumors, of course, but she had listened to them all, and had thought that they were right. People had been crucifying him, and no one had stood up for him.

Not even her.

She couldn't have known the truth, but still, it made her sick. She knew what it was like having people spread shit about you and not having any control over what they said or thought.

Her face flushed warmer still. She would've made a joke about needing to call the fire department to put out the flames in her cheeks, if she wasn't dying of embarrassment.

Jaxson let out a few choice swear words that made her eyes pop back up to his. She gaped at him.

"Sorry, miss," he ground out. "I…shouldn't have said that." He took a long, deep, shuddering breath and then said, "Coffee and donuts for the two of us, please."

Sugar nodded and quickly got to work, filling to-go cups and grabbing jelly donuts for them both. After Jaxson paid, he jerked his head in Sugar's direction. "Thanks, Sugar. Sorry again for…for letting off steam. It wasn't appropriate."

They headed for the door, the bell jingling behind them as

they crunched their way through the light skiff of snow on the sidewalk. It was snowing just enough to ice everything up.

January was a damn depressing time of the year. Dark and dreary and gray…the holidays were over, and now there was nothing to do but settle in and wait for spring to come.

Sugar sighed. Waiting was never her strong suit.

"You should've asked him out," Gage said at her elbow.

She whirled around, her hand over her heart. "Good Lord!" she said. "You could stop sneaking around, you know."

He gave her a long suffering look. "I wasn't. I clomped up here like I always do. You were just off in la-la land."

She sniffed. She wasn't about to dignify that with a reply.

"He likes you," Gage continued bluntly. "And based on how much you blush around him, I'm gonna guess that you like him."

Sugar glared at him. "I do *not* like him," she announced, a little too forcefully. "I just…it's hot in here. We should turn down the heat."

"You were freezing last week," Gage pointed out.

She glared at him even harder. "I cannot date him. I cannot date *anyone*. You know that."

"I know that you believe that. I don't believe that it's true."

"What?" she snapped back. "I think I know that better than you do! I can't date you, Gage!"

The words were out before she could stop them. Her hands flew up to her mouth and she stared at him, wide-eyed. She hadn't meant to say it. She was never going to be able to suck those words back in and stuff them deep down in her soul where they belonged.

"Sugar…" Gage breathed her name softly. His face was inscrutable as he stared at her. "Why did you say that?"

"No, I'm sorry," Sugar gasped, shaking her head. "I didn't mean to. Forget I said anything." She'd broken the number one rule of working at the bakery: Ignore the fact that Gage was in love with her. It wasn't ever spoken out loud or acknowledged at all, and…

She'd broken that rule. Stomped it into the ground, really.

"Why did you say that?" Gage repeated, a steely edge to his voice.

"Emma told me a long time ago," Sugar whispered, broken. "I just…I don't feel the same way. I'm sorry."

Gage started laughing. Sugar's head snapped up and she stared at him. Gage let out a howl of laughter. "You…she…" Gage was wheezing.

Sugar stared harder. Gage laughed more.

"I'm not in love with you!" he finally got out.

"You…you're not?"

"No. My sister…" Gage wiped his eyes with the backs of his hands. "Oh Emma. Always the matchmaker. I think she's spent her whole life trying to hook me up with someone. I knew that when we moved here, you'd become friends with her, but I didn't know that she'd decided that *we* oughta date."

The Dyer family had moved back to Long Valley when Gage's father had retired from the Marine Corps, but Gage had happened to graduate from high school the day before the big retirement, and he'd gone off to culinary school, rather than moving back to Long Valley with the rest of the family. This had put Sugar into the awkward position of being close to Emma, the younger son Chris, and even the parents, but Gage…

Well, he'd been a virtual stranger until Emma had pushed Sugar into applying for a position at the bakery. She had insisted that Gage needed her help after moving back to Long Valley himself to take over their grandparents' bakery. It wasn't long after Sugar had started there that Emma had started telling her that Gage was in love.

With her.

Which Sugar had believed.

Because...she was full of herself and thought that men would throw themselves at her?

No, that wasn't it. Sugar was many things, but cocky about men was *not* one of them. Emma had just been so believable, so earnest.

Sugar was mortified. She'd made an ass out of herself, she really and truly had. No thanks to Emma. Why, she was gonna wring her neck the next time she—

"I'm sure Emma thought she was telling you the truth," Gage said softly. "She's tried to set me up on more dates than I can count. She seems to think that I'm going to end up a bachelor for life. I remind her that I'm 29, but you'd think I was saying 59 instead."

"I'm so–sorry," Sugar stammered, staring at the floor. "I really thought..."

"That I've been waiting two and a half years to make my move?" She could hear the laughter in Gage's voice. "I may be a patient man, but that seems pretty damn long, even for me."

Sugar looked up from studying the tiles of the floor to glare at him. "You don't have to laugh at me, you know," she informed him.

"I'm not laughing," he protested. At her incensed glare, he added, "Okay, fine, I'm laughing, but not at you. Just this whole situation. Sugar, I'm glad that you don't like me, because if you were spending your days wondering when I was going to ask you out, I'd feel real bad. So let's be happy that this finally came out in the open."

She pressed her lips together. "Fine." She nodded her head abruptly. As her embarrassment subsided, though, she started to feel relief pour through her instead. *Gage doesn't like me!* The worry she'd had niggling at the back of her mind for months at how she was going to let him down gently when he finally got up the guts to ask her out...it all whooshed out of her, sucked away into the world, leaving behind peace and relief.

"We were talking about why you think *you* can't date," Gage said quietly.

And in flowed the worry and stress again. Sugar's back stiffened. "You know what happened with Dick. You know why I'm working here. I can't date someone else, for God's sake. One major catastrophe per lifetime. It's a rule. I read it somewhere."

She picked up her spray bottle and washcloth and began wiping down counters and the cash register and then started in on the display cases that seemed to show every smudge and fingerprint ever impressed upon them.

"I think you oughta rethink that rule," Gage said softly. "I can't tell you what to do, but as your friend, I want to say that I think you're making a mistake. It doesn't have to be Jaxson, of course – with the way things are going, he's not gonna be around for long anyway – but someone. You can't close yourself off from the world forever."

Sugar refused to look up from the display case she was wiping down and eventually, his footsteps faded away, towards the back again. She let out a huge sigh, slumping against the display case, smudging it and ruining all of her hard work. She couldn't bring herself to care, though.

She stared off into the distance, worrying her lower lip. Was Gage right?

No. He wasn't. He didn't know. He didn't know everything. He knew most of it, but not all.

Someone like her didn't deserve love or second chances.

She knew the truth, even if she'd never tell another soul.

CHAPTER 8

JAXSON

J AXSON PULLED UP in front of his ex-wife's house.

A house that was suspiciously dark.

He stared at it for a moment. This was *not* a good sign.

He heaved himself out of his SUV and through the snow to her front door. He knocked on the door once. Twice. He raised his fist to pound a third time, but with a sigh, he instead pulled his phone out of his back pocket. He could continue to pound on Kendra's front door, or he could give up and call her.

"Hello?" she answered on the fourth ring. It was noisy wherever she was at, and Jaxson could hardly hear her over the shouts of laughter and loud music.

He did an about-face and marched back to his SUV. Wherever the hell she was, it was *not* her house. He might as well get back into the car and warm up while having this conversation.

"Where are you?" he demanded, sliding into the driver's seat and slamming the door behind him. He probably shut it a little too hard, but he was too pissed to care at the moment.

"At Jumping Off."

"With the boys?"

"Of course with the boys," she snapped. "Do you think I'd come to this godforsaken place for *fun*?"

Jumping Off was a roller-skating rink, arcade, bouncy slide, pool of balls "funhouse" that served over-priced and over-cooked food at astronomical prices.

In other words, a place that every child would absolutely love, and every parent would absolutely hate.

"It's my weekend to have them, Kendra. Why are you at Jumping Off?" He tried to keep the anger out of his voice, but failed miserably. If his ex-wife was trying to intentionally piss him off, she was doing a damn good job of it.

"It's their friend Isaac's 9th birthday party. What was I supposed to do – tell Isaac that he was born on the wrong damn weekend?"

"No, but you could've told *me*. I drove 90 minutes, in the dark, to pick them up. You—"

"I put it into the calendar," she snapped. "Maybe you ought to learn how to read one of those!"

Jaxson ground his back teeth together as he started the engine. If he told her once, he'd told her a hundred times to tell him when she added shit to the shared custody calendar. She always somehow "forgot."

"I'm coming over there," he told her. "I can hang out and watch them play and *then* take them back to Sawyer for the weekend."

"Don't you dare. Ivan is here. You two would end up in a fistfight in ten minutes flat."

Jaxson ground his teeth together harder. She was right. He and Ivan…didn't get along. It might have something to do with the fact that he was drunk about 75% of the time. Or how he snapped his fingers whenever he wanted Jaxson's attention, like Jaxson was his puppy dog. Or maybe it was when he'd found Ivan and Kendra in bed together, signaling the end of his marriage to her.

No, he most definitely could not sit next to Ivan for hours on end without someone having a bloody nose by the end of it.

And it wouldn't be Jaxson.

"Fine. Tell the boys I love them."

He hung up before she could say anything else, and stared into the darkened residential street ahead of him.

He might as well go grocery shopping while he was there. Every time he went into the Shop 'N Go in Sawyer, he had a minor heart attack at the prices. He was going to drop dead at age 52 from grocery prices if that kept up.

A good run through Winco and Costco would be good. He could stock up on the essentials, then head back to Sawyer.

Alone.

Jaxson heaved the last of the groceries out of the backseat of his SUV. It was his eighth trip into the house, loaded down each time like a pack horse, which meant he'd had *way* too much fun grocery shopping.

It was possible that the sight of reasonably priced groceries may have made him go a bit overboard. Just maybe.

Turning to head to his apartment, he heard the jingle of a collar and looked up the street to see Sugar walking toward him with what looked like a small horse beside her. He did a double take. *What the hell?* He squinted.

Nope, Sugar wasn't taking a shetland pony out for an evening walk; just a Great Dane. Jaxson was willing to bet next week's paycheck that the dog weighed more than she did. Setting the grocery bags on the ground, he waved in greeting. It was surprisingly nice to see her; it felt like ages since he'd seen her last, even though it'd just been that morning.

It'd been a hell of a day, between inspecting fire hydrants and being stood up by Kendra and buying enough groceries to feed a small country…

"What are you up to?" he called out.

She smiled, her teeth reflecting the scant streetlight. "Taking Hamlet for a walk," she called back. Hamlet wagged his massive tail and began pulling her towards him, no doubt seeing Jaxson as another source of affection and attention that he could enjoy.

"*Hamlet*?" He blurted out the question. "You mean as in Shakespeare's *Hamlet*?"

They were now close enough that the Great Dane could begin nosing his way through the grocery bags. *Hmmm...* Maybe Jaxson wasn't a source of affection and attention, but rather, raw meat. Hamlet had gone straight for the bag with the t-bone steaks in it.

Sugar didn't ignore his behavior, nor did she yell at him. Instead, she simply tugged nearly imperceptibly on the thick leash and the giant dog responded obediently by immediately sitting down.

Jaxson was impressed.

"Yeah, Shakespeare's *Hamlet*," Sugar said, once her massive dog had heeled. "It comes from—"

"Hold on, don't tell me," Jaxson interrupted. Their breaths were coming out as puffs of fog in the brisk winter air. As he paused, the mist dissipated, allowing Jaxson to see those beautiful brown eyes sparkling in the dim light. "Is *Hamlet* the one where he says, 'There is something rotten in the state of Denmark'?"

"Good guess!" Sugar said. "Wowsers. A man who knows Shakespeare *and* how to fight fires." Even as she was saying the words, though, her body convulsed in a full-blown shiver, shaking from head to toe. She looked about a half-step away from having her teeth chatter loudly.

Before he could second-guess himself, Jaxson asked, "Wanna come up for a cup of coffee and warm up?"

Why had he said that? He shouldn't have said that. She was a girl, and last Jaxson checked, girls had cooties. Or at least cheated on you with the next-door neighbor and then made it out to be *your* fault.

Which was pretty much the same thing as having cooties.

But still, inexplicably, he held his breath.

She bit her lower lip, her eyes flicking towards the ground before she looked back up into his eyes.

"I would love to," she said, the regret obvious in her voice, "but Hamlet has been cooped up all day. I can't force him to go sit in your apartment after spending the day sitting in mine. Hey, actually, why don't you walk with us?" Her voice was eager with excitement at the idea.

"Well, I have to get the last of these groceries into the apartment," he said, suddenly realizing how complicated it was to be spontaneous. "Do you walk Hamlet every night?"

"Yeah," she said. "I have to walk him every day after work. In the wintertime, I end up having to bundle up in a snowsuit worthy of a snowshoeing trip in Antarctica so I don't freeze to death, but hey, it does get me out and about."

"Welllll," Jaxson said, thinking quick, "if you can wait for just a moment, I'll run these upstairs," nodding towards the bags laying in the snow and ice, "and then I can join you two."

With a shy nod, she softly said, "Okay."

Bounding up the stairs two at a time, Jaxson realized that he was feeling happier than he had all evening. He snatched the thickest coat he owned from the hook, swapping it for his lighter jacket he'd worn to Boise, and then on a whim, grabbed his Elmer Fudd hat. He looked ridiculous in it, but being warm was what *really* mattered. Plus, he figured it'd be a good test to see if Sugar was willing to be seen in public with him with it on. If she told him to march back inside and change hats, well, he might just march back inside and not come back.

He clattered back down the stairs. When Sugar caught sight of him, she immediately began laughing.

"Hey, Mr. Fudd," she called out through her giggles, "wanna go on a walk with me?" She bent over, gasping for air as she laughed, and of course, Hamlet took that to mean that it was kissing time, since she'd conveniently put her face within range. He began slobbering all over her face as she continued to laugh.

Jaxson struck his best bodybuilder pose when he reached the bottom of the stairs. This only made Sugar laugh harder as Hamlet laid on even more kisses.

Yeah, Sugar was pretty okay. Maybe she didn't have *quite* as many cooties as other girls.

Maybe.

CHAPTER 9

SUGAR

S UGAR STRAIGHTENED UP from her laughing bout, wiped her face clean with the sleeve of her jacket – damn, Hamlet was good at giving kisses – and shot Jaxson a smile. "Ready?"

She tried to hide the twerking butterflies in her stomach. She wasn't sure why Jaxson made her so nervous, but she'd be damned if she was going to let those nerves show.

He fell into step beside her while Hamlet proceeded to sniff every bush and dormant tree along the way, stopping to mark about every third object they passed. He was *such* a boy sometimes.

Sugar cast about for something to say.

"So…grocery shopping in Boise, huh?" she asked knowing full well that it was the lamest topic of conversation *ever*, but it was all she could come up with at the moment.

Jaxson smiled, but his shoulders seemed to tense up at the same time. She wondered what was going on in his head. She didn't have to wait long for an answer.

"I went to Boise to pick up my boys for the weekend," he started explaining. "My ex-wife made other plans with the kids and didn't bother to tell me. So I went shopping instead."

They had made it to the park and Sugar fished a ball out of her coat pocket. Throwing the ball into the darkness, Hamlet took off like a shot. Sugar figured Hamlet could see every ball within a mile radius. She used the time to think of what to say to Jaxson. He had kids?

He wouldn't want anything to do with her, then. People tended to shun baby killers. Especially people with children of their own.

She forced herself to smile.

"How old are your boys?" she asked, trying desperately to cover her inner turmoil.

"They're six and four," Jaxson replied promptly. "They're actually the reason I am here."

Hamlet returned the ball, now covered in slobber. Sugar bravely picked up the wet mess and threw it into the darkness once more.

"Wait a minute…" she said, surprised. "You moved to Sawyer for your kids?"

"Strange, I know," he said with a small chuckle. "My ex dragged me through the courts, telling the judge the whole time that I shouldn't have any rights at all because I'm a firefighter. I got called away quite a few times over the years. Boise is just too big and too busy, you know? She told the judge that if I had custody and I was called away on a fire, I wouldn't have anyone to watch the boys." He let out a bitter chuckle that was as icy as the air. "She was right, but that doesn't mean I have to like it. The judge told me I had to find a more stable job. I figured a small town like Sawyer would have a lot less call-outs, and I don't have to sleep at the station when I'm on duty. The judge said that after six months of stability, he'll revisit the issue. Until then, I get the boys every other weekend."

"Except when your ex stands you up?"

"Yeah, except then," he replied dryly.

Hamlet returned with his ball, dropping the sodden mess at

her feet. He flopped down, finally admitting that he was worn out.

Pulling the ziplock bag out of her pocket that she carried for just this reason, she slipped the frozen chunk of slobber and ice into the protective bag before placing it back in her pocket.

"You must love your sons a lot," she commented softly while clipping the leash to Hamlet's collar.

"Yeah, I do," Jaxson said, equally as softly. "I'll do anything for them. Including moving to the ass-end of the earth to impress a damn judge."

They walked for a while in silence. As they got closer to Jaxson's place, she felt her steps shorten. She wanted to stretch this time out as much as possible before Jaxson found out the truth about her and didn't want to be around her anymore.

Despite her sluggish pace, they reach the front steps of his apartment building all too quickly.

"Thanks for walking with me," she told him quietly. Dammit all, it was a hell of a lot more fun to go with Jaxson than it was to go by herself.

That was *not* something she was willing to spend too much time dwelling on.

He looked down at her in the semi-darkness, the sun having set long ago. The street lamp on the corner cast deep shadows across his face, making him look mysterious.

A stranger.

Which he was, really. In all the ways that mattered, he was.

He reached up and stroked his fingers across her cheek, and then ran his thumb across her lower lip. She wanted to nibble on his thumb. She wanted to flick her tongue out and touch it.

Actually, she wanted to do a lot more than that.

"You want that cup of coffee now?" Jaxson asked huskily. "I'm sure you could use a warm-up."

"No," she said, some part of her still sane. Still rational. Shaking her head and backing away from his hand, she pulled on Hamlet's leash. "Bakery hours are awful early. I need to get to bed."

Which was a lie; she didn't work on the weekends. Holli, a high school student, picked up all of those hours. But she needed something to protect herself, even if it was a small white lie.

She spun around, half walking, half jogging away from Jaxson. Away from temptation. Away from the pain that lay in choosing to be with someone.

CHAPTER 10

JAXSON

J AXSON STARED AT THE LIST in front of him. Hydrants with low pressure, or no pressure, or too much pressure that blew out fire hoses and caused damage…they all made the list. In comparison, the list of fully functioning hydrants around the city was…depressingly small.

Of course, it was all hearsay, based on what Levi told him. Fire hydrants couldn't exactly be tested in the dead of winter. Shooting streams of water out into the street so he could turn everything into an ice skating rink didn't seem like a great way to ingratiate himself with the locals.

And if there was one thing he needed help on, it was definitely befriending the locals. Moose, Dylan, and a few of the others were friendly enough, and after spending two days driving around town with Levi playing tour guide/hydrant inspector, Jaxson felt fairly confident that at least Levi was firmly on his side.

But the rest of the firefighters and townspeople…Jaxson just wasn't sure what to think about them, or what they thought about him. Probably nothing positive.

With a groan, he stood up. He was sick of going in circles in his head. He was a doer, not a thinker. If he didn't do *something* soon, he'd go stir-crazy.

With a half-formed idea swirling around in his mind, he headed for the door, credit card in hand. It was time to go shopping.

HE DROPPED the bags into the passenger seat and walked around to the driver's side, sliding in and consulting the map in front of him. *Hmmmm…*Since he was parked in front of the hardware store, that meant that the closest hydrant was just up the block.

Directly in front of the Muffin Man Bakery.

He ground his teeth in frustration. *Dammit!* He'd been doing a fine job of avoiding Sugar *and* the Muffin Man since she'd practically taken off running last week. It was hard not to take it personally when a girl was so intent on getting away, she ran like the hounds of hell were nipping at her heels.

It wasn't exactly good for a man's ego, that was for certain.

Well, he might as well start there first and get it over with. With any luck, she would stay inside and he'd stay outside and they could pretend the other one didn't exist. It was either that or march inside and demand to find out what the hell was going on in that head of hers.

He wasn't entirely sure that was a grand idea. He was real tempted to use some choice words as part of that questioning, and even he knew that wouldn't help.

He pulled his SUV forward a block and then began the preparations, laying out tarps to protect the ground and grabbing a few loose bricks piled against the storefront to hold the tarps down in the winter wind. It was miserable work, but he knew that if he didn't make sure to protect the sidewalk and benches, there'd be hell to pay for it, and rightly so. No one wanted black streaks of spray paint all over everything.

As Jaxson worked, he heard the bell above the bakery door tinkle, and then a whoosh of warm, wonderful smelling air washed over him. He stiffened even as he breathed in deep. That smell was the smell of heaven on earth…

And Sugar was the devil here to tempt him.

He turned, a smile shoved into place, when he saw it was Gage standing there, two cups of coffee in his hands.

"Thought you might want a little somethin' to warm you up," Gage said, holding one of the cups out.

Jaxson felt his shoulders relax as he sent Gage a real smile. "Thanks, man. I really appreciate it." He cupped his hands around the to-go cup, sipping at the warmth and letting it run through him. Oh, that felt good.

"What's up with the black spray paint?" Gage asked, jerking his head towards the pile stacked around the hydrant.

"This hydrant doesn't work," Jaxson said ruefully. "Honestly, half the hydrants in town don't work right. Too much pressure, not enough pressure, no pressure at all…It's the Goldilocks story of hydrants, except the ones that are just right are few and far between."

Gage cocked an eyebrow at him. "You trying to say that if my bakery caught fire, you wouldn't be able to use this here hydrant to put it out?"

"Yup, I'm saying exactly that. So do your best not to burn down your bakery before spring hits."

"Damn, there goes my plans for next week," Gage said dryly.

They both chuckled quietly as they stared at the worthless hydrant in front of them.

"I have to say, that makes me a bit twitchy," Gage finally said, taking another sip of his coffee. "You say most of the hydrants in town are dead?"

"About half have some sort of problem. Now, this is all based on hearsay, but it was Levi telling me, so I don't have any reason not to believe him. I can't test them myself till spring comes. Opening up a fire hydrant and spraying down Main Street, turning it into one big ice skating rink…Well, I think that sounds like more fun than it really would be. Especially when people came after me with pitchforks."

"Sounds like you already know Sawyer," Gage said with a small laugh. "Truth be told, I'm still learning my way around it. My grandparents started this bakery; it was the Dyer's Bakery before I took over. I was the only one in the family who wanted it. I graduated high school the day before my dad retired from the Marines. He moved our family back here to Long Valley while I took off for culinary school. I'd only visited Sawyer during the summer and holidays until my grandparents retired and sold the bakery to me. Suddenly, I was living here full-time and dealing with all of the bullshit that comes from living in a town where everyone knows your name, *and* your business. I will say this about Sawyerites – if they don't like you, they don't pretend otherwise. They'll tell you that you're an awful son of a bitch to your face."

Jaxson grimaced, remembering over the past couple of weeks. It was true that James and Robert hadn't exactly tried to hide their disdain for him. Didn't really make it easier to like 'em, though.

He shivered so hard from the frigid air whistling down the street, he scalded his bare hand with the piping hot coffee. "Shit!" he exclaimed, trying to suck the hot liquid off the back of his hand.

"Come on in. Might as well clean up in the bathroom and warm up a bit before you start into your painting project."

Jaxson looked down at the worthless hydrant and then back up at Gage.

It wasn't a real tough choice.

"Much obliged," he said.

They hurried into the warmth of the bakery. Prickles of heat shot through him, and Jaxson shivered again. He was gonna need to up his winter gear at this rate. Boise's winters just weren't as severe as Long Valley's. Even his warmest jacket and socks weren't cutting it.

"Oh, there you are!" Sugar said to Gage. "I'd wondered where—"

Jaxson looked up and their gazes caught. She sputtered to a stop, just staring at him, her chocolate eyes seemingly swallowing up her whole face.

Gage cleared his throat, mumbled something about his mixer needing cleaned, and disappeared into the back. Not exactly subtle, but Jaxson appreciated it all the same. He wasn't looking forward to the conversation ahead, and he sure as hell didn't want an audience for it.

CHAPTER II

SUGAR

S UGAR WASN'T QUITE SURE she was breathing right. After three days of jumping every time the bell over the door jingled, here was Jaxson. In the flesh. Staring right at her.

She gulped.

She'd spent since last Friday debating whether she'd been an idiot or a genius for running away. Because that was the only thing she could truthfully call it – she'd quite literally run from Jaxson, and more specifically, the desire in his eyes. She'd been afraid of that desire. Still was. Nothing good could come from it, and yet…

She walked around the counter, telling herself not to but her feet were moving anyway and then she was standing in front of the display case, staring up at Jaxson.

Like most men who were not midgets, he was much taller than her, and she had to crane her neck to meet his gaze. For the 4,278th time in her life, she cursed her parents, both of whom were on the short side of the measuring stick. She'd really had no hope of growing to a decent height, but even still, she couldn't say that she was thrilled that she'd only made it to a paltry 5'3"...and a *half*, when she was feeling particularly picky.

Which was most days.

She stared up at him. He stared back. Finally, he raised a to-go cup up in the air. "Gage was just tryin' to help me warm up," he said. "Mite bit chilly out there."

"It's a warm day for January," Sugar protested. It'd even gotten up past freezing at one point, although the light was fading fast and the thermometer was no doubt going to begin to drop like a stone.

"Standing outside in it, I beg to differ. Some things in this valley are *real* cold."

Her breath caught as he towered over her, glaring down. She had the sneaking suspicion that they weren't talking about coffee *or* the weather any longer.

He moved closer. Her neck craned up more. "Why did you run away the other night?" he asked. He set his coffee cup down on a nearby table and used his free hands to pull her up against him.

She struggled against him, resisting and fighting to break free.

Okay, fine, that was a lie.

She *wanted* to resist his pull, but didn't. She knew she should, but...somehow couldn't. She snuggled up against him instead, cradled in his arms. "I...I can't date someone," she told him breathlessly, every part of her burning that touched him. "Even fire chiefs."

He cracked a smile at that. "No exceptions even for fire chiefs, eh?" he said so softly, she probably wouldn't have heard him if his mouth wasn't inches away from hers.

Which really it shouldn't be and she was going to stop all this real soon. Any minute now.

Just not this very second.

She shook her head. "No exceptions," she whispered back.

"Funny, I have the same rule," he breathed.

"You can't date fire chiefs?" she said with a breathy laugh.

His eyes darkened with desire. "No room in my life for a girlfriend."

"Well, at least we're on the same page," she murmured, as his mouth swooped down to cover hers. She shivered as he pulled her hungrily towards him, his mouth and tongue working in concert to drive her crazy with desire. Some part of her brain was screaming for her to stop, but it was getting drowned out by the much louder part of her brain that was applauding every moment.

She ran her hands up his arms and across his shoulders as she groaned. She'd stopped being able to breathe years ago, it seemed, and yet, she wasn't missing the oxygen. She just wanted Jaxson. Nothing existed in the world except them.

He pulled back just a tiny bit, until only a piece of paper could slip between their lips, but not two.

"I've been thinking about this problem of ours," he whispered, as he began to kiss his way across her cheek and over to her ear. He nibbled on her earlobe as he murmured, "I think we ought to be friends. With benefits." He sucked her earlobe into his mouth and she felt a jolt of electricity shoot through her, setting her body on fire. She moaned.

"Real good friends, with *lots* of benefits," he whispered as he began pressing kisses against her jaw, his tongue flicking out and setting her skin ablaze as he kissed his way down her neck.

"I like...friends..." she gasped. "A girl...always needs...friends."

He pulled away and smiled down at her, his eyes lit up with passion and desire. "I like how you think," he growled.

Then he was dropping his hands and moving away towards the door. She stumbled and grabbed onto the back of one of the chairs, holding herself up as she watched him walk away.

"Best get back to work," he said over his shoulder, and then he was disappearing outside, the bell jingling overhead as he left her alone to stare after him.

CHAPTER 12

JAXSON

"W E'VE GOT TO GO AFTER ANGUS," Jaxson said bluntly, staring at the chief of police, the muscle in his jaw twitching sporadically. "I don't care if he *is* the mayor's son. Smoking before school is one thing. Smoking before school and setting fire to a local historical landmark is quite another."

The police chief laughed. "Listen, you're new here, and by all accounts, you aren't gonna last long anyway." Jaxson's spine stiffened so fast, he may've given himself whiplash. At the look on Jaxson's face, the police chief raised his hands in surrender. "Don't get all pissy with me. I'm just saying things the way they are, and one of those things is, you don't go 'round, arresting the mayor's son. Not if you still want a job next week. I happen to like my job, and screwing it all up to prove a point ain't gonna happen. That's a hill I ain't gonna die on."

"The thing is, Chief, people are blaming *me* for that damn fire, that I didn't put it out and instead watched it burn. You know that the hydrant didn't work and that's why I didn't do anything, but most people aren't getting the full story. If we charge the kid for smoking, maybe people will stop paying so much attention to what I did and did not do, and more attention to what the mayor's son did. If something doesn't change and soon, you're right, I won't have a job much longer."

He felt the panic build inside of him at the thought. It'd only been a couple of weeks since he'd started as fire chief. It was still half a year until the family court judge would hear his case again. He couldn't get fired. He couldn't let Kendra win.

He couldn't give up his boys.

"Well now, I don't see as how that's my problem," the police chief said, rocking back on his heels. "The mayor's my boss. He's your boss. I don't think endearing myself to him by arresting his only son is gonna be my smartest move."

"I don't give a *damn* what you think!" Jaxson shouted, slamming his hand down on the chief's desk. "You've got to do your job – *that's* what I think! And arresting underage kids for smoking a cigarette before school and causing massive property damage to a historical landmark in town is most definitely your job." He was breathing heavily by the time he was done, glaring at the chief, wishing that somehow, looks really could kill.

"Listen, kid," said the pot-bellied chief, hooking his thumbs into the belt loops of his jeans, "you're already in a heap of trouble in this town. Not only did you stand around and do piss-all to put out the mill fire, you've also been painting hydrants around town every color under the sun—"

"Each color means somethin'!" Jaxson burst in. "I'm not just picking random colors 'cause I think they're pretty! Black means—"

"All I know," the chief said, steamrolling right over him, "is that we here don't like our hydrants painted anything but red. A hydrant is supposed to be red, dammit. I don't know how y'all do it in your big city with your fancy rules, but here, a hydrant is fire-engine red. End of story.

"Also," he stood up a little more and glowered down at Jaxson, "you don't go around kissin' other men's girls."

"I'm sorry, *what*?" Jaxson stared at the chief, completely confused. He'd only kissed one girl since he came into town, and that was Sugar. She sure as hell wasn't somebody else's "girl."

"Sugar Stonemyer down at the bakery. Everyone knows that she's sleeping with Gage. You were kissing her last night. I wouldn't be surprised if Gage chose to rearrange a few of your teeth and frankly, I'm not sure if I could arrest him for it. A guy moving in on another guy's territory…well, it just ain't right."

"Sugar? Gage?" Jaxson stared at the chief wide-eyed, his mind spinning. That couldn't be right. Why would Gage leave them alone to talk if he were dating Sugar? Why wouldn't he have said anything to him? "Hold on a moment, how do you know I was kissin' Sugar?" Jaxson blurted out.

"The whole front of that bakery is nothin' but glass," the chief said with a shrug. "I think if Sugar sneezes, most of the town knows by noon. That's how we know they're datin'. I've seen 'em going at it more than once when I've driven by on patrol."

Jaxson staggered back, staring at the chief. He couldn't breathe. He couldn't think. He had to go.

He nodded once, then spun on his heel and headed for the door. He had to talk to Sugar. He had to talk to her *right now*. He felt the anger rolling off him in waves, although truth be told, he wasn't real sure why, because dammit all, they were just friends with benefits. The "benefits" thus far had only been a kiss in the bakery, but why the hell would she even want that if she and Gage were dating? Was Gage not man enough for her? Was she lookin' for more? Did Gage know?

His mind spun with questions that had no answers.

The chief may be wrong about a lot of things, but he was right about this. Movin' in on her, even if it was just as friends with benefits, wasn't right. Not if she was with Gage.

He slammed his way into his SUV and threw it in reverse, tires spinning on the snow and ice before gaining traction and shooting him backwards into the street.

None of it made any sense, and Jaxson was gonna find out the truth if he had to shake it out of Sugar.

CHAPTER 13
SUGAR

SUGAR SHIFTED FROM one foot to the other, smiling gamely at Mrs. Gehring as the elderly lady dithered over the choices. "Well now, I just don't know if I want another jelly donut or a cinnamon-and-sugar donut," she said, patting at her perfectly coiffed gray hair in distress. "They're both so good."

"You could always get one of each," Sugar suggested, putting a little extra oomph into her smile. It was either that, or jump over the counter and strangle the genteel older woman.

"Oh no, I couldn't do that," Mrs. Gehring protested. "I've got to watch my figure, you know." She patted her painfully thin waist with a little smile. "A girl can't lose her figure. Why, the men stop paying attention to you then!" She let out a cackling laugh, which made Sugar snort with laughter. Mrs. Gehring had to be pushing 90. Her husband had died years ago, and Mrs. Gehring had made it clear after his passing that she wasn't going to settle down with just one man after that. She was happy to play the field, and she played it well.

Just then, Sugar felt the hair on the back of her neck prickle. Like what happened when she was scared and creeped out while watching a horror flick, but this time, it was a good prickle. Which she didn't even know could happen, but there it was all the same. Her eyes shot up as the doorbell jingled and her gaze caught Jaxson's as he walked in. Like touching a live wire, her whole body lit up and her breath caught in her throat.

"Like that new fire chief fella that you've been kissing," Mrs. Gehring continued on, still studying the donuts in front of her intently. "He's a handsome one."

Sugar flushed a brilliant red as her gaze volleyed back and forth between Mrs. Gehring and Jaxson. *Please, don't let him know what she's saying. Please, let him be suddenly deaf and dumb.*

As she watched, a laughing grin spread over Jaxson's face.

He had not, in fact, gone deaf or dumb in the last 20 seconds.

Argh!

Sugar's face flamed an even more brilliant red, which she also didn't know could happen. *Dammit all to hell and back.* He probably thought that she'd been the one to bring his name up with Mrs. Gehring and had been drooling all over him while doing it (figuratively speaking, of course), and how exactly was she supposed to explain to him that she hadn't done any of that, without being inexcusably rude in the process?

"A maple bar," Mrs. Gehring said decisively. "I'll take a maple bar."

Sugar quickly bagged the donut, deciding to ignore the fact that a maple bar hadn't even been one of the choices Mrs. Gehring had been debating. She'd finally chosen something, and for that, Sugar was grateful. Maybe Mrs. Gehring would leave, the earth would open up and swallow the city of Sawyer whole, and then Sugar wouldn't have to talk to Jaxson ever again.

It could happen. It could *totally* happen.

Mrs. Gehring slid the money across the counter to her. "Good luck with your beau," she said in a stage whisper, loud enough for someone in the next county over to hear.

"Ummm…thanks," Sugar whispered back, a painful smile glued to her face.

She was pretty sure that the space under the counter wasn't big enough to actually crawl into and die, but that didn't keep her from wanting to try.

Mrs. Gehring turned to head out, cane in one hand and her donut in the other, when she spotted Jaxson. Her spine stiffened in surprise with a crack of old bones that made Sugar wince in sympathy, and then she began slowly making her way towards the door as if nothing had happened. She nodded her head regally in greeting as she passed Jaxson, and then ruined the effect by leaning over and whispering conspiratorially, "Good luck with your sweetheart." That time, Sugar would swear she was loud enough for *all* the world to hear.

Both of them watched Mrs. Gehring walk out the door, the bell jingling merrily behind her. Sugar hoisted a smile back onto her face. "How are you this morning?" she asked Jaxson casually. Yeah, she was cool. No awkwardness here.

None whatsoever.

Jaxson's smile for Mrs. Gehring slipped into a scowl as he stared at Sugar. "So I was down at the police station and talking to the chief about Angus setting fire to the mill."

Sugar nodded as she listened, a bit confused about where this was going. He seemed agitated, angry even, but it seemed directed at her, and that just did *not* make sense. She'd had nothing to do with that fire. He knew that.

Jaxson continued, "So while I'm there, the chief tells me that I'm making an ass out of myself by hitting on a girl who's already dating someone else. Is that true? Are you and Gage dating?"

Sugar's mouth gaped open in shock. "Now hold on a moment here, how did he know you were hitting on me?" she demanded. Which now that she thought about it, how did Mrs. Gehring know they'd been kissing? She'd been so embarrassed while Mrs. Gehring had been talking, it hadn't occurred to her to ask, but she was asking now.

"That was my question, too," Jaxson said, disgruntled. "Apparently, the next time we choose to make out, the bakery is not the place to do it."

At that, their gazes shot over to the huge plate glass windows lining the front of the bakery, and then back to each other.

Whoops. Well, shit. That was stupid, Sugar.

Dammit all, she could berate herself on the intricacies of dating – or not, as the case may be – in a small town later. For now, she was crossing her arms and glaring at Jaxson. She wasn't about to give an inch. "Well, I'm not dating Gage," she informed him tartly. "He's my boss, and he's my best friend's older brother, and he's even my friend, but he's *not* my boyfriend."

"Shit, Sugar!" Jaxson growled. "The police chief was real sure about this. Why would he lie?"

"Because the police chief is a gossiping old man who has nothing better to do with his time," Sugar shot back, "since he sure as hell isn't arresting people who're burning down old mills!"

"And he's prone to seeing things, too?" Jaxson retorted. "He said he watched you two make out plenty of times as he's driven by on patrol. He doesn't strike me as someone who sees shit that plain isn't there."

Sugar felt Gage at her elbow just as he spoke up quietly but forcefully. "Sugar and I aren't dating, Jaxson. We never have, and we sure as hell haven't kissed. I think that rumor is the product of the fevered imagination of a whole lot of people in this town. People just don't seem to believe that you can be simply friends with a member of the opposite sex."

Jaxson and Gage stared at each other for a few long moments, and then Jaxson slowly nodded. "I haven't been here very long and I can already see that," he acknowledged grudgingly.

"Now hold on just a moment here!" Sugar exclaimed, jamming her hands onto her hips and glaring up at Jaxson. "I tell you something and you don't believe me, and then Gage here tells you the exact same thing and finally, it's true? What, you only believe people with *dicks*?" That last part may or may not have come out in a half-shout. Sugar felt the color rising in her cheeks again, but this time, it was from anger, not embarrassment.

"I—" Jaxson started when Gage interrupted them with a fierce whisper.

"I think you two outta take this outside to discuss it further. In fact, Sugar, go home for the night. It's close to closing time anyway. You two need to discuss things, *minus* an attentive audience."

Sugar looked up to find half the bakery quickly looking away guiltily, while the other half were still openly staring at them, not embarrassed at all to be caught in the act. The bakery was quiet enough to hear a pin drop.

This discussion of theirs was gonna be all over town by morning, and it'd only take that long because of the shitty weather.

Sugar groaned, burying her face in her hands. She contemplated crawling under the counter again. It was stuffed full of straws, to-go boxes, and napkins, but right then, Sugar didn't care. She wanted to be anywhere but there. With a sigh, she jerked her head once in acknowledgment of Gage's advice, spun on her heel, and headed to the back to grab her jacket.

She jerked it on angrily, storming back up to the front as she announced to Gage, "I'm leaving. I'll be back tomorrow." She wasn't quite sure why she felt compelled to tell him that, other than to feel like she had some semblance of control over the situation.

She stalked out past the counter and the gawking stares,

and through the front door. Jaxson followed on her heels and they stomped down the sidewalk, side by side, both angry, and neither one saying a word.

"I—" they both said at the same time. Sugar blew out a breath in frustration.

"You go first," Jaxson said graciously.

Sugar wasn't about to lose her chance to talk, and let loose on him. "Why is it that you believed Gage and not me? I've had it up to here—" she gestured above her head, "—with men only listening to other men, like women don't matter." She folded her arms defiantly across her chest as she waited for his response, stomping down the street through the snow.

He grabbed her arm and spun her to a stop. "I – I'm sorry," he said softly. "It wasn't the fact that Gage owns a dick that made me listen to him."

The edges of Sugar's lips turned up momentarily at that. She was pretty sure the people of Sawyer were not going to let her forget that particular turn of phrase anytime soon.

"It was just...I guess it was hearing it from a second person, owner of a dick or not." They began to wander again down the street, this time at a more leisurely pace. "I know I have no right to say anything at all. We had agreed to just be friends with benefits, although, I'm putting this out there – one kiss does not equal a true *ahem* benefit in my mind." She laughed a bit at that as he continued, "Anyway, I don't know what came over me, honestly."

He heaved a sigh, and she could tell he was debating what to say, and what to leave out. She kept quiet, giving him the space to think things through.

Finally, he said quietly, "I should probably tell you that Kendra and I got a divorce because..." He sighed and then plunged in, "I came home early one day and found her in bed with our neighbor, Ivan. I'd thought something was going on between them for months, but she'd always denied it so believably, she made me feel like I was just seeing things;

making up stories to make her feel bad. That is, until I caught them, of course. There wasn't much point in denials then. I guess I'm just a bit more touchy on that topic than I realized I would be. Even if I have no right to be when it comes to you."

They stopped for a moment in front of the hardware store and Sugar stared sightlessly at the display in the window as she said softly, "That makes sense. People have been thinking for a long time that Gage and I have been dating, so I shouldn't have been surprised that the rumor made its way to you. Honestly, his sister pushed it more than anyone else. She had me convinced that Gage was desperately in love with me, and I was damn worried that she was right. I just don't see him that way," she said with a shrug. "I've tried, but…he's like the older brother I never had, you know?"

They began to wander down the street again when Sugar blurted out, "It's the flour."

"Flour?" Jaxson repeated blankly.

"I was thinking about it the other day and realized that it was the flour," she said with a firm nod. "He's the messiest baker I know. He spreads flour around like he's a damn fairy with fairy dust or something. It's hard to be attracted to someone who perpetually has a streak of white across his nose."

"What about charcoal from a fire?" Jaxson asked her softly as they came to a stop in front of her apartment.

"Well, I just don't know," she said teasingly. "I guess I'll just have to find out, won't I?" She opened up her front door to the joyous greeting of Hamlet.

Jaxson looked around, surprised. "Hold on, we're at your apartment?" he asked.

"Where did you think we were going?" Sugar asked, laughing, as she knelt to give Hamlet a big belly rub and chin scratch. He rolled over onto his back, growling in pleasure.

"Your car? I guess? I wasn't paying much attention, I suppose. Did we leave your car back at the bakery?"

Sugar shot him a grin as she continued to love on Hamlet. It was her favorite time of the day, and she was pretty sure it was Hamlet's, also. "No. I walk to work."

"Even in a blizzard?"

"*Especially* in a blizzard. Driving on snow and ice is a real pain, even more so because I only have to go a few blocks. It's easier to walk than it is to scrape off a car every morning, especially as early as I have to leave."

She got to her feet and Hamlet sprung up beside her and headed over to Jaxson for some lovin'. *Traitor.* She ignored that for a moment. "It's dog walking time. Want to head out with me?"

He hesitated for a long moment, and she started to panic. After the disaster that was their bakery discussion, he probably wanted nothing more to do with her. She hurried on before he could bluntly tell her that. "You don't have to, actually. It's pretty cold out there. I just thought I'd ask. No worries, truly. I'm just gonna bundle up a little more and then head out, so I guess I'll just see you arou—"

"It's all right!" he exclaimed with a small laugh. She sputtered to a stop. "Really, I'd love to. I was just trying to decide if I'm dressed warm enough or not. I got pretty cold just walking from the bakery to here."

"Oh. Right. Of course." She shot him a smile, trying to hide her unease.

It wasn't that she didn't like being around Jaxson. Quite the opposite, and that was the cause of her distress. The last time she'd liked being around a guy – well, she'd been branded as a whore and forced to marry him.

It did tend to make a person a little jumpy about trying it a second time, that was for sure. Even with someone as sexy-as-sin as Jaxson Anderson was.

Especially with someone as sexy-as-sin as Jaxson Anderson was.

CHAPTER 14

JAXSON

H E WALKED NEXT TO SUGAR as they headed for the city park again, her shoulders hunched against the biting wind as Hamlet trotted just ahead, his golden coat bright against the gray slushy snow and gray sky. His tail wagged with every step as he looked around, alert for any intruders into his domain.

Of course, Hamlet was so damn big, Jaxson wasn't sure any intruders would dare challenge him. It was a good thing Hamlet had a gentle soul. He was so gigantic, Jaxson was pretty sure he'd get knocked flat on his back if Hamlet chose to jump up on him. Turns out, his first thought upon seeing Hamlet – that Sugar was walking a miniature horse – really wasn't that far off the mark.

Jaxson's mind wandered back to what he'd told Sugar on the way to her apartment. As much as he didn't want to, he should tell her everything. He'd left out a few key details that she should know before she could make an informed decision about having a relationship with him of *any* kind, even the friendship kind.

It was only fair, even if the thought sort of – okay, totally and completely – terrified him.

They reached the edge of the park, lit up by street lamps and the fading sunlight from the setting sun. Sugar unclipped Hamlet's leash, pulled the well-worn tennis ball out of her pocket, and threw it as hard as she could across the park. Hamlet went bounding after it, chunks of ice and snow flying as he ran. They both laughed quietly; Hamlet chasing a ball was the very textbook definition of excitement and happiness.

"Sugar…that wasn't all that happened that night," Jaxson said quietly into the still of the evening. A car passed the park, the headlights catching the auburn streaks in Sugar's hair and then they were past and Sugar's face was in shadows once again.

As Jaxson stared down at her, he realized that this somehow made it easier to talk to her. If he couldn't see her huge brown eyes or the way she bit her full bottom lip when she was thinking, well then, he could pretend that he was just talking to a tree.

A very short tree.

A very short tree wearing the perfume of baked bread and glazed sugar.

Then she slipped her hand into his and squeezed, saying without words that she was listening, and that movement broke the short-tree illusion he'd been trying to sell himself on, but the comfort of her hand squeeze somehow made up for it anyway. She pulled her hand free to throw for Hamlet again, the dog's huge body streaking away in the dim lighting, and Jaxson found himself wishing for her hand back.

Instead, he made himself talk. The sooner he told her everything, the sooner he could put this behind him and pretend it never happened.

"I'd known for a while that Kendra wasn't happy," he started. "She's not exactly a subtle person, and she'd made it known that I wasn't there for her the way she wanted me to be."

He looked up into the dark blue sky, rolling his head from

side to side as he studied the barren tree branches stretching up into the evening sky, trying to catch the sparkling stars but never reaching quite high enough.

"She wanted to date a firefighter. That's sexy and dangerous and exciting. We'd only dated three months before we decided to get married. I'd really thought she was the one for me. Now, I realize that it was just hormones talking. I'd never had someone in my bed who was quite as…adventurous as she was. I saw what I wanted to see, and she saw what she wanted to see.

"Neither of us saw the truth.

"We'd only been married a month and already, we'd begun fighting almost daily. She didn't like me being on call all the time; being pulled away from date nights and family dinners on a moment's notice. She didn't like me sleeping at the firehouse for 24 hours at a time. She liked the danger I was in, in theory. Not so much in practice."

The evening light was completely gone now, but along with its disappearance, the wind died away, too. Strangely, despite it being pitch black except for the street lamps lining the edge of the park, it felt warmer than it had all day. Sugar threw the ball again and then looked up at Jaxson quietly, waiting for him to talk it all out. He could hardly make out her face in the semi-darkness, and was glad for it.

She was back to being a very short, amazing-smelling tree, thank God. It was safer that way.

"Then, she announced she was pregnant with Aiden, and I tried to be excited about it. I'm one of those rare guys who actually wants kids of my own. My marriage wasn't working out the way I thought it would, but I could still raise a child to be good and kind and help others, like I do when I go out to a fire. Our second boy, on the other hand, was a *complete* oops – the product of a makeup session fueled by alcohol, and so condoms didn't occur to us. I was even less thrilled with Frankie than I was with Aiden, but as soon as he arrived, squalling and face all red and fists balled up, I just fell in love with him. Newborn babies are some of the ugliest creatures on the planet—" Sugar let out a little chuckle at that, and Jaxson smiled as he continued, "—but you somehow love them even more because of that. Don't ask. Parenthood makes no sense."

She let out a full-throated laugh at that, and he pulled her up to him, wrapping his arms around her as she buried her face against his chest. The world felt so right in that moment, and he was about to destroy all of that, but he had to, and so he kept going, because he had to.

Because he must.

"But that night...*the* night...I'd arranged for another firefighter to cover the last of my shift, and arranged for a babysitter to come watch the boys. I was going to take Kendra out for a night on the town. Try to bring that spark back that'd gone missing years earlier."

"You're a firefighter," Sugar murmured against his chest. "You're supposed to be putting flames out, not lighting them." Sugar said it so deadpan, it took Jaxson a moment to register what she'd said.

He let out a belly laugh and said dryly, "Well, if I was an arsonist, I'd have even more job security."

"That's true! Hmmm...don't know what I was thinking."

He snuggled her tighter against him as Hamlet rested by their side for a minute, his panting and Sugar's breathing the only noise in the world at that moment.

"When I came home, the boys were sitting in front of the TV, watching some Disney channel show, and I asked them where Mom was. Aiden had a funny look on his face, but he told me up in our room and so I snuck up the stairs, trying to surprise her. When I saw them in bed together...well, let's just say that the surprise part was accomplished. I couldn't believe she'd been lying to me for months; that she was cheating on me; but most of all, that she'd do it with the kids in the house. She'd been telling the boys that she and the neighbor were planning a big secret party for me, so they shouldn't tell me that the neighbor had been over at the house, or that'd ruin it all.

"It'd been a well-kept secret, all right, although I can't say I exactly enjoyed the party."

His bitter words drifted out into the dark of the night and he just stood there, running his hands up and down Sugar's back as he stared unseeingly into the darkness. He felt her shiver, which yanked him out of his reverie. Wow, he was such a jackass; here he was, freezing her to death while he whined and complained about his ex.

He jerked back. "I'll take you home now," he said gruffly. The spell was broken. It no longer seemed like a good idea to finish the story. He didn't know what he'd been thinking. He didn't want to admit that he wasn't a good guy after all. He liked to think of himself that way, but he knew the truth, even if he didn't admit it to others, and certainly not to Sugar.

He quickly began walking back towards her apartment, away from her, away from the embarrassment of it all, until she grabbed his arm and pulled him to a stop. "I'm gonna make a guess," she said quietly, "that you've never told anyone else this story. Am I right?"

He stared off into the distance above her head, unwilling – unable – to look her in the eye as he jerked his head once in acknowledgement of her comment. "No one." The words were so soft, he could hardly hear them himself, but she understood them anyway.

"Then I'm honored that you've chosen to tell me. I've done some things that I'm not proud of. I'm not gonna judge you, I promise."

Jaxson let out a snort of disbelief. If Sugar had done anything more awful than kill a spider, he'd eat his shorts.

She didn't respond to his snort, but instead just stood there, her hand on his arm, waiting for him to speak.

He didn't know Sugar well; it wasn't like they'd been

dating for years, or even at all, really. But somehow, his gut told him that she could out-wait him – that if he didn't start talking, they'd still be standing still as statues on the edge of the park come morning.

He stared out into the darkness, willing his lips and tongue and lungs to do what he never wanted to do – talk about that night.

"I was angry when I found them. That sounds so blasé – people get angry all the time. Yell a little. Stomp around some. It wasn't like that. I was so mad, there was this film of red that covered the world. I could hardly see straight. I was operating purely on instinct. I picked Ivan up, who was a little larger than me, and tossed him out of the bed. He flew across the room and hit the wall, knocking a hole in the drywall. I hadn't even meant to throw him that hard. I was just trying to get him out of the way. I wanted to reach my wife. I wanted to hit her. To hurt her as much as she'd hurt me.

"A tiny part of my brain heard the neighbor on the phone, calling 911, but it didn't register. Looking back, there's this filmy haze over everything, like trying to remember a dream when you wake up the next day. I couldn't see, I couldn't think, I only wanted to hurt."

He pulled Sugar into his arms again, needing her warm, slim, calming presence against him, to help him make it through this. She slipped into his arms as if she were meant to live there, as if she'd always been there, and leaned her cheek against his chest. Hamlet settled down at their feet, curling up around them, sharing the warmth. A small part of Jaxson knew that they should go indoors to finish this conversation, but he instinctively rebelled against that thought. If they were inside, then he'd be looking at Sugar as he talked, and then…

He wouldn't talk at all. He knew it. There was no question in his mind about that fact.

This had to be done before he could wimp out.

"I'm crawling across the bed to get to my wife, to punch her or strangle her or something, I don't know, I didn't really have a plan in mind, and then…" He let out a shuddering sigh. "I heard my boys. They'd overheard the ruckus and had come running upstairs to see what was going on. It was quite the sight, I'm sure. The naked neighbor, slumped up against the wall, pleading with dispatch to hurry. My equally naked wife, clutching the sheets up tight, screaming at me – I still don't know what she was saying. I just saw her mouth move.

"And then me. There I am, about to murder their mom."

He let out a guttural laugh of pain and anger and hatred and surprise, but no humor.

There was nothing funny about this story.

"My boys saved me. They saved me from jail time, from the damn electric chair. If they hadn't shown up just then, Aiden shouting for me to stop, Frankie crying…I can't think about it. I just can't.

"The cops finally arrived but I was lucky, because the only person I'd even touched was the neighbor, and my wife – who was still in shock at the time – told him that under the circumstances, he probably shouldn't press charges. So nothing really happened, except it all got back to my chief at the fire station. I got pulled in and given a stern talking to about the proper behavior of firefighters. Part of being a public servant is that even private disputes aren't private. If I pulled another stunt like that, they'd start the proceedings to get me fired.

"Meanwhile, my wife quickly got over her shock and used that whole scene during the divorce proceedings to paint me as a violent man who couldn't be trusted; that I might harm or even kill one of my boys if left alone with them. She also emphasized how I was called out a lot, and how active the Boise Fire Department was. Basically, I wasn't a fit parent. The fact that she was screwing the neighbor, who was a drunk, while the kids were downstairs, and then asking them to lie about it to me…that didn't seem to matter much.

"Finally, the judge told me that I needed to get a more

stable job that would take me away from the kids less often, and that I needed to take anger management classes. I signed up for the classes that day, and started looking for a new job that night. I wasn't about to screw around with this. These are my boys. I love them more than life itself. I wouldn't harm a hair on their head for all the money in the world, and Kendra knows that. But that doesn't play well in court for her, so she conveniently forgets it every time we step into the courtroom. If she had her way, she'd get a check in the mail each month, and I'd never see Aiden and Frankie again.

"So I'm not going to let her have her way. I won't give them up. Not ever."

The conviction in his voice rang out strong and true. He may sometimes wonder if he really was the good guy that he liked to think of himself as being, but he never questioned being a good father, or how much he loved his boys. That was beyond reproach. Beyond doubt.

"All of that to say," he said with a small laugh, "that the idea of someone cheating is…a rough topic for me. There's a lot of things that I'd be just fine with, or at least calm about, but cheating ain't one of 'em."

Sugar mumbled something against his chest that he didn't quite catch. "Come again?" he said.

She pulled back with an exasperated sigh. "For a guy who only wants to be friends with benefits, you sure are possessive," she informed him. "That is, unless you've changed your mind?"

The words hung between them in the crystal cold air.

CHAPTER 15

SUGAR

S HE STARED UP AT HIM, her gaze steely-eyed even as her heart raced. She couldn't believe she'd actually had the balls to say that out loud to him. She hadn't meant to – it'd just slipped out, and then he'd wanted her to repeat it and she'd actually had the guts to say it *twice*.

Which was probably more surprising to her than it was to him. Jaxson didn't know that she'd gotten this far in life by being the most agreeable person in the room; by never causing waves, no matter the situation. The fact that she was trying to change this about herself didn't mean that the change was easy; only that she realized that she needed to try.

Although why she started with this particular topic was a mystery, even to her. As she stared up into his face, worrying her bottom lip as she waited for a response, she began to question her life choices. She shouldn't have said anything. It was a dumb comment to make. Why, he probably—

"Oohh!" she half shouted, getting dragged sideways by Hamlet. He'd apparently decided that he was done waiting for them to be ready to go home, and was going to take them there himself, whether or not they wanted to go. She stumbled for a few feet, finally regaining her footing and pulling her Dane to a stop. "You goofball," she said affectionately, patting his massive head. He wagged his tail, tongue lolling out of his mouth happily. "You could warn a girl before you take off walking, you know."

They started off, together this time, down the street towards her apartment and warmth and light. She didn't say anything, even as Jaxson took her hand and held it as they walked. It was a very un-friendlike thing to do, but since she was enjoying it, she wasn't about to complain.

It took another block before Jaxson broke the silence. "I think we oughta just stay friends," he announced. "There's a lot going on in my life, and you say that dating isn't a good idea for you either, so…friends with benefits it is. If you're okay with that." He pulled her to a stop and looked down at her, the street lamp throwing his face into shadows and light, his eyes dark and burning as they peered into her soul.

She didn't know what she'd wanted him to say in response to her probing question, but she was sure she didn't want him to say *that*. Some stupid part of her wanted…

Well, it didn't matter what she'd wanted. Friends with bennies was what she was getting. She smiled gamely up at him. "Of course," she said softly. "I just wanted to make sure that we're on the same page, is all."

"Good," he breathed, his mouth swooping down to cover hers. "I'd hate to think we weren't." And then he was kissing her and she wasn't breathing or thinking but only feeling as his firm lips pressed and molded against hers, and then his tongue was sweeping inside and electrical shocks were pulsing through her as she moaned, pressing herself against his hard body.

This may not have been exactly what she wanted, but for now, it was good enough.

He pulled away slightly, brushing a few strands out of her

face lightly before saying with a teasing grin, "I do believe you're gonna be more fun than any other friend I've ever had."

She let out a belly laugh as they turned to walk the last block to her apartment.

Yessiree, this was good enough for her.

CHAPTER 16

JAXSON

J AXSON OPENED THE FRONT DOOR and his two boys tumbled inside like puppy dogs, shouting and laughing as they went. His apartment wasn't much, but it had two bedrooms – albeit small ones – which met the court's requirement of giving the boys their own room. In a tight rental market, it was the most he could hope for.

"It's small," Aiden observed, his hands on his hips as he surveyed the minuscule living room. Jaxson had crammed a couch and entertainment center into it, but had to leave his coffee table behind in storage. There was no room for extraneous furniture here.

"It is," Jaxson agreed. "But, you guys have your own bedroom back here. Come check it out!" He led them down the short hallway to the bedroom across from his, and pushed the door open. A bunk bed was against the wall, one mattress covered with a Batman bedspread and the other with Power Rangers.

"Cool, Dad!" Frankie yelled, cannonballing into the lower bunk, directly on top of Red Ranger's face. "You bought this for us?"

"I sure did. I wanted you guys to have something here that

you loved. Plus, check it out!" He flipped on the Batman desk lamp, casting the bat logo on the ceiling and they both cheered.

"Wow!" Aiden yelled, throwing his arms around his dad's knees. "Wait until I tell Isaac about the lamp!"

Jaxson grinned. It felt good to give his sons something that they loved. It made him feel a little more like a dad, and a little less like a family friend or uncle just taking care of some kids for the weekend. "You guys put your stuff in the drawers and I'll go get started on dinner."

He headed back towards the kitchen/living room combo as they began arguing over who got which drawers in the dresser. He laughed quietly to himself. Some things never changed.

He pulled out the boys' favorite – mac 'n cheese out of a box and a package of hot dogs. He'd tried making high-end mac 'n cheese one time, thinking that real cheese surely had to have more nutritional value than orange powdered shit, but the boys just pushed the creamy, delicious noodles around on their plates, refusing to believe that this was also mac 'n cheese.

After that, he stuck with the fifty-cent boxes from the grocery store.

Just as the pot of water began to boil on the stove, he heard a knock on the door. The boys came running out, excitement boiling over at the idea of someone visiting, and Jaxson jerked his head towards the door. "You guys wanna open it?" he asked as he began dicing up the hot dogs. It was probably the neighbor, wanting to borrow a cup of sugar or something; whatever it was that neighbors borrowed from each other in small towns.

"Oh hi!" came Sugar's surprised voice, accompanied by a howl of arctic air swirling through the room. Jaxson spun and stared at the front door as Sugar stared back, her face white, her eyes wide with panic. "I'm so sorry, I thought you were supposed to have them next weekend..." She stumbled to a stop, just staring at Jaxson, clearly pleading for help.

He wiped his hand on the hand towel and hurried over,

plastering a smile on his face. "Since Kendra kept them last weekend, she let me have them this weekend," he said. "Come in and meet them, and let's close the front door."

Already, he could hear the furnace kicking on, struggling to keep the apartment a decent temperature against the onslaught of frigid air. Sugar hurried in, Hamlet trailing behind her obediently.

"Scooby-Doo!" Aiden and Frankie shouted in unison.

Sugar and Jaxson both watched closely as the boys threw themselves at Hamlet, making sure that he stayed calm throughout. Not surprisingly, he was gentle as always, letting them stroke his head as he wagged his tail, clearly thrilled to be the center of attention. He was sitting so he didn't tower over the boys, although Aiden and Frankie's faces were right within licking range, something Hamlet was happily taking advantage of.

Their squeals of delight could probably be heard a block away, and Sugar used the cover to whisper urgently, "I really am so sorry. I didn't mean to…I mean, your boys might think something else, and we're not dating, and I really shouldn't be meeting your children, and—"

He cut off whatever else she was about to say. "It's okay. Really." Which was a lie – a *huge* lie – because nothing about this felt okay. It felt exhilarating and terrifying and wonderful and puke-provoking.

The one thing it did *not* feel was simply "okay."

He sucked in a deep breath. "Why don't you hang out with the boys while I finish up dinner? It's nothing fancy—" which was the understatement of the century, "—but my boys don't exactly have refined palates."

She nodded, her eyes still wide with panic, her face still white, but she turned back to the boys and sat down on the ground with them, her diminutive size helping her to fit right in. Hamlet, overjoyed that Sugar was within licking distance, began giving her a thorough face bath.

Jaxson turned back to the rapidly boiling water on the stove, listening to his boys and Sugar chat as he finished up.

"So why did you get Scooby-Doo?" Frankie asked. "Do you like him?"

Sugar's laughter tinkled out. "Well, his name isn't actually Scooby-Doo," she informed them, to a chorus of, "Why not?"

"His name is Hamlet. But I do like Scooby-Doo. I grew up watching that show too."

"Really?" Aiden asked, surprised. "I thought you were old."

"Aiden!" Jaxson shouted from the stove, frantically trying to keep the mac 'n cheese from burning while also shouting sternly over his shoulder. "That is *not* polite!"

"It's okay," Sugar said with a laugh. "I am old, compared to you. But Scooby-Doo has been on TV for a long time."

"Ohhhh…" the boys said in unison, clearly surprised by this information. Jaxson grinned to himself. It was a lot of fun seeing his boys' minds blown.

"So you got Hamlet because you like Scooby-Doo?" Frankie persisted, clearly wanting to figure out why an adult would pick such a large dog. Kendra had always put the kibosh on getting any kind of dog, but was especially adamant about not getting a dog larger than a rat. Which was why they could never agree on which dog to adopt, and thus never got one. A small, yappy, obnoxious ankle biter? No thank you.

"Uhhhh…" Sugar stammered, clearly trying to buy herself some time to put her thoughts together. "Truthfully, I got Hamlet because my ex-husband is allergic to dogs, and I figured that after our divorce, if I was going to get a dog, I'd get the biggest one I could find. I figured it was only fitting. He used to come by my house a lot, but after I got Hamlet, he stopped by one time, couldn't breathe, and had to leave. He hasn't been back since."

"Are you Daddy's girlfriend?" Aiden asked. Inquisitive

little buggers. For the first time – but probably not the last – Jaxson cursed having such smart, observant children.

"Oh no!" Sugar exclaimed, a little too loudly. Jaxson was setting the table, and looked up to see that her face had flushed a brilliant red. He grinned to himself. There was something about watching her squirm that was *greatly* entertaining. "No, we're just friends," she assured the boys.

"Friends with benefits," Jaxson said under his breath. They should definitely get around to the "benefits" part of this equation, and soon.

"What does it mean to be friends with benefits, Daddy?" Aiden asked. Jaxson's eyes shot up and he saw his son standing directly in front of him. He'd just been over by Hamlet! How'd he moved so damn fast?!

"Uh, just that we go on walks together with Hamlet," Jaxson said quickly. "That's a big benefit to both of us. Sugar gets to have someone to walk with and Hamlet gets to have two people who will throw a ball for him."

He heard Sugar's laughter pour out of her, and decided to ignore it. There were some things just not worth dignifying.

"Oh," Aiden said, clearly confused. "Does that mean that I can be your friend with benefits too?" His eyes lit up as he looked at Sugar, doing everything but clasping his hands together in his begging efforts. Sugar was busy trying to decide whether she wanted to die from laughing, or die from embarrassment. "You'll let us take Hamlet for a walk, right?" Aiden persisted. He was not one to get sidetracked easily, which was both a blessing and a curse.

It was more on the curse end of things tonight.

"I'm okay with it if your dad is," Sugar said hesitantly, after her giggles finally subsided, looking up at Jaxson from her place on the floor.

"Dinner first," Jaxson decreed, "and then we can go for a walk with Hamlet."

The boys shot over to the table and threw themselves into

their chairs, clearly determined to eat their dinner in the quickest time possible. "Don't make yourself sick," Jaxson scolded, as Frankie began shoveling the orange-and-red conglomeration into his mouth. A four-year-old boy chewing with his mouth open was *not* something Jaxson could see and still have an appetite afterwards. Frankie slowed down just the tiniest bit, which made Jaxson want to sigh and laugh at the same time.

He caught Sugar's eye and they smiled together, and his stomach did flips at the sight of Sugar and his boys all sitting at the dinner table together, like they all belonged there.

No, he'd describe this terrifyingly wonderful situation with a lot of different adjectives, but *okay* was definitely not one of them.

CHAPTER 17

SUGAR

ONCE THE LAST OF THE NOODLES were gone from the plates, Frankie and Aiden shot out of their chairs and down to their bedroom to put on their warmest winter clothes. "It's going to be cold out there!" Jaxson called down after them. "Put on your scarves and hats!"

He began clearing off the table. "Here, why don't I do that?" Sugar said. "I'm already all bundled up and ready to go." Truthfully, she was a little too warm, which had to be a first for her. She was almost always freezing, so being hot was a feeling she wasn't exactly used to. Her thermal underwear clung to her sweaty skin and she tried to discreetly pull it away from her thighs. This had to be the least sexy move on the face of the planet, but Jaxson thankfully didn't seem to notice.

"Oh, sure!" he said, surprised. "I'm so used to doing everything by myself. Thanks!" He shot her a heart-stopping grin and then headed to his bedroom to change. Sugar loaded up the tiny dishwasher, trying to pretend that it was totally normal for her to be doing dishes at Jaxson's house.

Totally normal.

This was totally not normal.

She turned around to find Frankie had grabbed his plate

from the table and was placing it on the floor in front of Hamlet, who was eagerly licking it clean. "No, no!" Sugar yelped, hurrying over and snatching the plate off the floor. "Hamlet gets…gassy if he eats human food." Hamlet's massive head was following the arc of the plate as she tried to take it away – now that he'd had a taste, he wasn't about to let it go easily.

"Gassy?" Frankie repeated, confused. Hamlet sank down in despair when Sugar held the plate up over her head. He gave her a mournful look. She ignored him.

"Yeah. Ummm…" She searched for a delicate way of saying it. "You know…"

"She means that Hamlet farts a lot," Aiden announced as he came back from the bedroom, bundled up like an Eskimo, clearly having overheard the conversation. The boys broke down into giggles and Sugar rolled her eyes as she turned back to the sink to finish up. Turns out, boys were exactly the same, no matter the decade.

"You guys ready?" Jaxson asked as Sugar loaded the last of the dishes. She searched underneath the sink and found a box of dishwasher detergent, starting it before beginning the process of getting bundled up herself. She'd shed her hat, scarf, jacket, and gloves when she'd gotten there, but her Carhartt overalls had stayed on. She was so warm from the hot water, she was almost painfully thrilled to go outside. Anything to cool her flushed skin.

Jaxson smiled at her and she felt herself flush even warmer. Being around Jaxson wasn't good for her sanity, she decided. She should just go home and hide far, far away from this addicting man.

Before she could force herself to do it, though, she realized that if she left, the boys wouldn't be able to walk Hamlet. She knew they'd be horribly disappointed by that, so she decided for their sakes, she'd stay.

No other reason, of course.

After Frankie and Aiden argued over who got to hold onto Hamlet's leash – which Aiden won, by virtue of being the oldest – they set off down the street, Frankie hurrying to keep up with his older brother. "I really am sorry," Sugar said softly under her breath to Jaxson, her words puffing out into the bitter cold, sending clouds upwards. "I didn't mean—"

"It's fine, really," he reassured her. "After Kendra pulled her stunt last weekend, she felt guilty enough that she let me have them this weekend instead. She's right – I do need to get better about checking the custody calendar. I shouldn't have gotten frustrated with her for doing exactly what the courts said for her to do. I just got busy with everything happening here."

"Do you have kids, Sugar?" Frankie asked, slipping his hand into hers. She looked down at him, startled, but he was clomping through the snow, stomping every little pile of white stuff into poofs of white stuff. He'd obviously given up on being given a chance to hold Hamlet's leash. Sugar made a mental note to let Frankie do it on the way back. Hamlet had slowed down once he'd realized it was Aiden carrying his leash, matching his pace to Aiden's, and so the usually brisk walk to the park was taking a lot longer. Sugar was happy to see it, though; she hadn't been sure how Hamlet would react to children since he wasn't normally around them.

Which led her back to Frankie's question. "No, no kids," she said softly after a long pause. She felt, rather than saw, Jaxson stiffen beside her, and she knew he'd caught her hesitation. She knew he'd want answers.

She knew she wouldn't want to give them to him.

Finally, thankfully, they'd made it to the park, where throwing the ball for Hamlet could distract Jaxson from asking any questions. With any luck, he'd forget he ever had any to ask.

CHAPTER 18

JAXSON

J AXSON FROWNED AT A FORM the state was wanting him to fill out. Did they want the total training hours for each man on the firefighting team, or just the hours completed in the last year? He sighed. This was going to require yet another phone call to the Idaho State Fire Commissioners' Association. At this rate, he might as well put them on speed dial. As fire chief, firefighting seemed to involve more paperwork and less flames, which yeah, that was the whole point of moving up here – so he could tell the judge he had a more stable, less stressful job – but that didn't mean he had to *like* it.

The man door to the station opened and Jaxson looked up through the office window out into the bay, happy to have something to take his mind off the paperwork spread out in front of him. It was Moose, and he looked…upset.

Dammit. Maybe Jaxson wasn't happy to be distracted from the paperwork after all. Whatever was going on, it didn't look good.

"Hey, boss," Moose called out as he neared Jaxson's office door. He popped his head around the doorframe. "Can I come in?"

"Yeah, sure. Of course. Anything to save me from more paperwork." He pushed the papers away and settled back in his chair as Moose sank down into a chair across from him.

"Well…ummmm…Listen. I have something to tell you that you aren't gonna like."

Jaxson nodded slowly, his eyebrows creasing as he stared at Moose. The pit of dread in his stomach was growing by the moment.

"It's…well, it's James. James and Robert, of course, but since Robert doesn't eat breakfast in the morning without James' say-so, I think we can safely pin this just on James." They both grimaced at that all-too-true statement.

Jaxson hadn't told anyone this, but he'd started calling the pair JimBob in his head. He'd never once seen one without the other, and had never seen Robert speak without James' permission. He was fairly sure that medically, Robert was in possession of a spine – mostly because he was capable of walking – but emotionally, he wasn't quite so sure.

"What's JimBob doing?" The question slipped out before he'd realized it, and Jaxson bolted upright in his chair. "Shit!" he hissed. "I didn't mean to say that."

"JimBob, eh?" Moose sat back in his chair with a laugh. "Damn, I have to say that I'm jealous I didn't think of that myself!"

"I shouldn't be talking about the men on the force that way. Please forget I said anything." *No matter how true it is.*

Moose's smile slipped from his face. "That's what I wanted to talk to you about, Chief. I don't think you want James or Robert on the force any longer. They're…they've gone around to all of the guys and told them to stop carrying their radios with them. That way, if a fire happens, you'd be the only one to respond. They said that this would make you just look like an even bigger ass in front of everyone after the mill fire, and that it ought to get you fired, since you're not capable of fighting fires or even convincing other men to show up to fight fires with you."

"Oh damn," Jaxson said softly, as his mind whirled through the possibilities. People could get seriously hurt or even killed from a stunt like this, and the fact that JimBob seemed to think that it was okay to do this was disturbing, to say the least. *Shit.* There was no way Jaxson could continue to ignore the situation. He'd hoped that by giving JimBob the space and time necessary to get used to the idea of Jaxson being the chief, he could head off any problems. He thought they'd eventually work through this.

Instead, he was going to have to fire the pair. *Dammit, dammit, dammit.*

He looked back up at Moose. "Thanks for telling me," he said softly. "I appreciate it."

Moose jerked his head. "Sure thing. Good luck." He headed back out of the fire station, leaving Jaxson alone with his thoughts.

This could be laid squarely at the feet of James, no question about it. He could call them both in at the same time, but what was the point? It was a volunteer position. If James were forced to quit, Robert would too. It'd be better to just confront James without a sycophant nearby to egg him on. That'd only make a tough situation even tougher.

He'd start with James and go from there. He could always call Robert in tomorrow and talk to him. Alone. If such a thing were possible.

But for now, he'd better call James in tonight. It was better to just rip the bandaid off and be done with it. If he left it alone for the night, he wouldn't be able to sleep as he just lay in bed and worried about the coming confrontation. It wasn't going to be pretty, he was damn sure of that. He picked up the phone, hit 9 and then dialed the phone number for Frank's Farm and Feed. He got ahold of the secretary, who informed him that James was still out making deliveries.

"Tell him that he needs to come by the fire station tonight, before he goes home."

"Well, I'm supposed to be going home soon—" the woman protested.

"Then clip the note to his damn timecard!" Jaxson barked. He tried hard never to lose his temper – not after *that* night – but this whole situation was pushing him dangerously close to the edge. "And tell him that this is an order, *not* a request." He slammed the phone back down into the cradle before the woman could protest further. He stared at the stack of paperwork in front of him, forgotten now. Dammit all, he wished that his biggest worry was over how to count training hours for his men. Although it'd been just 30 minutes earlier when he'd been working on that problem, it seemed like a lifetime ago.

This was his first time in a leadership position like this. An insurrection…he'd never imagined his new job, his ticket to getting his sons back, would end up like this. Were all small towns this backwards? This stubborn? This difficult? Or had he just picked an extra special one that truly hated outsiders with a passion?

James showed up at 8:42 that night. Jaxson knew this because he glanced up at the clock on the wall just as the man door opened. There was exactly zero chance that James had actually been out delivering propane this late into the evening, and sure enough, he more stumbled than walked towards Jaxson's office. Jaxson watched the progress, his back teeth grinding together with every step. James must've hit the local bar before coming over, maybe hoping that a bit of liquid courage would help him out.

Shit. The last thing Jaxson wanted was a drunk-as-a-skunk employee in his office, especially a drunk-as-a-skunk employee who Jaxson then had to fire. This was shaping up to be epic, in a truly horrific way. The first time Jaxson had ever fired someone, let alone fired someone from a volunteer position, and the guy had to show up wasted.

He silently began questioning all of his life choices, beginning with his choice to be born.

He stood back and let James stumble into his office, shutting the door behind him. James didn't bother sitting down, and Jaxson didn't bother offering him a chair. They both knew what was coming, society's niceties be damned.

"Tell me about the radios, James," Jaxson said quietly, the ticking of the clock and James' labored breathing the only sound in the small office. James' eyes were bloodshot and half-lidded, as if he were barely able to keep them open as he glared at Jaxson from beneath his bushy eyebrows.

"This was supposed to be *my* job!" James slurred in return, completely ignoring Jaxson's question. He jabbed his finger into his chest. "Mine! I worked for 22 years for this damn department, and then *you* come along and steal the job, just like that!" He tried to snap his fingers for emphasis, but he couldn't get them to work right and after a moment of staring at them in confusion, he forgot all about it and looked back up at Jaxson. "Do you know what the money would've done for me and my family? And I would've been able to retire in *style* in five years! Instead, I'm gonna be stuck delivering damn propane until the day I die, and it's all—" he poked Jaxson in the chest, "your," *poke*, "fault!" *poke*.

Jaxson felt himself slipping back into it – that same haze that'd come over him the night of the fight with Kendra. *The night.* That same red film slipped over his eyes as he stared at James, anger pouring out of every cell. Before he could swing a punch and knock some teeth out, though, James began wandering away.

Jaxson took the space to remember what he'd been taught in his anger management classes. *Deep breathing. They only have the power over you that you give to them.*

He felt his overwhelming anger begin to subside. Just a bit.

"This! All of it! S'posed to be mine. Chief Horvath told me so when he retired. He said I was a shoo-in. And then the city council worried about some damn training hours through the state, as if what really matters is how many hours you *pretend* to be a firefighter, versus the number of hours that you actually *are* a firefighter! Stupidest damn thing I've ever heard!" He turned back towards Jaxson, stumbling a bit in the rotation. He steadied himself, staring at Jaxson through bleary eyes. "I'm gonna kill you, you son-of-a-bitch!" he roared, charging across the small office.

Time slowed down as Jaxson watched him come, debating his choices. He wanted so badly to swing a nice upper-hook and take the drunk man down. It would be so satisfying…Just one punch. That's all he wanted. It would be self-defense, right? Every jury in the land would see it that way.

And then the faces of his boys flashed through his mind. He couldn't take the chance. He couldn't lose them.

And so at the last moment, he stepped to the side and James plowed into the filing cabinet behind him in a spot-on linebacker tackle, which managed to knock him out and send a cloud of dust up into the air at the same time.

He dropped like a rock to the floor as Jaxson coughed and waved a hand in front of his face, trying to clear the air. He really needed to clean that filing cabinet, if only for the health of his lungs.

He stared down at the passed-out man at his feet for a moment, and then picked up the phone in his office, calling city dispatch.

"Sawyer City Dispatch," came a crisp female voice.

"Hey, it's Chief Anderson over here at the fire department," he said. "Can you send an officer over? I have an ex-volunteer who needs to be escorted from the building."

"Oh. Sure." The surprise was clear in her voice, but she didn't ask any further questions. "Officer Knittle is in the area. I'll radio him now."

Jaxson hung up, staring down at James as he waited for Officer Knittle's arrival. He knew what he was doing. He knew that calling the police over meant that this would go onto James' record. If Jaxson was going to be a nice guy, he'd carry the man out to his SUV, throw him in the backseat, and drive him home.

Jaxson was *not* going to be a nice guy, though. He'd been a nice guy since he'd moved to Long Valley, and what did that get him? A passed-out, drunk, ex-volunteer who had done his level best to take out the one and only filing cabinet in Jaxson's office.

No, he was going to let James suffer the consequences. After putting the city of Sawyer and its citizens at risk just because his pride was hurt and he wouldn't enjoy the retirement he thought he was owed, yeah, James deserved a little suffering.

That and the headache he was going to wake up with would be plenty of punishment, Jaxson figured.

Officer Knittle stepped through the man door and came over to Jaxson's office, whistling when he saw the prone figure on the ground. "What happened?" the cop asked, circling James and staring down at him.

"James has been causing some severe problems within the fire department. I called him over here tonight to let him go, and…he didn't take it well. Charged me. I stepped to the side and he rammed into the filing cabinet, taking a pretty hard blow to the head. Knocked him out cold."

Knittle looked at the cabinet and let out another low whistle. "Damn. You can even see where he hit it." Jaxson peered closer. Yup, there was a dent all right. He hadn't even noticed with everything else happening.

"Shit. No wonder he's still out for the count," Jaxson said, wonder in his voice. "Maybe you should take him down to the hospital instead of over to the jail; have him checked out. He might've given himself a concussion."

"Are you sure you want to do this?" Officer Knittle asked quietly. "If I take him in, I have to file a report on this. I imagine he was none too happy with you getting hired, but he *has* been a dedicated firefighter for years in the valley."

"He was staging a revolt among the men," Jaxson responded, looking Knittle straight in the eye. "Told everyone not to carry their radios with them so that when a fire happened, I'd be the only one to respond. He thought this would make me look bad, maybe prove I wasn't capable of being the head of the fire department. If a fire really had broken out, though, he could've put someone's life at risk. I don't care what kind of vendetta you're carrying around; letting other people die to prove your point ain't right."

Knittle's eyes grew big. "Yeah, you're right. I'm sorry to hear it. I always thought he was a good guy beneath all the gruff. I wouldn't have thought...well anyway, grab his hands and I'll grab his feet. We'll carry him out to the car and I'll drive him over to the hospital, then book him after that. You willing to press charges?"

"I am. I think it's the only way to get through to some of these men that they may not be happy to see me, but they can't pull this kind of shit."

Knittle nodded. "Yup. Someone's gotta stand up to them. Are you gonna fire Robert, too?"

"I am. I have to. Even though I'm sure he didn't start any of this, he did go along with it."

Knittle nodded again. "I always did wonder where Robert stored his backbone when he left for work in the morning," he said casually as they hefted James' dead weight up and through the office door, Jaxson walking backwards, craning his neck to look over his shoulder so he didn't do something truly dumbass, like run into a wall or something.

After they got James into the backseat, snoring softly, apparently taking the deepest, most restful nap of his life,

Jaxson looked at Knittle over the top of the squad car. "Thanks for your help. 'Ppreciate it."

Knittle jerked his head. "Hope your talk with Robert goes better."

Jaxson grimaced. "I'm sure it will." Which it would. Robert didn't have it in him to cause problems without James around, but all the same, it just wasn't going to be any fun. In fact, he was pretty sure that this job had a serious case of non-fun.

He walked back into the office and began turning everything off for the night – the buzzing overhead fluorescent lights, the ancient computer, the tired printer – and then locked the door behind him. He should go home, drink a beer, watch some TV, and pretend today never happened.

He stopped just as he began to climb into his SUV, one foot inside, the other still on the ground, his breath coming out in puffs of white.

No, no, as a matter of fact, he *wasn't* going to go home. He had a friend with benefits, and he'd never actually taken her up on the benefits part.

It was time to rectify that situation.

CHAPTER 19

SUGAR

SUGAR SNUGGLED DOWN beneath the covers, the weight of Hamlet causing the whole bed – including her – to shift to the left. She sighed. She could argue with Hamlet about where he slept, or just try to go to sleep. Considering she'd argued with him before and lost every time, she should just lose gracefully again tonight. Hamlet was a real sweetie, but he was damn sure of where he wanted to sleep, and it was *not* on the floor.

He shifted, causing the whole bed to shake and Sugar found herself snuggled up against his furry body, whether or not she'd wanted to be there. Happy to have her company, Hamlet lapped her face with his tongue and then settled back down. She stared up at the ceiling into the darkness, willing her mind to let her go to sleep.

Waking up at 4:30 in the morning was *not* natural to Sugar, and neither was going to bed at 9:00. Her biological clock dictated that she be a night owl, which meant that despite having worked at the bakery for coming up on three years, she still felt like she was being tortured every time her alarm clock went off. Getting up at 4:30 in the morning just wasn't natural, and she didn't care who thought otherwise, or told her that she'd eventually get used to it. Her body never would. Thank heavens she worked at a bakery that sold coffee. Gage let her drink as much as she wanted for free. It was pretty much the only perk that came with working at the shop, but Sugar was grateful for it anyway.

Just as her body began to relax into the mattress – and into Hamlet's warm side – she heard a knock on the door. She bolted upright, staring into the darkness. Who was knocking on her door at this time of night? Everyone knew she worked at the bakery, and not to come by her house after eight.

She pulled on her robe and then headed to the front door, Hamlet padding sleepily beside her. If it was Dick, coming over to argue with her again about her "poor life choices" that she'd been making lately – the one where she decided to divorce him, in particular – she'd be real tempted to sic Hamlet on him.

Which in Hamlet's case, just meant licking every inch of skin he could reach, but since Dick was severely allergic to dog hair, she figured that was revenge enough under the circumstances.

She pulled the door open. "What do–oh!" she said, staring at Jaxson. Instantly, her hands began tightening the robe around her body further. She patted at her hair. She probably looked like she had a rat's nest on top of her head. "What are you doing here?" she asked, surprised. "I have to get up in the—"

And then he was through the door and closing it behind him, and kissing her.

His movements were frantic as he pressed his lips to hers and explored. She felt overwhelmed, but in a good way that was completely foreign. She waited for the urge to panic and shove him away to wash over her, but it never came.

She let him guide her backward into the apartment. She let go of the death grip on her robe, instead wrapping her arms around him both as a response to her growing eagerness, and the need for his stability.

In a strange moment of clarity, she heard Hamlet's toenails clicking against the tile of the kitchen floor as he let out a little whine. Instinctually, she recognized the sound as his disappointed whine. Apparently, Hamlet was ready for bed and not happy about this interruption. She tried to feel guilty about keeping him from his sleep, but then Jaxson was kissing her, setting her body on fire, and she forgot all about it.

Jaxson finally stopped walking her backward and instead shifted his hands so that one arm encircled her around the waist, pulling her even closer to him, while his other hand held the side of her face.

Although she normally wore a nightgown to bed, tonight she'd just been wearing a pair of panties when she'd crawled in to sleep, and then, of course, the robe she'd pulled on when he'd knocked on the door. His hand snaked through the opening of her robe, pushing it off her shoulders and chest as he pulled her tightly to him. Her cheek warmed, the sensation perfectly outlining the shape of his hand on her face.

Sugar sank deeply into the moment. It pained her to admit how much she'd missed these feelings. Realistically, it hadn't been *that* long since she'd last felt the touch of a man, but this…this was completely different.

With Dick, it'd always been about him and the fact that she was the woman most readily available – the most convenient to help him take care of his physical needs – but she was never more than that. Never special. She'd often wondered if he cheated on her, but if he had, she'd never heard about it, and she would've only been grateful that his attentions were turned elsewhere.

Tonight, Jaxson sought *her* out. *She* was the woman he wanted. Sugar admitted, if only to herself, that there was something amazing about being the subject of his desire. Being special and wanted by a wonderful man was what she'd longed for her entire life, and tonight – if only tonight – it was true.

She melted into the feeling.

His thumb caressed her cheek as they continued to kiss. His lips massaged hers, adding pressure, enticing her to open her mouth. It didn't take too much convincing for her to let him in. His tongue was warm and soft, but forceful at the same time. She felt herself getting swept up by the intensity, and only wanting more.

With painful perfection, Jaxson held the kiss long enough that Sugar was feeling lightheaded when he finally released her.

"Hello," she managed to breathe out.

"Hi," he said quickly, before catching her mouth with another shorter but equally as intense kiss.

"You must've had a pretty good day," she said when they broke apart, smiling up at him, her neck craning way back to get a good view.

His whiskey brown eyes were blazing with need, and the sight made her catch her breath.

"Actually the opposite," he growled. "I needed something good to happen today, and when I realized that, all I could think of was you."

"Oh," was Sugar's breathy response, and then he was shoving her robe the rest of the way off her body, letting it pool around her feet. She was relieved to shed the frumpy flannel robe that was both supremely comfortable and supremely unflattering, but then suddenly felt self-conscious at being exposed.

She could never really reconcile her petite form with her comparatively large bust, to the point where she could see herself as attractive. In her mind, she'd always considered her body to be a collection of incongruous parts that by themselves were each attractive, but in concert, were somehow mismatched.

She chanced a glance at Jaxson, the panic starting to build inside of her. What if he didn't like what he was seeing?

"Oh my God," Jaxson said in a hushed tone. "You are stunning."

"Really?" she blurted out, unable to contain her surprise.

"Yes," he managed to say, his breath coming in halting gasps.

She felt his hand slide from her cheek, down her neck and over her shoulder, finally coming to rest on her breast. He lifted the weight of it as the pad of his thumb brushed lightly over her nipple. Her flesh was already hard from the cooler air of the apartment. The roughness of his calloused thumb caused short tantalizing jolts of electricity to course through her body.

She pressed her body tighter to his, finally enjoying the difference in her size compared to that of a man. This was no longer a feeling of intimidation or shame at being weak. Jaxson's size, his height and strength, radiated security through her. She reveled in the new contrast as she let him support her.

With stunning speed, he dropped his hand from her breast and encircled her body. He lifted her slight form into the air so they were eye to eye. Her legs instinctually wrapped around him, just above his hips, her arms tightening around his neck, drawing their lips together for another long kiss.

Then suddenly, he was leaning forward, startling Sugar with the sensation of falling in slow-motion. She clung tightly to him until she finally felt the soft touch of the blankets on her bare back. She relaxed her arms just a bit but her lips, ever eager, kept reaching for his. She sunk into the mattress as Jaxson pulled away, her legs untangling themselves from around his body and draping over the end of the bed instead.

Her heart raced as she watched him unbutton the dark blue shirt of his uniform. He tugged his arms free and then, like a magician, his hands blurred as he pulled his white undershirt over his head in a movement so fast, she didn't consciously register the action. He stood there for a moment, towering over her, his body such a contrast to hers – hard where she was soft. Large where she was small.

She was surprised when she didn't panic at their size differences. Instead of worrying about how he was going to use his strength to hurt her, she could only focus on how he'd use it to bring heaven down to earth. She hadn't expected to have that reaction – she actually hadn't been sure *what* reaction she'd have, really – and let out a tiny sigh of relief that her body and mind were all in agreement on this one: Jaxson was perfect.

Speaking of perfection…his chest. She couldn't help drooling over the strong, square plates of muscle that stood guard over a contingent of smaller tightly packed muscles. His entire body rose and fell with his intense breathing under her watchful gaze.

He dug a hand into the pocket of his pants, retrieving a condom that he put on the edge of the bed for easy access.

Her body began to tingle in earnest as his hands worked the buckle of his belt. In no time, his Wranglers were falling to the floor and she began to see the outline of him through the tightly stretched fabric of his dark red underwear. With as much speed and dexterity as he had used to tug his shirt over his head, he removed the jockey shorts.

There was no mistaking how he was feeling in that moment. She only had a second to take in the sight as he ripped open the small square package and rolled the condom over his length, before he was leaning over her.

A tickle of fear formed in the back of her mind, the first inkling of it since he'd shown up that night, but it wasn't a fear that he'd hurt her, at least not intentionally. In the brief moments that she'd had to examine Jaxson, she realized that he was *much* bigger than Dick.

His dick was bigger than Dick's dick?

She made a mental note to chuckle about the unintentional

joke later. For now, she was torn between enjoying this experience and admonishing herself for the constant comparisons. She couldn't keep contrasting every moment, every movement, every part of Dick against Jaxson. It wasn't fair, even if Jaxson did keep coming out on top…

She wrestled her mind into submission and gave herself over to the moment. To him.

His perfectly delectable chest pressed against her. She felt like he might start her on fire, his skin was so warm. His lips found hers once again as he settled his weight on her. Instead of being scary, it was reassuring.

This was so erotic, too. She'd never been desired like this before. It felt wonderful to be viewed with such want and need, and even more amazingly, feel that way towards him. She'd known that Jaxson was sexy, but not like this. She'd known that fact with her mind, not her soul.

Not like she knew it now.

He pulled back from the kiss and her skin cooled, raising goosebumps across her entire body. He slipped his fingers under the waistband of her panties. She brought her legs up, resting her heels on the footboard of the bed, as he pulled the fabric towards him. She lifted her hips, letting the soft satin slide free.

He wound the tiny collection of purple satin and elastic over her thighs, past her knees and feet, which she lifted into the air with perfect timing. Neither of them concerned themselves with where he flung it.

He reached down, grasping her ankles and guiding her legs over his shoulders.

She trembled with excitement. Her mind screamed, *Yes! Please! Yes! Please!* Over and over. Nothing was left but desire.

He placed his hands on the tops of her thighs and, with a pull on her and thrust of his hips, he entered her.

Her eyes slammed shut as colors exploded across the backs of her eyelids. The sensation was all-consuming. She was certainly not a virgin, but she might as well have been one, in all the ways that mattered.

He was touching parts of her that had never received attention before, filling her in an entirely new way. The combination of the physical sensation of Jaxson moving in and out of her slowly but firmly, and the emotional overload of being with a man that she *wanted* to be with, caused a flash of bright white light to explode in her mind. She felt her body tense with a completely foreign sense of joy, her body responding by going rigid. She felt him slip deeper inside of her as she pressed herself against him.

She heard a sound. It seemed to be a faint echo of a grunt that had traveled a hundred miles to reach her ears.

He continued to rock back and forth as her body lurched in unrestrained pleasure.

Finally, her muscles relaxed just a bit. Her back flattened against the bed once more and she managed to open her eyes. Jaxson's face was tight with concentration as he kept his rhythm going.

Feeling her relax, he released his grip on her ankles, something she'd failed to notice until that point. Pulling back, he freed himself of her body. She felt her face contort into a look of disappointment.

He reached down placing a hand on each of her hips and, using his impressive strength, lifted her off the bed just enough to roll her over. He repositioned his hands on her hips and lifted her once again. Her knees bent automatically and he lowered her onto the bed once more so that her knees rested on the end of the mattress.

She braced herself with her arms and bowed her back before turning her head over her shoulder to look at him. His face had taken on a look of focused desire, his lips turned up on one side.

She felt his fingers curl into the soft flesh of her hips. Once again, he combined a pull and a thrust, entering her. And just like the moments before, she was taken with sensations that were alien. She fell in love with these new feelings. She became addicted to these new feelings.

He moved with her, back and forth, back and forth, her mind cataloging in meticulous detail the way he felt both entering and leaving her. Her mind greedily soaked up every detail, as if it was worried that this may be the only time this would ever happen to her. This feeling, this emotion...

This love.

She felt his fingers tighten against her skin as he pulled her body roughly, holding her tightly to him, as he came, shouting his relief into the darkness of the apartment. She felt his breathing through every cell in her body, his muscles tensing and relaxing sporadically. She was lost in the idea that she was giving this man as much joy as he'd given her.

Finally, his fingers relaxed. He slumped forward, bending over her so that his chest rested against her back. She could feel the pounding of his heart through her spine. Everything was so close. So raw. So perfect.

She felt him slip from her, and wanted to cry at losing that connection.

There were a few disorganized moments as they crawled forward together onto the bed. Eventually finding their way under the blankets, she climbed on top of him and curled into a ball, pressing her slight frame against his heaving chest.

Her eyes slowly closed as that feeling of security enveloped her. For perhaps the first time in her life, Sugar felt completely relaxed, completely safe, completely content. She slipped away into the welcoming embrace of slumber.

CHAPTER 20

JAXSON

J AXSON WOKE UP to a heavy weight pushing inexorably down on his legs, trapping him in place. He was being crushed to death as some terrible retribution for wanting to kill his wife and now, they'd decided he should—

Then Hamlet let out a long snore, shifting his weight across Jaxson's lower half, and Jaxson sank back into the mattress, scrubbing at his eyeballs with the palms of his hands. Good Lord Almighty, that was one way of waking up. He was plenty awake now, even if Sugar and Hamlet were still snoring beside him...and on top of him.

Having Sugar use him as a human mattress would be one thing – he was quite happy when she'd fallen asleep on top of him last night, actually – but having Hamlet do it was quite another. He shifted his legs one at a time, working them out from underneath the massive dog, until he could swing them off the bed and sit up, staring out through the window to the cold predawn world outside.

Last night had been nice. Real nice.

He grimaced to himself. Who was he kidding? Last night had been more than "nice." It had been stunning. Amazing. The best sex he'd ever had, and wasn't that just something? He and Sugar were supposed to only be friends with benefits, and last night was definitely one hell of a benefit, but…

It was more than that. It'd been much, much more than he'd expected. More wonderful, more mind-blowing, more… everything.

He felt a cold sweat break out all over his body at the thought. He wasn't supposed to love last night like that. It was just supposed to be a way to let off steam, not change his whole world.

He stood up and began searching for his clothes, strewn every which way in the darkness. He didn't want to wake up Hamlet or Sugar; he just wanted to leave. Sneak away. Get some breathing room. Think a little. Screw his head on straight.

Something.

He pulled his jeans on and then shoved his feet, sans socks, into his boots. He couldn't find them in the darkness and anyway, they were too complicated to operate at two in the morning. Yanking on his Sawyer City Fire Department shirt but leaving it unbuttoned – buttons were too complicated also – he grabbed his jacket from the back of the couch and headed for the door, trying to keep the clomping of his footsteps to a minimum.

He'd go home and sleep in his own bed, letting Hamlet have his domain back, and in the meanwhile, he'd think. A lot. And decide just what in the hell he was gonna do about a certain Sugar Stonemyer.

CHAPTER 21

SUGAR

BEEP. *BEEP. BEEP.*

Her obnoxious, way-across-the-room alarm clock was going off, and dammit all, it was way across the room so she couldn't just beat it into submission. She cracked one eyelid open, trying to decide if she'd somehow acquired new superhero skills during the night and could now turn off her alarm clock with a one-eyed glare across the room.

Alas, her superhero skills seemed to be lacking this morning, as they were sadly lacking *every* morning. She rolled off the bed and crashed to the floor, then crawled across to the side table where – blessed be! – the alarm clock was finally within reach. She promptly whacked it until it shut up. She sat back down on the floor and scrubbed her eyeballs with the palms of her hands. She was even more tired than normal, and she couldn't remember why. There was something weird. Something off. Something wasn't the way it was supposed to be.

She squinted in the semi-darkness, trying to see by the light of the waning moon and a street lamp streaming in through the window. It was 4:30 – a quick glance at her alarm clock said 4:36, actually – in the morning, which is when she always woke up when going to work. Hamlet was snoring at the end of the bed, completely and happily oblivious to the alarm clock routine. There was a wool sock on the floor, long and thick and halfway turned inside out, sticking out from underneath the bed. That was weird. She didn't own any socks like—

Oh.

Oh.

Jaxson. Jaxson Anderson had happened last night. And again early this morning.

She dropped her head into her hands and sighed. She shouldn't have done that. She really, really shouldn't have done that. Despite their official status as Friends with Benefits, last night had felt like a lot more than that.

Her head shot back up, whacking it up against the wall. She rubbed it gingerly as she looked around the bedroom again. *Hold on a moment. Then where the bloody hell is Jaxson?*

She scrambled to her feet, then back down onto her hands and knees to look under the bed – because Jaxson would hide underneath there? She didn't know why she was looking there. She knew it was ridiculous even as she was doing it. Once she discovered the mate to the wool sock at the end of the bed, she snatched them both up and stood up, tossing the socks onto the bed and heading through the rest of her small apartment, on the hunt for Jaxson.

He was gone. Disappeared. All just a figment of her imagination…except for his socks.

It seemed like if she was just going to conjure this shit up, she could've at least chosen something better for him to leave behind than sweaty, used woolen socks.

She stumbled into the bathroom, brushing her teeth as she stared at her sleep-rumpled reflection in the mirror. She was a bonafide idiot. She should've known that she couldn't do FWBs. She thought she could be all suave and city girl and chic – have a no-strings-attached fling with a sexy man.

She could not.

She felt a wave of depression roll over her. With Jaxson sneaking out, trying to pull a disappearing act on her, it was clear he didn't even want FWBs status, let alone anything else. She'd allowed herself to fall in like with a guy – a guy she barely knew – and even worse, fall into bed with him. What the hell had she been thinking? She'd only ever slept with one guy in her entire life, and the debacle that was her first marriage – and the too-awful-for-words circumstances leading up to it – should've been her clue that this sex idea shouldn't be repeated.

No matter how amazing it felt.

She made herself go to work, and then made herself smile at customers, and then made herself not cry when, hour after hour, Jaxson didn't appear. No coffee and donut for him today. This would be the first time he'd skipped coming by since the last time he'd freaked out and quit coming by, which just cemented it into her mind: He was avoiding her. Staying far, far away from her. Maybe, the horrific thought occurred to her about three in the afternoon, the sex had been awful for him, and he'd just been pretending the whole time!

She was concentrating hard on not letting the pain of that thought show on her face, when she heard his name. Her head shot up so fast, she'd probably need to go see the chiropractor after work for it, but she ignored the pain and zeroed in on Mr. Behrend and Mr. Maddow, who were there for their weekly piece of pie and coffee, just like every Wednesday afternoon.

"Can you believe the nerve of that man, firing James?" Mr. Behrend snorted. "James has been with the department for over 20 years. You can't fire him any more than you can fire the tanker. The whole thing is ridiculous. He's a damn volunteer who has risked his life more times than I can count for this here community, and this is his thanks? That city slicker needs to go back to where he came from, before he sets the fire department on fire, too. Why, he's so lazy, he'd probably just stand there and watch that burn to the ground also!"

Mr. Maddow guffawed at his friend's witticism. "Never seen anything like it. I knew them people from Boise weren't the brightest bulbs in the bunch, but I didn't expect this. No siree bob. And to think that we're paying lots more in taxes every year for this dumbass. If he's still there by summer, I can tell you who ain't gonna be – the city council! I say we get every one of 'em kicked out. Teach 'em a lesson."

Sugar looked down at the counter, making ever-smaller circles with her rag. They were right – Jaxson didn't fit in here. Never had.

Which meant that soon, he was gonna leave and head back to Boise anyway. Falling in like with him was even dumber than she'd realized. She'd started to like the one man in town who was guaran-damn-teed to be on his way out the door.

Yeah, Sugar was an idiot, all right.

CHAPTER 22

JAXSON

PAPERWORK. How had his life been reduced to nothing but paperwork?

He stared bleary eyed at the grant paperwork in front of him. After Chief Horvath had secured the new fire truck through a grant, everyone in town congratulated him on a job well-done, not realizing that there was still a step two left in the process – getting all of the upgrades for their brand-new stripped-down fire engine.

The city council had been pretty clear on this topic during their last meeting together – it was Jaxson's job to find the money to get a decent-sized tank on the truck, longer hoses, and a ladder on top. *This* was why they were paying him the big bucks.

Well, that and the state insurance fund was requiring it. Hiring him full-time, that was, not upgrading their truck. If the City of Sawyer didn't hire a full-time fire chief in this year's budget cycle, the state's insurance would start charging them a stiff penalty. The state had made it clear: Full-time staff meant faster response times, better equipped personnel, more training, and thus, less damage and injuries in the case of a fire.

Which meant that despite what James seemed to think,

there had been roughly a zero percent chance of him being hired, not with the level of training that he had. The state insurance company would've been fit to be tied if the city had tried to hire him.

Even though James had been with the department for approximately a million years or so, he'd apparently done his level best to avoid every training session he could, and so after looking through the personnel records, Jaxson saw that even Moose and Levi, who'd both only been with the department for a handful of years, had more training than James had ever acquired.

Jaxson's stomach rumbled, jerking him out of his thoughts and reminding him that he hadn't bothered to feed it yet today. He thought back, trying to remember, and couldn't recall eating yesterday either, although he may've popped a piece of toast into the toaster at some point. It was hard to remember if that was yesterday or the day before, though.

His stomach rumbled again, like a freight train coming through his office, and with a groan, Jaxson threw on his jacket. He'd go down to Betty's Diner and eat something. Shut his stomach up.

It was a damn good thing he was taking a break from Sugar so he could screw his head on straight. Otherwise, he might be tempted to eat his way through a baker's dozen of donuts instead of a proper meal, and even in his starved state, he knew that wasn't healthy.

It sure sounded good, though.

Or maybe it was just the idea of seeing Sugar that sounded good. As he got into his SUV for a long overdue lunch break and headed over to the diner to eat, he had to admit – if only to himself – that the idea of seeing Sugar again made his heart lurch with happiness. Or maybe was causing him to have a heart attack. That could totally be it.

Didn't matter. He'd loved last week way too damn much. He couldn't allow himself to do it again.

"Hi Jaxson!" said Chloe, one of his favorite waitresses. "Head on back to your booth – it's open. I'll be by with a glass of Pepsi in a minute." Her platinum blonde hair bobbed as she headed into the back to fetch his soda.

Well, he had to admit that there were perks to living in a small town. Like waitresses who memorized your favorite booth to sit at, and your favorite drink, and your favorite meal to eat.

He wasn't sure what it said about him that he was so regular in his habits, though. Was he really that boring?

Before he could work himself up into a full-blown existential crisis, though, Chloe reappeared at his elbow, a glass of brown, carbonated liquid in her hand. She put it down on the booth table and put her hand on his shoulder. "Meatloaf and mashed potatoes?" she asked.

"Yes, please," he mumbled. He was sure tired. He tried to remember if he'd slept well the night before, but gut instinct told him probably not.

She shifted around until she could look him square in the face. "Why Jaxson, when was the last time you ate? Or slept? Or shaved?" She put her hands on her hips and stared at him. He ran his hand over his jaw, scrubbing at it. It did feel a might bit stubbly to him. When *was* the last time he'd showered or shaved? He stared blankly ahead, trying to remember, and… not.

"You look terrible," she informed him bluntly.

"You should tell me what you really think," Jaxson said dryly. "I'd hate for you to hold back on account of my tender feelings."

She glared, not appreciating his humor one whit, and leaned against the side of the booth bench seat opposite him. "Is this because of that mill fire?" she asked. "Or the firing of James? Or something else?"

"Yes."

"My oh my, you're talkative today," Chloe said with a small

laugh. And then, like a true woman, her eyes narrowed even as a grin spread across her face. "The 'something else' is Sugar, isn't it? I heard you two were going at it – you even spent the night at her house – and then…nothing. For a whole week. Something happen?"

"How do you know I spent the night at her house?" Jaxson retorted hotly. Damn small towns. He just couldn't believe them. Didn't people have something else to do, other than gossip about him?

"Your SUV. It's bright green. No other Ford Explorer in town is that color. You might want to look at getting it painted if you want to go incognito."

Jaxson grunted. Maybe he'd start walking everywhere like Sugar did. The idea was starting to hold more appeal by the moment.

His stomach rumbled loudly before he could think of something witty to snap back, or at least something appropriate. Witty might've been above his mental capacity just then.

"Let me go put in your order. I'll be back."

Chloe disappeared into the kitchen and seemingly just moments later, reappeared with homemade rolls, steam wafting up from them. She slid the small plate in front of him, along with some homemade jelly. "Eat," she urged him. "I don't know how long it's been since you ate anything, but I'm gonna guess a minute or two."

His stomach rumbled again, this time loud enough that a table two booths over all turned to stare. Jaxson ducked his head and began spreading jelly on a fat, fluffy roll. Biting into it…heaven. He hadn't tasted anything this good since…

Well, since the last time he ate a donut from The Muffin Man.

He ignored that thought and shoved the rest of the roll into his mouth. Maybe if his mouth was full, Chloe would take the hint and not ask him any questions.

She sank into the booth opposite him. At his cocked eyebrow, she shrugged. "I told Betty that I needed to take a 15. She said that was fine. She expected me to step outside or something, but I'm free to sit out here in the dining room if I want. And I do. Because you're going to tell me everything."

It was official – his stuff-his-mouth-full-so-Chloe-wouldn't-ask-any-questions plan had not exactly worked out the way he'd intended.

CHAPTER 23

SUGAR

S UGAR SLID GAGE'S LATEST CREATION – a peanut-butter-and-dark-chocolate swirl cheesecake, topped with chocolate shavings – into the refrigerated showcase. The man was wickedly good – or terrible, depending on your point of view – at whipping up creations that'd tempt a saint. It was a damn good thing that Sugar liked salty, crunchy snacks, not sugary ones, or she figured she'd be about as round as she was tall by this point. But even to her, this cheesecake was temptation incarnate.

Maybe she'd just watch to see if anyone bought it. If it was still there by the end of the week, well, she'd just have to buy it so Gage wouldn't wonder if maybe his latest creative idea wasn't a good one. That would be a tragedy, she figured.

The bell over the door jingled as a blast of cold air whooshed in. "Be right there!" Sugar called out over her shoulder, scooting the cheesecake to the right just a smidge before shutting the door and wiping her hands in satisfaction. She turned, a smile firmly planted on her face, when she saw Jaxson standing there, his Elmer Fudd hat in his hands, turning the brim of it around and around as he stared back.

Her stomach hit somewhere around her knee caps as she stared at him. "Uhhh…" she croaked.

It'd been nine days since he'd come into the bakery. Nine long, painful days.

Not that she'd been counting or anything. She hadn't. She just happened to remember how long it'd been because she had an amazing memory.

"Uhhh…" she croaked again.

Truth be told, she had a terrible memory. She'd always chalked it up to how shitty her life had been up to this point, and figured this was a self-defense strategy her brain employed to keep her from slowly going insane.

Before she could do something dreadfully embarrassing, like croak again, Gage came out through the swinging doors. "Sugar, have you seen the—" He stopped short when he saw Jaxson, and his whole body stiffened up. "What are you doing here?" he growled, acting for all the world like a papa bear protecting his cubs. He was only three years older than her, but some days, he acted more like it was twenty.

For once, she didn't mind, though. She would've demanded the same thing if her body had done something more useful than begin an imitation of a frog croaking in the wilds of the swamps.

"I wanted to talk to Sugar for a minute," Jaxson said quietly. "I wanted to apologize."

Gage swung around to look at Sugar. "Are you okay with that?" he asked quietly, clearly ready to throw Jaxson out on his ear if she said no. For the last week, he'd been supportive, listening to her whine and cry and complain about being an idiot. He'd quite literally been the shoulder she cried on.

She couldn't ask for a better friend.

"I am," she said, nodding firmly, sounding much more sure of herself than she actually felt. And she did want to hear what he had to say. *Then* she'd tell him to get lost. Not only because of his disappearing act for the last nine days – not that she'd been counting – but also because she was incapable of just being friends with benefits. It was an impossibility for her. She'd tell Jaxson that…

Right after she listened to whatever it was he had to say.

"All right," Gage said, the note of disapproval clear in his voice. "Well, it's close to closing time. Why don't you just head on out? I'll close up tonight."

Sugar headed into the back and snagged her jacket off the coat rack. Gage followed her, stopping her for a moment. "You sure?" he asked softly. "I could throw him out if you want me to. After the bags of flour I throw around, I don't think he'd be too much harder."

She let out a little laugh at the thought. "Thank you," she said softly. "I appreciate it – I really do. I'll be fine, though. See you tomorrow?"

Gage gave her a one-armed hug. "Good luck," he said gruffly, and then turned back towards the mixer bowl.

She headed back out front. "Ready?" she asked, overly cheerful. He nodded and they stepped out into the bitter cold, the temperature surely hovering around zero, *without* the wind chill factored in. "Let's hurry," she said, already speed-walking down the sidewalk. "I have to get out of this before I turn into an icicle."

Jaxson's long legs helped him quickly catch up, and then they hurried down the sidewalk together, ice and snow crunching with every step, no sound passing between them otherwise. It was too bitterly cold to meander and chat. It was too bitterly cold to breathe, really. The icy air stabbed her lungs, making each breath an agony, but she hurried on, her eyes stinging and watering as they went.

Finally, they burst into her apartment and she shut the door behind them, shivering and shaking with cold as she stood there, trying to hurry the heat back into her bones.

"Wowsers," Jaxson said with a laugh. "Why is it that we live here again?"

Sugar sent him a painful smile. "No idea!" she said cheerfully.

Hamlet came bounding into the living room, yipping and growling with pleasure, flopping over onto his back for a belly rub. "Hello, you handsome boy," Sugar said, stripping her gloves off and loving on him. "Did you have fun today?" He yipped and howled a little more and she laughed. "I see. Sounds like you had quite the day." Hamlet's tail whipped across Jaxson's boots, thumping with every pass, his lips pulled back in the most doggyish smile she'd ever seen. She knew it was just the gravity at play, with him lying on his back and all, but it still made her chuckle.

She finally stood up and Hamlet heaved himself to his feet, hurrying to Jaxson's side for a dose of loving from him. "I need to take him on a walk," she said. "I'll put a jacket on him to help him keep warm, and then bundle up myself. Are you coming with us?" She had a challenge in her eye when she asked him that, and he met it with a level stare of his own.

"Planned on it. Put on long johns and wore my thickest coat. And of course, my hat." He pointed to his Elmer Fudd hat, planted squarely on his head. She laughed a little.

"I should get me one of those. Do you think they make Elmira Fudd hats? Pink camouflage with rhinestones?" At his chuckle, she said, "Well anyway, let me change. I'll be right back. You keep loving on Hamlet. He needs some attention after me being gone all day."

She'd almost said "we" instead of "me." Now wouldn't that have been the damnedest thing to let loose.

She was awfully glad she didn't make that particular mistake.

CHAPTER 24

JAXSON

H E PUSHED HIMSELF to his feet when Sugar came back out of her bedroom. "Ready to…" He stumbled for just a moment as he took in her Michelin Man outfit; she had so many layers on, she appeared to be waddling. "To go?" he finished weakly, forcing the smile off his lips. He couldn't laugh, he just couldn't. She'd never forgive him, and he already had enough to ask for forgiveness about.

She spun in a clumsy circle, a smirk on her lips. "This is all the rage, you know," she informed him. "In Antarctica."

He did burst out laughing at that and she grinned up at him for a moment, before taking off on a hunt for a leash for Hamlet. Finally finding it, she clipped it to his collar. "Oh!" she said in surprise. "You found his jacket. Thank you."

Jaxson shrugged. "It was right in with the rest of his stuff and it gave me something to do while waiting." He liked the big smile she sent him. It made him feel real good. Like he'd accomplished a huge feat – slain a dragon or climbed a mountain to pick a star out of the sky just for her.

She had a way of making a man feel ten feet tall, and it wasn't just on account of her being on the short side, either.

They headed out towards the park, the wind still howling

and biting at them, but Sugar seemed to take it a little better this time. With all of those layers on, he imagined the cold was barely touching her. She sniffled – her nose must be running – and he smiled to himself. Okay, maybe she was feeling the cold on her face. Without donning a ski mask, there wasn't much in the way of being able to protect one's face from the biting wind.

It was too hard to talk and walk into the wind at the same time, so Jaxson just matched her shorter strides as Hamlet darted this way and that, smelling everything along the way, his huge golden head shining in the winter dusk.

They reached City Park in record time, and Sugar unclipped Hamlet's leash and lobbed his ball, hurrying to get the chore done and over with. It went sailing away, and then she turned her back to the wind, huddling up against its piercing power.

Jaxson snuggled her up against his side, figuring that body warmth was a good thing to be sharing right now. He stared off through the frozen, icy park, wondering how to start, when Sugar did it for him. "Why'd you sneak off like that?" she asked, her voice thick with pain. "And then, not show up for nine days to the bakery? Not that I was counting or anything," she said quickly. "I just happen to remember, is all. But...I thought you'd enjoyed that night between us. Did I do something wrong?"

He pulled her tighter against his side, the pain in her voice cutting through him, hurting more than the icy wind ever could. "No, Sugar, you did nothing wrong. I...I screwed up. I was wrong."

Hamlet came bounding over, dropping his ball at Sugar's feet, backing away, his tail wagging madly. She stooped and picked it up, launching it as far as she could, before snuggling back up against Jaxson's side. He continued on as if nothing had happened. "I can't be just friends with you, not even friends with benefits, and I was stupid to think I could."

She stiffened against his side. "I see…" she said, a suspicious quiver in her voice.

Grand. He'd made her cry. Wasn't *that* just the cherry on the top?

"No!" he said, harsher than he'd intended. She began to pull away, and he yanked her back, tilting her head up, forcing her to look at him. Her eyes were bright with tears, and a lonely trail wandered down her face. He wiped it away with the pad of his thumb. "I can't just be friends with you, Sugar. I…I want so much more than that."

Her mouth made a perfect O, but no sound came out. She gulped as the tears began streaming down her face faster. Jaxson felt panic hitch his breath in his throat. "I *shouldn't* want more and I'm sorry that I do. It's selfish of me. I thought I learned my lesson with Kendra – I shouldn't jump into relationships so quickly. Especially not with everything going on with this job and my boys and…" He shut his eyes for just a moment, and then opened them again. Pleading with her to understand. "But this past week – nine days," he amended quickly, just to tease her, "has been downright miserable. It was Chloe down at the diner who showed me the error of my ways; she told me to pull my head out of my ass. She's not one for mincing words."

Sugar laughed weakly. "She moved to Long Valley years ago – she's a transplant from Arizona, actually – but the way she talks, you'd think she'd been here her whole life. She fits right in."

Hamlet was nudging them then, obviously over trying to wait patiently for someone to remember to throw his ball for him. Jaxson picked it up this time, a ball of grime and slobber and ice, and hucked it, Hamlet taking off eagerly into the darkening twilight after it.

"Fitting in…it's not something I've managed to do real well yet," Jaxson admitted with a grimace. "I had no idea there'd be such a culture shock, moving up here. It's only 90 minutes away from Boise, but it might as well be on the other side of the world in some ways. I stick out like an Eskimo at a beach party."

She let out a full-fledged laugh at that one and he grinned down at her, back to feeling ten feet tall again. He loved making her laugh. "You know how much this job means to me," he said softly. "I can't screw it up. I can't lose it. My boys mean too much to me. But I'm starting to realize that I don't have to choose between them and a relationship. I thought I had to, but I…I don't."

He cleared his throat and said formally, "Sugar, will you be my girlfriend?" He felt stupid asking it; he felt like he was in junior high all over again.

But he wanted to know.

The edges of her mouth quirked up and he knew she'd had the same thought about junior high, but before he could properly build up a blush on his cheeks from embarrassment, she said quietly, "Yes. Yes, please."

He grinned, his mouth muscles aching from the cold, or maybe it was just from grinning so wide. "It seems like we ought to seal this with a kiss," he said, lowering his face to just above hers, hovering over her mouth. "You always need to seal a bargain somehow."

His lips danced lightly over hers as her breath, soft and light, whooshed out. "Bargain, eh?" she whispered against his lips. "Who do you suppose got the better end of the deal?"

"Hamlet. Now he has two people to love on him."

Her laughter tinkled out into the bitter cold air but Jaxson wasn't feeling the cold any longer. Nothing existed in his world except for her. He settled his lips over hers, feeling their softness and creases as his tongue flicked out, begging for entrance, and then she opened her mouth, moaning with pleasure as her fingers dug into his shoulders, clinging to him with everything she had.

It was right about the time that Jaxson was trying to unzip

her jacket so he could reach her body that he was jerked back to the present. They were standing in the middle of City Park, in sub-zero temperatures, and he was trying to *undress* her?

"Sorry," he mumbled, jerking his hand back. "I don't know what I was thinking."

She laughed shakily. "I don't know what I was thinking either, because you'll notice, I wasn't stopping you."

He looked around the park. "You know, I keep complaining about how small towns know your business, and then I kiss you like that in the middle of City Park. No wonder people know everything that we're doing."

She laughed again, melting against him. "Welcome to small towns," she said breathily, looking up at him. "Where you're living out a real-life episode of *Cheers* every day."

"*Cheers*?" he repeated blankly.

"Remember the theme song? 'Where everyone knows your name'? That's Sawyer for ya!"

"Well, I think we oughta give 'em somethin' to talk about," he said, another grin spreading across his face. "Ready to go? Your place or mine?"

"Yours," she said, scooping up Hamlet's ball from the ground and shoving it into the Ziploc baggie in her pocket. She snapped Hamlet's leash on. "It's a little closer, and at this point, I don't want to wait."

He let out a belly laugh. "C'mon, girlfriend of mine, I love how you think." He grabbed her mittened hand and they hurried down the blustery, wintry street together, heads bent against the wind, hearts as warm as the wind was bitter cold.

CHAPTER 25

JAXSON

IT WAS THE MOST infuriating thing in the world. He'd known that Sugar was dressed in layers while out on their walk, but frankly, this was beyond that. She was *buried* in clothing.

It all began when Jaxson nearly ruined everything by trying to shut the door before Hamlet was completely inside the apartment. *That* would've destroyed the mood. It's a very good rule to never slam a door on the tail of your girlfriend's dog if you actually wanted to, you know, get some.

Then, Jaxson couldn't seem to get his gloved fingers back around the pull of the zipper on her coat. He'd had no problem back at City Park, but now that it was time to actually follow through, he couldn't manage to get a grip.

Literally.

He began pulling at his gloves and couldn't seem to get them off either. Sugar laughed as he grunted in frustration and then, in the grips of pure desperation, stuck the tips of the gloves into his mouth, bit down, and yanked mercilessly at them.

He wondered for a moment what he'd done in a former life

to deserve gloves like these. Surely, he couldn't have done something *that* awful.

Meanwhile, Sugar'd somehow managed to work the zipper of his coat without any problem at all.

Magic. She was magic. Or very, very good in a past life.

Finally free of his thick ski gloves, he returned to removing her parka. Her clothing – apparently hellbent on making things as difficult as possible on him – began snagging on itself, the zipper catching on the fabric of her puffy coat several times, further delaying him from his ultimate goal.

She shoved at his coat and he stopped his work long enough to shake the sleeves free of his arms. Her hands immediately attacked the buttons of his flannel shirt.

Jaxson finally won against the dastardly zipper and as his prize, slid the arms of her coat over her shoulders, causing Sugar to pause her assault on his clothing.

Jaxson leaned down and their lips met again. Their tongues battled for position and he felt the heat of excitement rising inside of him. His hands increased their frantic exploration of this wonderful woman's body.

Sweaters, shirts, boots, snow pants, socks (three pairs on her tiny feet alone) were shed and flung recklessly about his living room.

Finally, he was left wearing only his stretchy jockey shorts that felt like they were at the limit of their structural integrity. Sugar was still covered in her long underwear, though Jaxson didn't really mind because the thin black layer clung to her curves tightly. The midnight fabric was silky to the touch and transparent enough to show off her lacy bra and matching panties.

He felt the tugging at his jockey shorts as he looked at her. He knew he was going to have a wardrobe malfunction of his own if he didn't get this woman into bed quickly.

Taking her by the hand, he ran the ten feet down the short

hallway of the apartment, tugging her along with him, her magically melodic giggle propelling him along. Dashing through the door to his room, he swung his arm and flung her toward the bed.

Amazingly graceful, Sugar followed along with his direction, spinning around him and jumping lightly backwards onto the bed in one movement.

Jaxson was on top of her as soon as she landed, her body warm against his. His soul felt like it was molding into him as he leaned in to kiss her again. Despite the frantic undressing, he allowed them the time to soak in the moment. There was something different about the intimacy of commitment, and Jaxson reveled in the change. It was both comforting *and* exciting to know that this was more than just temporary entertainment.

"Mmmmm," Sugar moaned into his mouth and then pulled away to admire him. "I need you."

Jaxson did not disagree with the idea and let his hands answer her. He slid them over her silk-covered body until he found the edge of her top. His fingers slipped under the thin fabric and pressed against her skin. She was on fire and he soaked in the feeling of her body rising and falling as her breathing increased rapidly.

He worked his hands further up her body, feeling the light fabric gather around his wrist as he moved. He found his way between her marvelous breasts, exploring the rise and fall of her body. She sucked in a breath at his touch and he grinned to himself.

She was, undoubtedly, the sexiest woman he'd ever known.

His calloused fingers rubbed over her hardened nipples lightly as he moved his hand. He loved the way she shuddered.

Finally, Jaxson slipped his other hand under her delicate back and helped her to a sitting position. Pulling his hand from under her bra, he managed to keep hold of the fabric he'd gathered. Sugar lifted her arms as he pulled the thin base layer off over her head. Once again, the clothing went flying to parts unknown as Jaxson focused his attention on the lacy bra that was slightly askew over her tits.

He encircled her with his arms as his fingers worked the set of small hooks with surprising dexterity.

His body responded to the sight of her freed breasts. He wanted to devour her. He wanted to take her right then and there, but he contained himself. She would want this to be a slow and romantic moment, and he needed to be willing to oblige her, no matter how painful it was. And God, was it painful. He began slowly making his way across her body, dropping little nibbling kisses here and there, trying to slow himself down.

He could do this. He *would* do this. He'd give her what she needed, and nothing less.

Sugar reached out, her hand flashing as she caught hold of his shaft. "Baby, this slow parade is great and all, but sometimes, a girl wants to ride her firetruck across town at a hundred miles an hour with the siren blaring."

Jaxson laughed at her ultra-specific metaphor before pouncing on her; hands, tongues, legs, and arms intertwining at a frantic pace. The touches were too many and too frequent to catalog. They kissed passionately and rolled from one side to the other until finally, Sugar won out, straddling him triumphantly.

Pinning his shoulders to the bed with her hands, she lifted her hips. The look on her face was that of pure, unadulterated, sinister glee. Jaxson watched her eyes, the brown color taking on a flaming quality as she lowered herself back down. She slid over him, her aim perfect and confident as she captured his entire length in a single motion.

Jaxson's eyes closed as he took in the sensation of heat

radiating through his skin, her body holding tightly to him. Despite wanting to ride her "firetruck" across town, he allowed himself a moment to fully appreciate this feeling.

Sugar was on her own schedule, though, and began lifting and falling on top of him. She slid perfectly over him until her full weight – not that it was much – rested on him. She then lifted off him again. Each set of movements was quicker than the one before.

Jaxson reached out, placing his hands on her hips and letting his arms match her rising and falling. His eyes were fixed on her amazing tits that bounced and jiggled in time to the rest of her body.

He'd never seen such a glorious sight in all his life.

"Oh yes. Oh yes, oh *yeeeesssss!*" Sugar screamed as her body went rigid. He could feel her thighs tightening against his hips. He let her have the time she needed, enjoying her experiencing pleasure.

Finally, she relaxed and collapsed against him. She panted for breath and her skin stuck to his as their sweat mingled together.

Jaxson waited for a couple more moments. When she began to lift her hips up and down in small strokes, he took it as his cue. He rolled to the side and Sugar giggled as he unseated her.

She looked confused for just a moment when he grabbed her hips and rolled her back toward the middle of the bed, putting her on her belly. He lifted her hips and her legs immediately folded into place underneath her.

Propping herself up with her arms, she looked over her shoulder with that same fiery look and then shook her ass at him.

He felt the same devilishness overtake his face as he gripped her and pushed his hips forward into her.

"Oh hell yes," Sugar screamed as he slid inside of her. He flexed his fingers, digging into her. "Oh God yes, baby please!"

He'd never been with a woman who talked during sex. Her open indication that she was enjoying herself heightened the experience.

He slid himself back and then forward again.

"Harder," she begged and he responded. He pulled her quickly to him and shoved his hips forward with more power. "Harder," she pleaded again, and once more he obliged.

This continued. With each thrust, she begged him to be rougher with her. He continued to increase the strength he used until it felt like he was hammering away at her tiny body. Their bodies moved so fast, the room filled with the sound of skin slapping against skin.

Each smack spoke to a primal part of him. This was the one woman he wanted. He wanted to know her. To feel her. To protect her. She was becoming everything to him and each thrust cemented the feeling firmer and firmer within his being.

Jaxson felt the tension building inside of him. He mentally begged himself for the sweet release he knew was imminent. One or two more thrusts, and he would be there.

"Yeeeeessssssss!" she hissed through gritted teeth. Her head flung backward as her body tensed, his body following suit. Their muscles tightened and they were pinned together as the waves of joy crashed over them.

Finally, they slumped forward, collapsing onto the mattress and each other. Once again, their bodies stuck together as the sweat of their exertion mingled.

"Don't let me…" Sugar panted, "ignore my alarm in the morning. Whatever you have to do, make me get up."

"Okay," was all he could get out before she was asleep. Jaxson didn't know where her phone was and hoped it wasn't buried in a pocket of a coat out in the living room, because then he would never hear it.

His eyes were heavy and his soul was calm as he lay there, half covering her body with his. He felt the warm weight of sleep stealing over him when his nose perked up.

The telltale smell of smoke tickled his nostrils and his eyes flew open.

Jaxson took another sniff of the air. He forced himself to have a full grasp on the situation before he went into "action" mode. It was a light smell. It was like the dust burning off the heater the first time a furnace was fired up for the year, but the heat had been on for months now.

He sniffed again. The smell was a bit fuller now. He gently pulled himself away from Sugar, certain that he could handle this without waking her. He found his feet and followed his nose. He didn't have to go far.

In the corner of his bedroom, Jaxson had a lamp next to the dresser. It was a fake-brass thing about five feet tall that he'd found at a thrift store. Sugar's silk base layer shirt had landed on the shade and was starting to smoke from the heat of the bulb.

Jaxson pulled the thin fabric off the lamp and inspected the small hole that had started to form. *Pleasure has its price*, he thought to himself, grinning as he dropped the shirt to the floor.

He took one more look around the room and was about to head back to bed when he realized light was spilling through the door from the living room. He gave an internal sigh and walked out to shut off the light.

He found that in all the excitement, both he and Sugar had forgotten there were *three* people in the apartment – technically Hamlet was a dog, but pets were family, too. The Great Dane had occupied his time by gathering all of their winter clothes into the center of the living room and making himself a bed. His usual spot on the left side of Sugar's sleeping form was not going to be, and Hamlet had obviously realized that.

Jaxson smiled at the dog's ingenuity and stepped into the small kitchen. He grabbed a large bowl and filled it with water. Hamlet looked up from his makeshift bed with a grateful look as Jaxson set the bowl on the floor.

Heading back to the bedroom, flipping the light switch as he went, Jaxson made a mental shopping list. *Gigantic dog bed, enormous bag of dog food, and massive water and food bowls.*

Crawling back into his bed, he found that Sugar had curled into a tight ball. Jaxson wrapped himself around her, falling in love just a little more with how well her size complimented his. He felt his soul relax, and he let sleep take ahold of him.

CHAPTER 26
SUGAR

THERE WAS A NOISE and Sugar couldn't figure out what it was and she was hitting, slapping, thumping to make it go away, and then she was drifting in a sea of warmth and happiness, snuggled up against this hard, long, warm thing...

"Sugar..." Someone was whispering, shaking her shoulder, and she burrowed down further under the covers. It was so perfect, right where she was at. She never wanted to move. She could stay here forever.

They were asking her something and she couldn't understand the words. "The heat is in the covers," she explained. There, now they'd leave her alone.

Except, they were shaking her again. "Sugar, you gotta wake up." This time, she realized it was Jaxson's voice. Why was Jaxson talking to her?

Hold on, why was Jaxson in her bed?

She shot straight up, clutching the sheets to her as she looked around the room, completely disoriented. "Where... what...?" She shoved her hair behind her ear and looked over at Jaxson. "Where are we?" she asked.

He used the pad of his thumb to wipe some dried drool off

her cheek. "My apartment. You spent the night." He handed her phone over – he must've retrieved it from her jacket after it started going off – and she groggily took it from him.

She looked around again, things slowly starting to come back to her. "Oh. Right. We came back here after our walk…" She trailed off as she remembered everything that had happened the night before, a blush climbing in her cheeks.

He sent her a lascivious grin, obviously remembering too. "Your alarm went off, and you told me last night to tell you this morning that if you ignored it, that you'd have to do the walk of shame to work, wearing the same clothes as yesterday, and to not let this-morning's-Sugar get away with that."

She sank back into the mattress, stretching and smiling drowsily. "That sounds like me," she mumbled, her face sinking back into the pillow. Jaxson had the *best* pillows. She needed to ask him where he got them from. In just a minute, she would. She just needed to close her eyes for a moment longer…

Then a whoosh of cool air flowed over her as Jaxson threw the covers back, exposing her naked body to the brisk morning air. "Aack!" she yelped, jackknifing upright in bed again.

He grinned at her unrepentantly. "I'm just following orders, ma'am," he drawled. "*Your* orders."

Her eyes drifted closed again as she stuck her tongue out at him. She felt for the edge of the bed, deciding that she could edge towards it with her eyes closed safely enough when suddenly, she was hitting the floor with a crash, her eyes popping open with surprise. His face appeared above hers, peering down at her worriedly. "You okay?" he asked.

She rubbed her elbow where she'd smashed it on the floor. She really ought to start trying to get out of bed in a way that didn't involve a face-plant. She reached over and grabbed a couple of scattered pieces of clothing so she could start pulling them on.

"You're one of those dreadfully cheerful people in the

morning, aren't you?" she mumbled as she pulled the first of her many layers on. She'd come here dressed with more layers than a trip to the North Pole would require, and putting them all back on seemed…exhausting. "The kind I love to hate?"

He was still hanging over the edge of the bed. "Yup!" he said cheerfully, rubbing it in. Sugar glared at him, but before she could force her brain to come up with some sort of response, Hamlet showed up. He wasn't much more of a morning person than she was, but having finally realized that they weren't going to shut up and let him sleep in peace, he trotted over and began giving her face a bath, happy to welcome her to the land of the living.

"Hammllleeeetttt," she chided him, pushing him away. "We are brushing your teeth tonight. I do *not* have enough coffee in me to deal with that much doggie breath."

He wagged his tail excitedly. Come to think of it, he wagged his tail excitedly about almost everything. It was one of his most awful personality quirks.

Granted, Sugar loved this personality quirk when she was more awake, but at…she peered at the alarm clock on Jaxson's nightstand…4:48 in the morning, she quite hated it.

And didn't feel even slightly bad about it.

Finally, after an expedition into the living room where she retrieved the rest of her clothing from Hamlet's makeshift bed, she managed to get all of her layers on. She was quite proud of herself for that minor miracle, really. She looked over to see that Jaxson was dressed too – when that'd happened, she wasn't quite sure. She was sad she'd missed seeing his naked body in the process. And then they were heading out the door, Hamlet happy to find a bush to do his own morning routine.

"I'd drive you back to your place," Jaxson said ruefully, "but I left my Explorer at the bakery all night. If the rumors weren't swirling before, they're surely full steam ahead now."

"If it wasn't such a bright green, it wouldn't stand out so much," Sugar pointed out as they began heading back to her place. For once, she was very glad to live in such a small town. Nothing was too far from anything else. The bakery, her apartment, his apartment, the park…in a normal-sized town, each destination could be a half hour away from each other, instead of just a couple minutes' walk.

There were benefits to living in a small town, even if they weren't always readily apparent.

"Chloe told me the same thing," Jaxson said with a laugh. "In Boise, it didn't really matter as much. Around here, a person's vehicle really seems to matter to people."

"Oh yeah," Sugar agreed. "Like the fact that you even own an SUV is strange. I can't name another guy in town who drives something other than a truck." They were nearing her apartment now and despite the bitter cold air, Sugar still didn't want to hurry. She was enjoying herself, which she didn't think was possible before her third cup of coffee.

"Trucks aren't real practical for kids," Jaxson said, shrugging. "There are those quad cabs, of course, but they're monsters. When you're in heavy traffic, you don't want to drive something that big."

Sugar cocked an eyebrow at him. "Exactly my point," she drawled. "Sawyer isn't exactly bursting with cars whizzing by."

He looked around, surprised. "You know, I don't think we've seen a single car since we started on our walk," he said, the surprise evident in his voice.

"It's five o'clock in the morning," she pointed out. "Where do you think people would be going at this hour of the day?"

Jaxson shrugged. "Even at three in the morning in Boise, there was always someone out on the road."

"Like hookers and drug dealers?" Sugar asked dryly.

"Hey, *you're* the one with a name like 'Sugar,'" he protested. "That makes you the closest I've ever been to a hooker."

She let out a belly laugh at that, and then sobered up and punched him in the shoulder.

"Oww!" he yelped, rubbing the bruised spot dramatically. "What was that for?"

"My name is *not* the name of a hooker," she informed him primly, as she opened her front door and Hamlet shot inside, happy to be home. "And you best remember that if you ever want to get laid again."

She shut the door in his surprised face and then leaned against it with a small giggle. It was rather fun messing with Jaxson Anderson's mind, turned out. He was going to spend the day worried that he'd somehow offended her, when the truth was, she'd long ago quit being touchy about her name. One couldn't be "blessed" with a name like Sugar, be touchy about it, and still retain their sanity. It simply couldn't be done.

But that didn't make it any less fun to mess with Jaxson's mind over it.

CHAPTER 27

JAXSON

JAXSON WANDERED up the street to the bakery to retrieve his SUV. He'd scoot back home for a quick shower and change so he wouldn't do the same thing that he'd teased Sugar about – the walk of shame by wearing the same clothes to work two days in a row.

Sugar…dammit all, was she really upset with him about the hooker joke? She seemed to have such a great sense of humor and he'd only been teasing her. She'd laughed, and then… suddenly she was pissed.

Women. If they didn't come with such delicious body parts and didn't make him feel so damn good, he might just quit them altogether.

Unfortunately, they did.

As he began heading back to his apartment in the still-defrosting Explorer, he decided to take a detour over to Betty's Diner along the way. He normally didn't eat out for breakfast – although he was a regular at the diner at lunch time – but he had time to kill before he had to be at work, and a nice plate of pancakes and sausages sounded good to him right then. Chloe, his favorite waitress at the diner, hadn't come in yet but he enjoyed a leisurely meal anyway, downing more than his fair share of coffee.

Finally, full and content, he headed back out and towards home to actually get ready for the day that he'd already been up for, for hours – *how did Sugar do this every day?* – when he spotted a small curl of smoke coming from the back of the burned-out shell of a mill.

The Horvath Mill.

And not the cloud of smoke that comes from breath on a cold winter morning – this was a long, thin tendril. Like what one would get if they were smoking a cigarette.

He slowed down, his heart rate accelerating in tandem. Surely the same damn kids wouldn't set fire to the mill a second time, right?

He turned the corner at a crawl, peering through the driver's side window at the backside of the mill. There, he spotted a group of boys, talking and hanging out. He glanced at the clock on the dashboard. Same time as last time – ten minutes before school started.

They'd honest to God decided to do it again. Jaxson shook his head in bewilderment. Was he this stubbornly dumb when he was a teenager? He hated to think so, even if he was afraid it was true.

He put his SUV in park and strode across the deserted road to the backside of the mill, black streaks from the fire permanently etched into its brick walls. "Are you kids trying to do it again?" he demanded when he got close enough, reaching out and grabbing the lit cigarette out of the mouth of the mayor's son.

They'd never met, of course – their social circles weren't exactly the same – but Moose and Levi had pointed him out one day so Jaxson could keep a close eye on him. Considering how much trouble this punk kid had cost him, Jaxson had appreciated the help.

"Hey, man," Angus protested, tossing his dyed black hair

out of his face as Jaxson ground the cigarette out under the sole of his boot. "I have to go to class. I can't make it through without—"

"You're 16 years old, and you're trying to tell me you're already addicted to cigarettes?" Jaxson demanded, cutting off his protests. The kid shrugged nonchalantly, the other kids mimicking his gesture. Too cool for rules, the lot of them.

"What does it matter to you?" Angus tossed back insolently. He looked closer at Jaxson's face. "Hold on, you're the new fire chief, aren't you?"

Jaxson grabbed his arm and pulled him out of the group of teenage boys, starting back across the street to his vehicle. "Yup, I am," he said grimly.

"Where are you taking me?" Angus howled. "My dad is your boss. He's gonna hear all about this! I'll have you fired by tonight!"

"I'm performing a citizen's arrest," Jaxson informed him, opening up the back door to his Explorer and pushing the kid inside. "You've got another year until it's legal to smoke, no matter who your dad is."

"What?!" Angus burst out, staring horrified at Jaxson's reflection in the rearview mirror. "You can't take me to the police station! I...I...I can't miss class!" he announced. "I'm supposed to be in school."

"You also aren't supposed to be smoking, so I think we're even."

Jaxson tuned out the begging and pleading from the backseat after that. It was only a couple of blocks down to the police station and for a moment, he wished he had sirens on his personal vehicle like he did on a firetruck. Turning on the lights was half the fun of putting out a fire.

He marched Angus inside, holding tight to his elbow. Officer Knittle looked up from the front desk, his eyes widening at the sight of Angus being dragged into the building. "What…what's going on?" he asked, shooting to his feet.

"Angus here was smoking outside the mill. Again. I've performed a citizen's arrest on him. Now, you can either book him or call the mayor and I'll explain to him why you're not doing your duty as a police officer of this town. But either way, the kid's ass is going into a jail cell."

Angus was back to his babbling bluster, trying to appeal to the city officer. "You can't arrest me! My dad will have your head. Plus, I'm supposed to be going to school right now. You're gonna get in trouble for keeping a minor out of school."

The officer's gaze shot back and forth between them, like he was watching a tennis match on TV, and Jaxson held his breath. He'd never done a citizen's arrest and really didn't know the proper procedure for it. For all he knew, what he was doing right then really was illegal, but dammit all, he wasn't gonna back down. Not now. Not after everything this kid had done – intentionally or not – to Jaxson's career.

The officer reached down and picked up the phone. *Dammit, dammit, dammit.*

His bluff had been called.

"This is on your head," the officer said, shoving the phone into his hand. Jaxson took it, along with a deep breath.

You got yourself into this. Now the only choice left is to see it through.

"Hello?" rumbled the sleepy, gruff voice of the mayor.

CHAPTER 28

SUGAR

SUGAR STRUGGLED WITH the giant bag of flour, pushing and shoving the thing across the floor with all her might. The damn thing weighed as much as she did, and moving it was like trying to push a damn boulder across the kitchen.

She had it balanced on its edge and after a moment's contemplation, began trying a new tactic of waddling with it tucked between her legs like some bizarre impersonation of a penguin with an egg on its feet – she'd watched way too many nature documentaries at this point, she decided – when she heard a burst of loud laughter come through from up front.

It startled her and she lost her tenuous grip on the edge of the bag of flour. In slow motion, she saw it begin to tumble and she was grabbing for it but it slipped through her hands and exploded in front of her, flour shooting out of a split seam in the top and all over the tiled kitchen floor.

Sugar began choking and waving her hand in front of her face, trying to clear the air enough to breathe. She heard more laughter and looked up at the swinging doors separating the front shop from the kitchen, to see Gage and Jaxson there, leaning up against the wall on either side of the opening, wearing matching grins.

Of *course* they'd witnessed that.

She wanted to curl up in a little ball and hide – preferably for the next year or so – but instead decided that it'd be much less embarrassing if she simply did her best to play it off as a joke.

"So…" she said casually, leaning against the stainless steel counter as if she didn't have a care in the world, "how's your day going?"

The effect was sadly ruined by another coughing fit as the flour did its best to worm its way inside of her. Jaxson hurried over and began patting her on the back, which only sent up clouds of flour into the air. She waved his "help" away as Gage began the task of trying to sweep the mess up.

Realizing that she probably didn't want to discuss the flour fiasco in any sort of detail – pretending it had never happened was a much better idea in Sugar's estimation – Gage spoke up. "Jaxson here performed a citizen's arrest this morning on the way to work. You know, after he came here and picked up his car."

Sugar ignored that last comment.

"Who did you arrest?" she asked, turning to him, eyes wide.

"Angus."

Sugar was pretty sure that announcement was more surprising than her dropping the bag of flour on the floor. Her mouth gaped open and she just stared up at him. A part of her wanted to panic, but he seemed so calm about it. So…unfazed.

If he'd been fired, he wouldn't be calm, right?

Jaxson, reading the panic on her face, shot her a saucy grin. "The mayor thanked me."

The kitchen was quiet for a moment, and then they all began laughing. "Are you freakin' kidding me?!" Sugar yelped, when she could finally breathe enough to talk.

She knew Angus. Everyone knew Angus. He was an asshole. A troublemaker. He spent most of his free time thinking of ways to bully other people around, and didn't hesitate in telling them that they couldn't touch him because he was the mayor's *son*.

A hell of a lot like her ex-husband, actually. What was it with guys demanding to be treated special because of who they were related to? Ridiculous, really.

Jaxson shrugged as if it wasn't a big deal, but the quirk around the edges of his mouth told Sugar that was just an act. "Said that he's been struggling with Angus for months now, and it was about time someone stood up to him. Teenage boys are apparently less than saintly and perfect. Who knew!"

Sugar walked over to the large trash can on wheels and shook her hair out over it, trying to get most of the white dust into the bin and not just onto the floor.

"Did he arrest…" Sugar started to ask Gage, but he was already shaking his head no.

"Who?" Jaxson asked, looking between the two of them, confused.

Gage went back to sweeping up the mess. "My younger brother, Chris. He happens to be Angus' best friend. He was probably there when you picked up Angus this morning. Did you see a tall, skinny kid, bleached blond hair combed forward into his eyeballs, acne, with skinny jeans on?"

"Yeah, I did," Jaxson said, surprised. "But Angus was the only one smoking, so he's the only one I focused on."

"I wouldn't be surprised if my brother had taken up smoking," Gage said with a bitter laugh. "If you catch him smoking, feel free to do a citizen's arrest on him, too. He…" Gage shook his head. "My parents had wanted a third kid for years and years, but couldn't seem to get pregnant. When Chris finally came along, they were getting a little older, you know? They should've been planning for their golden years, not diapering a baby. I think they were just too tired to take him on like he needed. Seventeen years later, and he's only matched in assholishness by his best friend. They make *quite* the pair."

Sugar wasn't sure what to say to that. It was true – every last bit of it. She and Emma had spent a lot of time dissecting where Chris went wrong, and they both agreed that it came from an upbringing where insolence was thought of as being "cute," and laziness was excused with, "He's just a baby," even when he was hitting his early teens. Unlike Emma and Gage, who'd been put to work at an early age, Chris had been coddled every step of the way.

And damn did it show.

Gage had tried to get his brother into the bakery to work and make some extra money on the side, but Chris had shrugged him off, and their parents had told him that Chris needed to focus on his school work. Which would've been fine…if that's what he was actually doing.

But Chris wasn't about to graduate as valedictorian of his class.

Sugar sighed in sympathy, and then turned back to Jaxson, trying to take the spotlight off Gage. "So where is the mayor's son at now?" she asked brightly. "Cooling his heels in a jail cell?"

"Yup. The mayor told me to have him hang out there for a day. Maybe it'd give him the time to think through his priorities."

Sugar snorted with laughter. She'd been kidding with the jail cell comment, but was starting to realize that Jaxson didn't mess around. "Remind me not to get onto your bad side," she said dryly.

He shot her an unrepentant grin. "You know, I still haven't gone home and cleaned up," he told her in a low rumble, his voice vibrating through her as he pulled her against him. "I never got that far. It looks like you could use some cleaning up, too." He patted her hair, sending up a small cloud of flour into the air. "We could go clean each other—"

"Some of us have to work 'round here," Gage interrupted drolly. Jaxson shot him a disgruntled look.

"Fine, fine. Well then, I'm here to pick up a dozen donuts."

"You have another training meeting?" Sugar asked, leaning over the trash can again, wiping at her shirt and jeans. She sure was a disaster. She didn't even want to look in the mirror.

"Nope. I'm taking them over to the jail."

She stopped in her cleaning efforts to gape at Jaxson.

"I thought I'd talk to him. See if I could make some headway."

She felt a smile spread across her lips as she stared at him. She couldn't be more impressed if he'd just announced he'd won a gold medal at the Olympics.

He wasn't going to make any headway, of course, but it was sure nice of him to try.

What a difference from Dick. It was hard to believe they were the same species, really. She tried for a moment to imagine her ex-husband reaching out to someone who needed guidance and direction, and snorted in disbelief. If Dick was going to guide anyone anywhere, it was towards the bar and alcoholism.

"Donuts are on the house," Gage said, sweeping up the last of the flour. "If that's all it takes to get through to Angus and my brother, you can have as many as you want."

Yeah, it was naïve of Jaxson to think that this would work, but as Sugar led the way back up front to pick out a box of donuts for him, she couldn't help but wish it was the way the world worked, anyway.

CHAPTER 29

JAXSON

H E PULLED UP in front of the city jail, a second time that day, and after patting his hair to get the remaining flour out of it, he swung out of his Explorer, donuts in hand. Officer Knittle looked up when he came in, surprised. "Can't get enough of the Sawyer Jail?" he asked sarcastically.

Jaxson laughed. "Something like that. Can I go back and see Angus for a minute?"

"Sure," Knittle said, coming around the desk. He led Jaxson to the back and pulled his keys off his belt to unlock the jail cell door. There was only one cell there; it looked like the city used it as a holding tank until they could shuffle people off elsewhere.

Jaxson walked into the small cell, holding the opened box of donuts out to Angus. "Want one?" he asked, Officer Knittle swinging the door almost closed behind him, leaving it slightly ajar so Jaxson could leave when he was done. He appreciated the thoughtfulness.

The kid reached out and grabbed one, hiding beneath the long fringe of his dyed black hair as he began eating it. No *thank you*, no *appreciate it*.

Was Jaxson this rude when he was a teen? He liked to pretend those years hadn't happened because they hadn't exactly been wonderful ones, but looking back, he grimaced to himself.

Yeah, he probably was this rude. Maybe even more.

"When I was a kid, I was mad at the world," he said softly, sitting down on the twin bed across from Angus. The springs squeaked beneath his weight as he took his time, carefully selecting a sprinkle-covered donut out of the box to eat before continuing on. "Didn't know who my dad was. Mom refused to tell me. The way I looked at it, he obviously didn't love me enough to show up when I needed him, and so every guy I met, I pretended it was him. I got into more than a few fights."

He turned sideways and settled up against the gray cinder block wall, licking his fingers between each bite. Angus just stared at the floor, hiding beneath the shock of hair he carefully brushed forward into his face every morning. *Who is he hiding from?*

"My mom's got early Alzheimer's," he continued. "She's in a nursing home now, and doesn't even recognize me when I go to visit her. Chances are, she doesn't even know the name of my dad at this point. Till the day I die, I'll never know who my dad is. Made me angry enough to hit and kick and punch and do drugs—" Angus snorted at that, still staring at the floor, "—and make a lot of other really stupid decisions. Firefighting saved me. Not Jesus, although I don't have anything against the man. No, it was fighting fires. It gave me a purpose. I could finally help people, instead of always hurting them.

"And the strangest thing was, I found that once I stopped trying to hurt everyone else, I stopped hurting myself. I went straight, and I never looked back."

He paused, waiting for Angus to say anything – anything at all – but he was still just staring at the cell floor, refusing to make eye contact or utter a word.

"Is there someone or something that's hurting you?" Jaxson

asked quietly. He knew it was a long shot – teenage boys didn't tend to open up to strangers after five minutes of talking and a free donut – but still, he sighed when Angus didn't say anything. Didn't move. He'd become a statue on the bed, a monument to anger and identity crisis and pissedoffedness at the world.

Jaxson stood, leaving another donut on the bed next to Angus. Finally, some movement – the kid grabbed it and began eating again. Still no *thank you* or *appreciate it*, but Jaxson hadn't expected any. It'd take a while until Angus got to that point, if ever.

"Smoking as a teen is a punishable offense. I'll talk to your dad about it. See what we can work out." He walked out of the cell, closing it behind him with a clang, and still, Angus said nothing, just sitting morosely on the bed, staring at the floor sightlessly.

Jaxson gave the remaining box of donuts to the police officers on duty, knowing that if he kept the box to himself, he'd just eat all of them. He wasn't sure how much more his waistline could take. He knocked on the partially open door to the mayor's office, and opened it up fully at the barked, "Come in!" He stepped in, closing the door behind him quietly.

"Oh, Chief Anderson," the portly mayor said, easing his considerable bulk up from his chair and hurrying around his desk to shake his hand. "Thanks for stopping by. And thanks for your help with my son. Take a seat."

He gestured to one of the chairs angled in front of his desk, moving back around to sit behind its polished surface. Jaxson noticed the unspoken body language – the mayor was, consciously or not, using his desk to emphasize his position as mayor. Did he equate power with his political position? Or was he in it to help others?

Jaxson hadn't interacted much with the mayor up to this point – he just hadn't been in town long enough, really – so he simply slotted the body language away for later analysis.

"I wanted to talk to you a little bit about your son," Jaxson said evenly, keeping eye contact with the mayor as he spoke. "I ran with a pretty rough crowd as a teen, and made a lot of mistakes. I was angry, and was taking it out on the world. Is there anything going on at home to cause Angus to act out?"

The mayor shook his head, his jowls swinging with the movement. "No, everything's normal at home. He just hit those hormonal years, I guess, because he's been near impossible for a while now."

Jaxson wanted to pry more, but he wasn't exactly a family therapist, and even if he was, the mayor wasn't his client. It was best to leave any further discussion about difficulties at home out of it.

"Well, there's a program across the nation called the National Junior Firefighter Program," he told the mayor. "Basically, it's the firefighter version of the ROTC. Usually, you can start training to become a firefighter when you're only 16. You don't get paid – it's strictly volunteer work when you're in high school – but it's a good way of trying out the field before deciding to become a full-time firefighter. Plus, it keeps you busy and out of trouble. You can't smoke pot if you're at a training meeting and learning how to put out fires."

"You think Angus ought to do this?" the mayor asked.

"I do. I'd like to expand the program to more teens over time – truth be told, our firefighting department is suffering from the same thing that most volunteer departments are suffering from: Our average age of volunteer firefighters is hovering around the retirement age. When the older men age out and can no longer serve, we only have a handful of guys left who can take a call in case of a fire breaking out. Moose, Levi, Troy, Dylan, and Luke are all younger but most of the rest of them are old enough to be my dad, or even my grandfather. Building up this program could only be a good thing for this community. We can sell it as your son being the trial run, rather than this is punishment for destroying one of the historical landmarks in town."

The mayor grimaced at that. He'd told Jaxson over the phone that morning that no one had dared to tell him that it was his son who'd caused that fire; according to the mayor, he'd never been told they'd caught the culprits. He had no idea his son was involved.

Jaxson wasn't entirely sure he believed that line; it was possible, of course, but he also wondered if it was a small-town case of "Don't ask, don't tell." No one told the mayor the truth, because they knew the mayor didn't want to hear it.

Jaxson was just enough of an outsider to upset this delicate balance, and just obstinate enough to be willing to do it. Chances were, this was going to eventually cost him, but on the other hand, ignoring the situation and trying to lay low got him a deputy chief who he had to fire, a burnt-out shell of a building, and a town full of people who thought that he didn't know his ass from his head.

He was done playing nice. If he got fired, at least he'd be able to leave town with his head held high, knowing he did his best.

"Let's do it," the mayor said. "My son can start after school next week. Do you think we ought to let him out so he can get to class?" He asked the question with a hopeful note in his voice, and Jaxson ground his back teeth in frustration.

"Well, he's your son," Jaxson pointed out. *Captain Obvious, reporting for duty.* "But I think maybe a day to cool his heels and think about things wouldn't go amiss."

"Right, right." The mayor bobbed his head in agreement. Jaxson wondered again about the dynamic between father and son, and if anyone else at home played into the picture. The mayor swore up, down, and sideways that he didn't know about his son's behavior and was appalled by it, but when it came to actually punishing the kid in any fashion, he seemed reluctant to do so.

Jaxson stood. "I better go get cleaned up." He gestured at his rumpled clothes, flour dusted on them. "Been…a rough morning." He decided to leave out the part where he was wearing his clothes from the day before, hadn't taken a shower yet that morning, and then had ended up in a flour bath because of Sugar's baking skills.

He figured that was a story he could leave out for the time being.

He headed out of City Hall and back to his apartment. He could get cleaned up, head back to work – hopefully with no citizen's arrests along the way – and then tonight, he got to pick his boys up. They were back to their regularly scheduled weekends, and it was his turn.

Should he introduce Sugar to the boys as his girlfriend? His gut twisted at the thought – from excitement or sheer panic, Jaxson couldn't be sure. They both felt about the same to him at the moment.

It was a pretty fast move, considering they'd just officially started dating about twelve hours ago, but on the other hand, the boys were damn in love with Hamlet. They'd spend the whole weekend asking when they would get to see "Scooby-Doo," as they insisted on calling him, if he didn't have her come over. And if he had her come over and she was within arm's reach, he didn't figure he'd be able to keep his hands off her, even if it just meant holding her hand.

No, it was time to tell the boys, caution be damned.

CHAPTER 30

SUGAR

SUGAR TOOK A DEEP BREATH. She was terrified, which was ridiculous. These were small children, not serial killers.

But she'd never officially met someone else's kids as their father's girlfriend before. She steadfastly refused to acknowledge the last time she'd come over to the Anderson's house with Hamlet in tow – that hadn't been intentional. Plus, she really hadn't been dating their dad at the time.

Now she was.

She raised her hand and knocked on the door. She heard a scramble of feet and indistinct voices, then a shout of, "I'm older!" before the door flew open to reveal Aiden.

"Hi, Aiden the Elder," Sugar said with a laugh. He shot her a confused look, clearly not understanding the reference, and then spotted Hamlet next to her.

"Scooby-Doo!" he yelled, launching himself at Hamlet. Hamlet's tail was wagging a million miles an hour, and she swore he had a doggie grin on his face. Maybe she wasn't the only one who was getting lonely at night.

"We better come in before we let out all the heat," Sugar said, tugging once on Hamlet's leash. He obediently moved forward into the small apartment, dragging Aiden along with him as if he weighed nothing at all. Once inside, he sat down to patiently receive all of the happy, adoring love the two boys could pour on him.

With the kids sufficiently distracted, Sugar unclipped Hamlet's leash and walked over to Jaxson, looping it around him and pulling him towards her. His eyes lit up and he looked down at her like a famished man at a banquet table.

"Hey there, beautiful," he murmured, pulling Sugar into his arms. She snuggled up happily against him, then leaned back, daring him to kiss her. She shouldn't – she knew she shouldn't – but she couldn't help herself.

His eyes shot over to the boys, still loving on Hamlet, and back down to her. "With an invitation like that," he breathed, and then his mouth covered hers and he was pulling her against him, his hands cradling her head, a low growl of pleasure in his throat.

"Daaaaadddddd!" one of the boys howled. Sugar was too dazed to pin the voice down. She jerked her head back, her face already a brilliant red. She spun on her heel and gave the boys a weak smile.

Before she could figure out what to say, Jaxson said softly, "I changed my mind, you guys. I'm dating Sugar after all."

Frankie began jumping up and down. "Does this mean we get to pet Scooby-Doo every weekend?" he cried, a huge grin practically swallowing his face whole.

"Every *other* weekend," Aiden corrected him, as only an older brother would, and then turned back to his dad. "Does this mean she's going to start sleeping here?" he demanded, crossing his arms in what could only be described as a miniature version of Jaxson. She'd seen that exact same disgruntled look on his face more than once.

"Well now, I'm not sure," Jaxson said. "We hadn't talked about it. Do you want her to?"

Aiden shook his head furiously. "You're *our* dad. I don't wanna share."

Frankie, picking up on the cues from his older brother, struck a similar pose. Sugar's heart twisted inside of her and she felt slightly ill. After they'd had so much fun together the last time, she'd somehow convinced herself that they would be excited to have her there.

Turns out, she'd been wrong.

Jaxson dropped to his knees in front of his boys and put a hand on each of their shoulders. "Aiden, Frankie, I want you to hear me. Listen closely and remember, okay?" At their nods, he continued. "I'm always going to be your dad. No matter what happens, no matter who I date, or even someday, if I marry someone. None of that matters when it comes to being your dad. I love you two with all my heart and soul, and that's never gonna change." They both nodded slowly, and Sugar's gut twisted. They shouldn't have moved so fast. The boys were obviously worried about this, and she wasn't happy that she'd caused them so much concern. "But guys, that doesn't mean that I can't date someone else. Dating Sugar doesn't mean I love you less."

Aiden screwed up his mouth and Sugar could tell he wasn't buying this line of logic.

Maybe she shouldn't get involved. These weren't her kids. She didn't have any kids at all. But she felt like she could connect some dots between what Jaxson was saying and what Aiden was hearing, so girding up her loins, she knelt down beside Jaxson.

She looked Aiden in the eye and said quietly, "Some people think that love is like a pie – if you love someone, that takes up a portion of the pie, and you can't love anyone else with that part of the pie. But it isn't true. You two love your mom, right?" They both nodded eagerly, their eyes fastened on her as she spoke. She swallowed the fear inside of her, and plunged on. "Just because you love your mom doesn't mean that you can't love your dad, right? You love them both."

Aiden's eyes began to light up with understanding. "I love my best friend Isaac, too," he told her.

"And the more time you spend around Hamlet, the more you're going to love him," she said with a grin. "Just because you love your mom and your dad and your best friend doesn't mean you can't love Hamlet too, right?"

"He's the nicest dog in the whole world," Frankie said loyally. He'd draped himself over Hamlet, and her dog was taking it stoically, as if his weight was barely noticeable.

Of course, Frankie was so small, his weight probably *was* barely noticeable.

"He really is," Sugar agreed. "So you see, your dad is the same way. He can love you guys and other people too." She didn't dare say "and me," because wouldn't that just be presumptuous. He hadn't told her that he loved her, and even if he felt that way, it was way too damn early in the relationship to say it.

"Do you love Sugar, Daddy?" Aiden asked.

Of *course* he asked that. Sugar wanted to bury her head and groan.

"Sugar and I have just started dating," Jaxson told his sons. "I'll be sure to tell you if we get to that point."

Aiden nodded, accepting that idea without further question. Sugar swallowed hard, her stomach finally loosening up. The first hurdle was over, but with such brilliant kids, she was pretty sure there were more questions to come.

She could only fervently hope to be absent the day they started asking where babies came from. Maybe she could pretend a bakery emergency had happened – *Batman, we've run out of muffins! Quick, to the bakery!* – and run out the door.

They were four and six years old. She figured that was totally believable.

Speaking of…

"You guys want to visit where I work?" At the boys' skeptical looks, identical down to the arched eyebrows, she clarified, "The Muffin Man. It's a bakery in town." They still just stared. "Where we make donuts and cakes and stuff."

"Ohhhh!" they exclaimed in unison. "Can we, Daddy? Please?"

It was Saturday morning, which meant that Holli was manning the front counter. A high schooler, she could only work on the weekends, but Sugar was happy to give her the hours. It seemed like Sugar lived there as it was. It was nice to have the weekends off.

"I have an employee discount, so it's my treat," Sugar told Jaxson. She left out the part where she was doing her damndest to buy the boys' affection. She figured that was probably obvious to Jaxson anyway. Never let it be said that she was above bribery, because she totally wasn't. Not that Jaxson would have much room to complain, Mr. Bring Donuts to the Jail to Bribe Angus.

Jaxson's mouth quirked up around the edges, but he didn't protest. Quite the opposite, actually. "I think I can be persuaded to eat some of Gage's baking," he said, patting his perfectly flat stomach. "If I keep this up, I'm gonna be as big as Hamlet soon, but at least I'll be happy!"

The boys laughed hard at the ridiculous idea, and Jaxson reached out and ruffled their hair. "Go on and get dressed," he said. "It's cold out there, and since Sugar has convinced me to walk everywhere, I figured we'd just walk on down to the bakery."

"I get to walk Scooby-Doo!" Frankie yelled, scrambling to his feet.

"I get to walk him on the way back!" Aiden countered as they ran down the hall to their bedroom to change.

"Nice save," Sugar said, turning on her knees to face her *boyfriend*.

Boy, that had a nice ring to it.

"Thanks. I wish I could say that your obvious ploy to buy my sons' love and affection through sweets doesn't have an ice cube's chance in hell of succeeding, but hey, they're my kids. They're easily bought."

"Is that how I won you over?" Sugar whispered, leaning forward, licking her lips, staring at his mouth hungrily. He wasn't the only one easily won over. Jaxson was a hell of a kisser, and she was quickly learning that she just couldn't get enough of him.

"It mighta helped," he admitted, and then began kissing her, his tongue sweeping inside, growling in possession and lust.

As Sugar kissed him back, her fingers curling into his dark brown hair, she figured that it didn't really matter how she won him over. The point was, he was hers, and that was all that mattered.

A small voice asked ever so quietly, "But what happens when he finds out the truth about you?" She'd gotten so good at ignoring that question, it was hardly a challenge to push it away and ignore it. With any luck at all, he never would.

And Sugar figured she'd be just fine with that.

CHAPTER 31

JAXSON

"Okay, you're going to use the back of your hand to feel the door, like this," Jaxson said, laying the back of his hand up against the door.

"Why the back of my hand?" Angus asked, tossing his dyed black hair to the side to get it out of his eyes. Jaxson wasn't sure what the attraction to this haircut was – it dropped all of Angus' hair into his eyes, and then he spent half of his day trying to get it back out of his eyes.

Jaxson had to say that he was glad he wasn't a teenager anymore. Shit that made perfect sense to him then didn't make a lick of sense to him now.

"Because the palm of your hand might have calluses or something else to block feeling. If the fire isn't very large yet, the door may only be slightly warm. The smallest thing can keep you from being able to sense that, and you could be in trouble because of it."

Angus nodded, his mouth screwed up in concentration as he laid the back of his hand against Jaxson's office door, mimicking his movement.

Just then, the man door to the fire station opened up, and Sugar popped her head around the corner. "Oh hi, Angus!" she called out when she spotted them. She came hurrying in, shutting the door to the wind and snow blowing in behind her. "I didn't know you were here." Her ponytail swished as she made her way over, and Jaxson pulled her to him, wrapping his hand around her silky dark brown hair to trap her in place.

"Why, hello Ms. Sugar," he growled, and leaned down to kiss her. After a few quite amazing spit-swapping moments, Sugar pulled back, a delightful blush covering her cheeks.

"We have an audience," she murmured, embarrassed. Jaxson looked up to see the man door close behind Angus. He'd made a run for it.

Jaxson laughed. "Not anymore!" he said. Sugar looked around, startled to realize that Angus had left. "Teenage boys are allergic to adults kissing," he told her. "They break out into hives at the first sign of it."

She rolled her eyes, laughing. "Hmmm…you might be right," she said with a wicked grin. "I never realized what power I held."

"Oh, you hold all sorts of power in your hands," Jaxson said, lifting her hands to his mouth to kiss the backs of them. He swore he could practically see her melt into a puddle in front of him. His chest puffed out with pride. Making her feel good made him feel good.

"Want to go out to dinner with me in Franklin?" he asked impulsively. "I don't have the boys this weekend, so we could actually go to a restaurant that doesn't serve hot dogs or pizza." He waggled his eyebrows suggestively.

She giggled. "I do like how you think. Should I go home and change?"

He looked her up and down, taking in her jeans and sweatshirt. She looked gorgeous, of course, but then again, she'd even managed to make the Michelin Man outfit look good, so he probably wasn't a great judge when it came to her outfits. "You look good to me," he said with a shrug. "Plus, it's snowing outside. You probably don't want to wear a dress anyway."

She considered that for a moment. "Yeah, probably not," she agreed. Practical to the end. "I guess we'll just have to wait until spring for you to check out this dress that I have."

He began moving around the fire station, flipping off lights and shutting down his computer. As he came back to her side, she gestured to mid-thigh. "It comes up to here," and then pointing right to her glorious tits, "and down to here."

He gulped. Hard. His vision might've gone a little double. He breathed in deep, trying to quell the surge of blinding lust at the vision dancing in his head. It'd been three weeks since they'd officially started dating, and he was starting to realize that rather than scratching an itch and then moving on, the more time he spent around her, the more addicted he became.

She batted her eyelashes at him innocently, and he realized that she'd just been messing with his head. "You!" he growled, and pulled her against him, mock-glaring down at her. "You're enough to drive a man wild, you know that?"

She grinned all-too-innocently. "Who, me?" she asked in her best Old West twang. "Why, I just don't know what you're talkin' about."

Shaking his head, he pulled her out the man door. "C'mon, woman, let's go. If you're not gonna show me this dress, you might as well accompany me to dinner. I should get *something* out of this here deal." Her laughter tinkled out as she followed along behind him, her short legs hurrying to keep up.

THE MAÎTRE D' walked them to a table stuffed back in a corner. "Will this do?" he asked imperiously, staring down his nose at the two of them. It was probably the sweatshirts and his baseball cap that were unimpressive to the man, but Jaxson didn't really care. He had Sugar there with him. Nothing else really mattered.

"Looks great," he said graciously. The man nodded and moved away to go stare down his nose at someone else.

"He doesn't seem to appreciate our choice in attire," Sugar whispered to Jaxson, her eyes wide with worry. Jaxson pulled out her chair for her, and then slid into his own across the tiny table from her. He hoped the plates wouldn't be too large. There wouldn't be room to put them on the table if they were. Jaxson had visions of holding his plate in his lap as he tried to eat snails or something else equally as disgusting.

"It's fine," Jaxson assured her. "All maître d's are assholes. It's in their bylaws. If they're too nice, they get kicked out of the Maître D' Club, which would just be a tragedy."

Sugar laughed, her shoulders loosening up. After ordering appetizers and drinks – thank God they had normal finger foods on their menus, no snails in sight – Jaxson looked around the upscale restaurant, candles flickering on every table, a live three-string orchestra in the corner playing elevator music. Sadly, whether it was live music or not, it was still dreadful, but Jaxson couldn't bring himself to care. Not with Sugar there with him.

He spotted a heavily pregnant woman being led to her chair by a doting husband. She looked about ready to burst. Jaxson mentally reviewed his EMT training on what to do if he were forced to help a woman give birth without anesthesia.

This could be a long night.

He jerked his head towards the woman while grinning at Sugar, deciding to make a joke out of the situation. Better that than worry about where he'd have the woman lay if she were to give birth right there in the middle of the restaurant. "You know, you have the perfect face structure for pregnancy," he said mock-seriously. "Your cheekbones are exactly right – the way they curve down. I bet you'd be the cutest woman this side of the Mississippi if you were nine months pregnant."

Instead of laughing and modeling her perfect pregnancy cheekbones – as if such a thing existed – Sugar's eyes got wide and she simply nodded, staring down at her menu. "What are you going to order?" she asked, eyes glued to the menu.

Jaxson quirked an eyebrow at her. Hmmm…not exactly the reaction he was expecting, but okay. "Anything that didn't previously live in a shell is fine with me," Jaxson muttered under his breath as he picked up his menu.

Sugar didn't respond to that, either.

He looked up and studied her face. Her mouth was pinched and she was staring at her menu like it contained the code to eternal life.

"You okay?" he asked, reaching out and touching her hand.

She looked up and back down again so quickly, he was a bit afraid she'd just given herself whiplash but she was smiling as she stared down at her menu. "Of course," she said to her menu. "Just fine."

Which had the undesired effect of not being the least bit believable. He stared at her several moments longer, mentally willing her to look up at him, but she wouldn't, so his eyes dropped back down to his menu. The words swam in front of him as he stared down, his world swimming around with it.

Something weird had just happened, and he'd be damned if he could begin to guess what.

CHAPTER 32

SUGAR

J AXSON HELPED HER into her coat and they left the restaurant, not saying a word as they headed for his SUV.

Which was exactly the amount of conversation they'd had through dinner.

Okay, so they may've exchanged a few words. Sugar couldn't remember, to be honest. The whole thing went by in a haze of pain and worry and she'd be hard-pressed to even say what she'd ordered for dinner.

Jaxson helped her into the passenger seat of the SUV and then hurried around to the driver's side. Instead of starting the vehicle, though, he turned in his seat and demanded, "What in the bloody hell is going on?"

He was shouting.

She slid down in her seat, staring at the front dashboard, wanting and wishing and hoping with all her might to just die.

She waited a few heartbeats. Dammit, she was still alive.

Now what was she going to do?

"Sugar, you need to talk to me," Jaxson growled. He put his hand under her chin and forcibly turned her head to look at him. "I need to know what's going on in that gorgeous head of yours. You were fine, and then...you were not. What happened?"

She looked at his face, open and trusting and so damn handsome, and choked back a sob. He wasn't going to be looking at her like that much longer.

Not after he heard what she did.

He just continued to stare at her, unblinking, and she knew deep down inside that they'd still be sitting in the parking lot of the most expensive restaurant in Franklin come morning, matching ice blocks frozen to their seats, if she didn't start talking. She knew she was stubborn, but she was pretty sure Jaxson had her beat by a mile.

She looked out the front windshield. It was easier that way.

"I was pregnant. Before. With Dick, my ex." She whispered the painful truth because if she whispered it, then maybe Jaxson wouldn't hate her so much. She began shaking from cold and worry and pain, and Jaxson started the vehicle, realizing that she was quickly losing body heat in the cold winter air. He backed out of the parking spot and pulled out onto the road, wandering through the darkened streets of Franklin. He didn't say anything. He simply drove, and listened.

Listened to a story she'd only ever told Emma.

"I didn't want to be. Dick and I had been married for almost five years by that point, and our marriage was pretty much destroyed. But I missed a period, and after spending a couple of weeks internally freaking out, I finally went to a doctor here in Franklin. I didn't want to go to a local doctor for fear that he'd tell Dick.

"Anyway, my worst fears were realized – I *was* pregnant. I came home in a daze. Dick was...he was a horrible husband. He'd make a horrific father. I'd have to shield the child from him, both physically and emotionally. Also, I knew that if we did have a child together, Dick would never let me go. I'd wanted to divorce him for a long time, but without any family support and no money of my own, I couldn't. Didn't mean I'd given up on that dream, though.

"So a child…it would be a life sentence for me and I knew it. I would never be free of Dick Schmidt. Not as long as I lived." She took in a deep, halting breath, trying to make herself just focus on telling the story, and nothing else. Like reciting a poem in English class. She could do it. Just pretend it all happened to someone else.

"So I get home, and I'm in a daze. Upset, you know? I know now that I was in shock, but of course, you never recognize it when you're in it. I'm trying to cook dinner and I'm not paying attention, and I burn it. Black as tar, and about as tasty.

"Dick came home, drunk like always. He smells the burnt food, and starts yelling at me. We start to scuffle – I'm worried that he's going to hurt me and then…I lose my balance."

The tears come then, trailing down her cheeks as she stared out of the darkened windshield at the frozen world around them.

"I don't know, really, if I lost my balance, or if Dick 'helped' me on my way. I've replayed that moment over and over again in my head, trying to remember, but it's all a blur. Either way, no matter how it happened, there I was, tumbling down the stairs to the basement. The entrance to the basement was right off the kitchen, and I hadn't even noticed how close I'd gotten to the stairs until I was falling…

"I'm lucky I didn't break my neck, honestly. I should have, by all rights. Or a leg or something. But instead, as I sat up, even more dazed and confused than before, I realized that there's blood spreading everywhere – coming out of me like the world's most over-the-top period. Dick was running down the stairs – stumbling, actually, 'cause he's still drunk as a skunk – and when he saw the blood…he thought I was dying. From internal bleeding."

The tears were still coming then, trailing down her cheeks, flowing out of her like the blood that night at the bottom of the stairs. The tears should've been stained red, but somehow were clear as always.

Some things just didn't make sense.

"Instantly, he was sweet as pie," she said, her voice shaking. "He thought he'd almost killed me, and if he didn't get me medical help right away, I *would* be dead, and as everyone knows, the police always look at the husband first. Even with his father as the judge in town, and even as stupidly drunk as he was, he knew he couldn't get away with murdering me. So there he was, helping me up, strapping me into the car, and driving to the hospital here in town, and the whole way, I'm terrified that I'm going to die because Dick is *still* fall-down drunk and I'm just sure he's gonna plow us into a telephone pole or something…

"But we make it. There's Dick, thoughtful and worried about his wife after her terrible, terrible tumble down the stairs, and the staff are only kinda buying it because Dick is well known around town as being a dick," she smirked to herself for a moment at the pun, the only smile she'd managed to muster up in quite a while, "but then, my worst nightmare happens. The doctor delivers the 'bad' news to us: I've lost the baby."

She took in a shaky breath, looking out the windshield as ever-growing-in-size snowflakes began to pelt it. The storm had died off while they'd been in the restaurant, but appeared to be growing in strength again. She wondered for a moment if the Explorer was a 4x4 or not, and thought to ask Jaxson, but then the thought disappeared again, as ephemeral as the flakes hitting the windshield.

She was back in the hospital again, mentally begging the doctor not to say anything in front of her husband, pleading, and then he did anyway, and Dick pretended sorrow and shock, until the doctor left them alone.

"Pregnant?" he'd hissed at her. "You're *pregnant*?! When were you planning on telling me about this?"

"It started almost right away," Sugar said aloud. "Dick began saying that this had been my plan all along – that I hadn't told him the news because I knew that if he knew, then he would be more careful around me. That I'd *wanted* to lose the baby, so I'd hid it from him so he'd hurt me and cause me to lose the baby. Then I could blame it all on him, you see." Hysterical laughter spilled out of her and then she stopped laughing and she was whispering, "He was right."

Jaxson drew in a sharp breath at that, and she laughed again, sharp and cold. "Not about everything, of course," she clarified. "But that part about me not wanting the baby. I didn't. I really didn't. And when I lost it, instead of being saddened, I was glad. Not happy – not joyful – but glad. I didn't want that baby and all that came with it. Losing it was a blessing, and I'm an awful human being for thinking that, but I can't help it."

Before he could tell her that she was right, that she was awful, that she deserved all that happened to her and more, she rushed on, eager to get to the end of the story. "It was too early to be able to tell if I was gonna have a girl or a boy, of course, but Dick became convinced that it was a boy. Someone to carry on the Schmidt line. Which made my conniving even more awful. If it'd 'just' been a girl, well, that'd almost be forgivable. But it was gonna be a boy, Dick just knew it, and therefore…I deserved all that I got. And I got a lot at his hands."

She realized that they'd pulled up in front of her apartment and were idling in the guest parking spot. He was probably trying to get rid of her, now that he knew. He wouldn't want to be around someone like her. No one would. That's why she'd been so smart and had kept every guy who came around at an arm's length.

Except Jaxson. She'd let him in, and she'd told him the truth, and now she couldn't bear to look him in the eye and see the judgment registering there. She'd break into a million little pieces for sure. "I'll go now," she whispered, her throat raw, and she opened the passenger-side door and tumbled out into the snow, scrambling up and heading towards the safety of her apartment. Away from Jaxson and his hatred of her.

She could grab Hamlet and some food and clothes and leave. She could drive to Denver, where Emma lived. She could move in with her best friend and start over again and this time, not screw it up by dating some man and telling him the truth.

Telling a man the truth was never a good idea. Then he'd just use it against her to hurt her more. Hadn't she already learned that lesson?

So dumb. So stupid.

Her hand was shaking as she tried to get her key into the lock, scraping the paint on the door in her haste and then Jaxson's hand was on hers, holding it in place, and he was standing behind her, trapping her in and she began fighting, punching and twisting and jabbing to get free, away from a man who would hurt her yet again and she couldn't breathe and she was sure the smell of alcohol was in the air and Dick was back again, here to finish the job this time...

The world swirled, the white snowflakes dancing in front of her eyes, and she couldn't see and then they swirled less as the blackness overtook her.

CHAPTER 33

JAXSON

FOR SOMEONE WHO PRIDED himself on being able to act in cases of emergency – basically the very definition of a firefighter – he'd sure been damn slow to react when Sugar had thrown herself out of the vehicle and into the snow, stumbling towards her front door. He'd been frozen in place, staring out the windshield, shocked into doing nothing. She'd been in the middle of telling him the worst story he'd ever heard, and then she'd been running through the snowstorm.

His mind was still processing what that son-of-a-bitch Dick Schmidt had done to Sugar, trying to understand how anyone could hurt someone as sweet and kind as her; how anyone could do the kind of screwing with her head that he'd done, and still look himself in the mirror in the morning.

He remembered then why Sugar owned Hamlet – to ward Dick off. How many times had he come by after she'd left him? How hard had he pushed her to take him back?

It was her keening, high-pitched wail that jerked him back to the present; back to reality. He yanked his seatbelt off and practically threw himself out of the SUV, running through the snow to Sugar, who was scratching at the door with her key, nowhere even close to the keyhole, and making the most heart-wrenching sound he'd ever heard in his life.

He put his hand on hers, wrapping his body around her, trying to show her how he would be there for her, protect her from the world, and instead, she was fighting him – kicking and jabbing backwards. She got a lucky hit to his solar plexus that knocked the wind out of him but she otherwise wasn't able to do much damage. She was probably too distraught to aim for any…important body parts.

Then she began melting in his arms, sagging against him, and through his gasps for air, he realized that she was fainting on him, literally.

He felt along her arm until he got to her right hand, pulling the key from her grasp and putting it into the keyhole. As he turned it, he realized that the door was already unlocked; she hadn't bothered to lock it before she left to find him at the fire station. In the midst of all that was happening, he couldn't help but let a small quirk of the lips pass across his face. Such a small town thing to do, leaving her door unlocked like that.

He pushed the door open, a swirl of snow and cold entering along with him, and found Hamlet on the other side, frantically waiting for Sugar. He must've heard the noises, and knew she was in pain. He whined as he licked her face, his tail wagging not out of happiness but worry. Jaxson carried Sugar over to the couch and laid her down, and Hamlet followed along every step of the way, glued to his mistress' side.

"I know, buddy," Jaxson said softly. "I'm worried, too."

He sat down on the floor, leaning against the front of the couch, Sugar's hand clasped in his, as he stared into the dark of the living room. What kind of man would be willing to do something like this?

Dick Schmidt…

Jaxson turned the name over in his mind. It seemed like he'd heard it somewhere, but damned if he could remember where. He'd met too many new people in the last six weeks to pin the name down.

What if he'd actually met Dick himself? Jaxson shuddered at the idea. He could've shaken the man's hand and not known who he was, or what he'd done to Sugar. A general feeling of disgust covered him from head to toe, like he'd just taken a bath in a mud bog.

Sugar began to stir behind him, and Jaxson flipped around, hovering over her, pushing her hair out of her face. He saw then that her eyes were leaking – she'd still been crying, even passed out. His heart twisted with pain.

Her eyes fluttered open and she wiped at them with the backs of her hands. "Where…what…" she said weakly. She tried to move, so Jaxson helped her sit up, putting a pillow behind her back so she could settle against the armrest of the couch comfortably.

He knew the moment it all returned to her. Her pliant, warm body became stiff and unyielding, like she'd touched an electrical outlet. "Oh my God," she cried, staring up at him in horror. "I can't believe…I'm so sorry…you have to go. Why are you here? Go away!" She began beating at him with her fists, trying to punch and push him out of her life.

He held his arms loosely around her, trying hard not to smother her, but also not leaving her alone. He wouldn't move a muscle. Not when she needed him.

Eventually, she wore herself out, and she sagged against him, defeated and exhausted. Hamlet whined his worry, nudging her leg with his nose, leaning up against the couch with his massive body weight. It was probably a good thing it was already shoved up against the living room wall, or no doubt his weight would've pushed it there anyway.

"I'm here because you need me, and because despite what you think, nothing of what you told me has made me think less of you."

Dazed, Sugar stared up at him, winded and defeated. "You

don't have to lie to me. I'm a baby killer. You don't have to pretend to be nice to me anymore."

He chuckled quietly at that. "Sugar, I've never pretended to be nice to you, and I'm not pretending now. You're not a baby killer, darlin'. You were in an impossible relationship with an evil man, and you reacted how almost anyone would, I think." He stroked her soft, straight brown hair away from her face as he looked down at her, taking in her bloodshot eyes and red nose and stark white cheeks in the dim lighting.

He'd never seen such a beautiful sight in all his life.

"Do you remember me telling you about my reaction to Kendra being pregnant?" He paused, waiting for her to respond. He wasn't going to let that question go by as a rhetorical one. He wanted to make sure she remembered.

She finally nodded quietly, staring up at him, not saying a word.

"I didn't want my boys, Sugar, and if Kendra would've lost Frankie at only a month along, I swear to you, I would've been glad for it.

"I love my boys with all of my heart, but I'm not gonna lie and say that having them with Kendra has been easy. A part of me wishes that I could've waited to have them with someone more stable. Someone who I could love for the rest of my life.

"But I can't change what happened, so I just live with it."

"But you love them," she protested, her voice cracking with pain. "I didn't love my baby. I wanted it gone."

"I didn't love them a month into Kendra's pregnancies, though." Jaxson picked up her hand and held it against him, trying to convey his admiration for her through his touch; by pushing it through his hand and up her arm, and into her heart. Could she feel how impressed and amazed he was by her? Her strength? Her kindness, despite all that had happened to her? The joy with which she looked at the world?

He'd never met anyone like her, and he had to get her to understand that. He had to.

"They were nothing but some cells floating around in my wife's stomach at that point. I didn't have an emotional attachment to them. I know it seems callous and cold, and maybe to someone who hasn't been in those shoes, it *is* callous and cold. But you learn to love someone over time. Their very existence doesn't guarantee that love. You'd known for sure that you were pregnant all of what, a couple of hours when you lost your baby?"

She nodded, staring up at him, her eyes so large, they seemed to take up most of her face.

"You can't build an emotional bond in a couple of hours, Sugar. It just can't happen. You felt what any human being would feel – trapped and in pain and worried about what this would mean for your future."

She was nibbling on her lower lip, still staring up at him, still not saying a word. He decided to switch tactics.

"I've seen you with Hamlet. I've seen you with my boys. And I've seen you with me." She laughed a little at that last nonsensical statement. "You are more loving than ten other women combined together. There's nothing wrong with you. Tell me straight: Do you want to have kids? Someday in the future?"

He was holding his breath, waiting for the answer to that question, and he didn't know why he cared so much, because he sure as hell wasn't ready to marry her, let alone have kids with her.

But still, he wanted to know.

"If someone can look past what I've done…I want to. I love children. Not teenagers so much – the mayor can keep his surly son," Jaxson chuckled at that, "but I *do* want kids. I'll just do my best to forgive them for turning into teenagers at some point."

Jaxson grinned at her, the first feeling of lightness since this whole debacle had started sweeping over him. "It is a lot to forgive them for," he said dryly. "I like Aiden at this age. I figure he can just stay six forever."

"It would be nice." Sugar smiled up at him, and he brought her hand to his lips, kissing the back of it, pouring his love into that kiss.

"There's nothin' to forgive, baby," Jaxson whispered, meaning every word of it. "Unless someone needs to forgive you for having *awful* taste in men, and actually marrying Dick to begin with. I suppose that's something pretty difficult to overlook."

Instead of making her laugh like he'd been trying to, Sugar's face shut down again. Like a curtain sweeping forward, her eyes went dark, the light that'd just started to reappear fading away into nothing.

"What's wrong?" he asked, confused. She shook her head, smiling the most painfully fake smile he'd ever seen in his life.

"Nothin'," she said. She leaned forward to pet Hamlet on the head, and the dog's huge body shook with happiness, licking and nudging her hand, whining with joy that she seemed to be better.

Better in Hamlet's eyes, maybe, but not better in Jaxson's. There was something still wrong. Something she was hiding from him.

"What is it, Sugar? You're lying to me, and I don't know why. You don't need—"

"Have you ever thought that maybe enough is enough?" she snapped. Her back was rigid and she was staring at him, anger vibrating out of her. "We've talked enough today about Sugar's messed up past. Can't we pick another topic, one less painful? Maybe discuss the AIDS epidemic or the state of politics right now?"

Jaxson snorted involuntarily with laughter at that one.

"I'm tired, Jaxson," Sugar said, less defensively this time. "Can we just leave this alone for now?"

He smiled, trying to show through it alone how much he

cared for her. "Of course," he said softly. "I'm here, whenever you want to talk."

"Well, right now, I think we ought to at least let Hamlet out into the backyard. He's probably in pain by this point."

Her loyal dog was simply sitting there, watching them talk, his body half lying against the couch as he took them in. He wouldn't whine and scratch at the door until the situation was dire, not when Sugar was in distress. Jaxson already knew that about the giant-hearted dog.

"C'mon, boy, let's go outside," Jaxson said, standing and heading for the back door. Hamlet padded along beside him, excited to be able to relieve his bladder. Jaxson heard Sugar running the water in the bathroom as he shut the back door behind him and Hamlet. She was freshening up, which meant she was doing better.

Which was good.

Her refusal to tell him what was wrong gnawed at him, but as he watched Hamlet sniff through every snowdrift, looking for just the right one to christen, he told himself that she was right.

Today had been a lot of pain. Too much pain, probably, for one day. Why hadn't she gone to a counselor to get help dealing with all this? Why hadn't she had any family support in leaving Dick's sorry ass? How was it that Dick controlled all of the money – surely Sugar had worked, right?

And being the judge's son – was Dick like Angus? Did he use his father's position in town to wreak havoc on it? Angus had an excuse – he was a teenager. Teens liked to wreak havoc no matter who their father was. But Dick was way past that stage, at least chronologically even if he wasn't emotionally.

He needed to find out more about Dick and the Schmidt family. There was a lot going on in this quiet mountain town that he didn't know yet, but he planned to find out.

CHAPTER 34
SUGAR

"I T'S SO GOOD TO SEE YOU," Emma whispered in Sugar's ear as they embraced long and hard. Sugar pulled back and grinned, her eyes shining with tears – tears of joy.

"It really is," Sugar admitted. "Why is it that you live all the way over in Colorado again?"

Emma took her arm and they began wandering down the hallway towards Emma's bedroom, Hamlet following along behind them. Emma's parents had left her room alone (except for moving a sewing machine and several hundred yards of fabric into it) when she'd left for college. She still had a place to stay when she came home to visit, all these years later.

Sugar tried to ignore the comparisons to her own family, although she was hard-pressed to do so, since they were so stark. It started and ended with Emma being loved by her parents, whereas with Sugar…

Well, she wasn't. There was no beating around the bush with that one.

"There isn't exactly a plethora of architecture jobs here in the valley," Emma said with a laugh. "Unless you count potato cellars, which I absolutely do not."

"Have you even *tried* to find a job in Franklin?" Sugar

persisted, settling down on Emma's fluorescent orange bedspread. Sugar hated the color with a passion, but since Emma hadn't exactly put her in charge of choosing her linens back when they were in high school, she'd always kept that particular thought to herself.

She was just grateful that Emma was using her week's vacation time to come home and visit, instead of going somewhere exciting, like New York or Paris. Having her home was simply too wonderful for words. Although Sugar loved being around Jaxson, and of course it was fun to hang out with the boys when they came up to visit, they were no replacement for her best friend.

"Franklin is too small," Emma said with a wave of her hand. "So, I hear through the grapevine that you're *not* madly in love with my brother." She shot Sugar a pouting look, and Sugar let out a strangled bark of laughter.

"You are as subtle as a nuclear bomb, you know that?" Sugar said dryly.

"With just as much tact," Emma agreed freely. "So who's this firefighter dude giving my brother competition?"

Sugar held up her hand, ticking off fingers as she talked. "For roughly the 472nd time, your brother and I are never gonna happen. He doesn't like me that way, and I don't like him. We're friends, and *only* friends. Two, the firefighter dude's name is Jaxson."

"Like Jackson Hole?" Emma asked, leaning over the side of the bed and petting Hamlet's massive head. He'd conveniently kept it in reach, in case anyone wanted to take advantage of all of this free-hand time, and Emma had apparently fallen for his sad puppy-dog eyes that said no one was using their hands for the betterment of the world. At the touch of Emma's hand, his eyes closed blissfully and his tail began thumping against the hardwood floors.

Hopefully Chris wasn't in his bedroom in the basement,

listening to that racket. Sugar sent out a silent apology to the teen if he was.

"Close. J-A-X instead of J-A-C-K," she told her best friend. "Jaxson Anderson. He was a firefighter for Boise and then moved here to become the new fire chief."

"And raise everyone's taxes in the process," Emma said with a small chuckle.

"Damn, you really don't miss a beat in Denver, do you? Is there a special Gossip Express that instantly sends every bit of Long Valley gossip hurtling across the US?"

"You only get the secret password when you have the guts to move out of this place," Emma said, laughing.

Sugar shook her head in mock-disbelief. This town really was unbelievable.

"I guess Chief Horvath was volunteer only," Sugar told her, "he was paid $100 per call-out and paid a couple of hours a month to do paperwork and whatever, but yeah, pretty much just volunteer. So when the city council voted to bring Jaxson in full-time…you should've heard some of the customers in the bakery. You'd think Jaxson had gone house to house, robbing people blind just because he hated them."

Emma wrinkled her nose. "I can imagine. To be honest, I'm surprised the Sawyer City Council did it. Are they sick of the job and just want to be booted out of office already?"

"Jaxson said that the state pushed them to do it; either they hired someone full-time, or started paying huge fines every year. Apparently, Sawyer was the largest town in Idaho to have a volunteer fire chief. Most towns this size had gone to at least a part-time chief well before now."

"I have to say, Sugar, I've never seen you take such interest in the politics of a small town before." The words were teasing, but Emma's tone was not. She was staring at Sugar seriously, her brow wrinkled in confusion.

Sugar shrugged, staring down at her hands. She only had a high school diploma, and as Dick had reminded her many a-time, she was too dumb to go to college anyway. Not like Emma.

It was true that it was strange for her to notice city politics at all, but then again, she'd never dated a fire chief before, either. "Well, obviously I'd know this sort of thing," she protested lightly. "It's all just information that has to do with Jaxson, you know?"

"You were married to the judge's son previously," Emma pointed out reasonably, "and at that point, I'm not even sure if you could've named the mayor, let alone discussed what the state policy is on the employment of fire chiefs."

"Jaxson just talks to me when he comes over after work, and I listen. It's not like I'm some political genius." *It's not like I'm smart like you are.*

Those words stayed unspoken, hanging in the air between them, pushing the air out of the room. Sugar studied her hands intently, hoping that Emma would leave the topic alone.

She couldn't.

She wouldn't be Sugar's best friend if she weren't just as stubborn as Sugar was.

"You could go to college now," Emma said quietly, urging her on. "I know you'd do well. Just because Dick says that you're too dumb to make it at college doesn't mean it's actually true. He said a lot of things that weren't true."

Sugar shook her head, looking up and smiling slightly at her best friend of ten years. "Truthfully, I don't know what I want to be. You've always had these grand ideas and dreams of constructing elaborate bridges and beautiful buildings. I haven't." She shrugged. "I'd thought I'd figure out what I wanted to be when I went to college, but of course, that didn't happen and…I guess I'm just past that stage in my life, you know? I'm happy now. Being with Jaxson, getting to know his sons, working with your brother, walking Hamlet…it's a quiet life, but that doesn't mean it isn't fulfilling."

Emma screwed up her mouth, not believing her but clearly not wanting to argue any further.

"What about you?" Sugar asked, wanting to change the subject. "Your texts have been sorely lacking in male details. Any hotties in Denver?"

"There was this one guy," Emma said, a scowl flitting across her face, "and I was just sure he was the one, you know? And then…turns out, he was married."

"Bastard!" Sugar yelped, staring at her best friend in horror.

"Pretty much. He even talked about marrying me. One night, he got all serious and I was *sure* a proposal was coming, and then he starts telling me about his wife and kids and how he feels so much guilt for cheating on them with me, but if I'll just hang in there, he was *totally* planning on divorcing his horrible wife and then he'd marry me.

"So it was a marriage proposal of sorts, but not exactly the kind I was looking for."

"What did you do?" Sugar breathed.

"Kicked him in the nuts, told him to never call me again, and walked home."

Sugar burst out laughing, throwing herself backwards on the bed. "Of *course* you did," she said through the laughter, wiping at the tears welling up in her eyes. "Oh Emma…"

Emma shot her a naughty grin. "But there is this one guy…"

As Sugar and Emma chatted through the night, only getting up occasionally to let Hamlet out into the backyard or get a snack to eat, Sugar couldn't help but compare herself to Emma. Emma wouldn't have put up with Dick's bullshit; not for one minute. She was bold and brash and didn't hold back. She wasn't a people pleaser. She saw what she wanted and she went after it.

Sugar was never going to be that way, no matter how hard she tried, and that was a fact.

CHAPTER 35

JAXSON

J AXSON OPENED THE FRONT DOOR to the bakery, letting the smells and warmth wash over him like always. Damn, he loved this place.

It was 7:30 in the morning on a Saturday, which guaranteed that Sugar would be nowhere around. Exactly as Jaxson planned.

Holli, a red-haired teen, looked up from stocking a display case of muffins. "Oh hey, Jaxson!" she called out. "Sugar isn't here." She looked slightly confused by him being there, looking for Sugar. Holli knew that Jaxson knew that Sugar wouldn't be there on the weekends, so…what was he doing?

Jaxson grinned to himself. Holli was as transparent as Saran Wrap.

"I was hoping to chat with Gage for a minute."

"Oh. He's in the back," she said, jerking her head towards the swinging doors, and going back to the muffin display.

Jaxson headed around the counter and through the doors, into the industrial kitchen, gleaming stainless counters everywhere. Gage looked up from a recipe, his muttering cutting off mid-sentence as he spotted Jaxson. "Hey!" he said, surprised. "Sugar has today off."

"I know. I…came to talk to you."

Gage's eyebrows shot up, but then he shrugged. "As long as you don't mind me baking as we talk, come on back. I'm trying out a new recipe, and thus far, it's kicking my ass."

Jaxson walked over and leaned against the counter as Gage went back to measuring out cupfuls of sugar. "So what did you want to chat about?" he asked, leveling off yet another cup and dumping it into a giant mixing bowl.

"Sugar." Gage didn't say anything, just continued to measure ingredients out, so Jaxson plunged on. "More specifically, her ex. What's the deal with Dick Schmidt?"

Gage cocked an eyebrow as he began meting out tablespoons of spices, humming a little under his breath as he went. "Dick is a dick, figuratively and literally," he finally said. "First, you should know that only Sugar calls him Dick. He hates that name with a passion, which is *exactly* why she calls him that. It's her way of defying him and standing up to him, after all he's put her through. I just thought I should let you know, in case anyone else in town calls him Richard, and you're confused.

"Well anyway, he still lives here in town. He used to stop by the bakery until Sugar filed for a restraining order. He used to go to her house, too, until she got Hamlet. He's obsessed with having her back, even though he tells her regularly that she was the worst wife in the history of wives." Gage snorted in disbelief. "He even had Sugar mostly believing that one, until she'd finally been away from him for a while. It took a bit for the cobwebs to clear, you know? He messed with her head big time."

"Was there anything special about how they ended up together? Why they started dating, or got married, or something?" Jaxson asked, coming to the heart of the matter. That was what got Sugar freaked out a month ago, and Jaxson figured that something pretty awful must've happened at the beginning of their relationship.

Which just didn't make sense. Why marry someone *after* something awful had happened?

He was missing parts of the puzzle but dammit all, he was trying to put it together without the box; without even knowing if he had all of the pieces, and with the additional handicap of Sugar intentionally hiding everything she could from him.

That got Gage's attention. "She hasn't told you about that?" he asked Jaxson carefully, staring at him, one eyebrow raised.

Jaxson shook his head. "I was joking last month about how she had awful taste to even marry Dick, and she freaked out on me. She acts like everything is fine now, but...it's not. She's hiding something big from me, but I don't know what."

Gage went back to the recipe. "Jaxson, I like you. But if Sugar isn't going to tell you that story, then I'm not either. It's her story to tell, not mine. Everyone in town knows parts of the story, but only a couple of us know all of it, and if she ain't sharing, then that's her choice."

Jaxson nodded grudgingly. Gage was right to say that, no matter how much it drove Jaxson crazy. He wanted to know what on earth was going through Sugar's mind. But on the other hand, the fact that Gage kept Sugar's confidences made Jaxson like him even more.

"Yeah. You're right. I shouldn't be asking you. I'm just getting desperate." He let out a laughing groan. Gage shot him a grin.

"Sugar makes granite seem malleable. She's a real people pleaser, which has gotten her into a spot or two in her life that haven't been good ones, but once she decides something...it's almost impossible to get her to move. The good news is, that extends to her loyalty and friendship, too. Once she decides that she likes you, she'll defend you to her dying day. You'll never find someone more loyal than Sugar."

"Someone once told me that if you want to know what a

person's like, just look at their dog," Jaxson mused aloud. "Hamlet is loyal and sweet and friendly as the day is long. My boys climb all over him like he's a freakin' jungle gym, and he just sits through it all, gentle as can be. The first time Aiden took Hamlet for a walk, there they were, Hamlet taller than him even on all four legs, but he realizes that Aiden doesn't walk as fast as Sugar usually does, so he slows down so he's not dragging Aiden down the street behind him. I even trust him with Frankie, who's only four. He's a hell of a dog."

"And Sugar is a hell of a woman," Gage finished for him, and they smiled at each other.

"I'm sorry I got all hot and bothered about you and Sugar dating," Jaxson said. He didn't apologize often, but he'd made an ass out of himself that day, and it was a big enough screw-up that he deserved to eat a little crow for it. "I didn't realize what Sawyer was like back then. Ahhh…the bliss of ignorance."

Gage laughed a little at that. "It's no biggie. A lot of people thought it. Hell, they probably still think it. Being a single guy in a small town isn't an easy thing. Every date you go on, you get scrutinized for. By the end of the date, if the rumor mill is to be believed, you're either banging her or marrying her. Sometimes, if the rumor mill is really on a tear, both at the same time."

Jaxson let out a belly laugh and Gage shot him another self-deprecating grin. "We ought to go down to O'Malley's Bar sometime after work. Are you free tonight?"

"Not tonight. At least, I hope not. But I'd love to take you up on that offer later. Hey, what's Sugar's favorite kind of bread to eat with soup, do you know?"

"My sourdough bread, especially with the potato bacon soup from Betty's. She eats those two together a lot during her lunch breaks."

"Much 'ppreciated," he said, nodding goodbye as he

headed back up front to find a loaf or two of the bread. He heard the mixer come to life behind him as Gage got back to work.

It was time to pry some answers out of a certain Sugar Stonemyer, by hook or by crook.

CHAPTER 36

SUGAR

S UGAR WAS AT THE BAKERY, serving up coffee and listening to Mr. Behrend and Mr. Maddow argue again over what the weather was going to be like this spring, when suddenly, she was at her apartment and hearing someone knock on her front door. She'd changed somewhere along the line into a gorgeous ball gown with a slit so high up her thigh, it actually made her look like she had long legs. She grinned with pleasure at the beauty of the dress, when she heard a knock again. Oh. Right. She'd gotten sidetracked. She hurried over to the front door to find Jaxson standing there.

He whistled. "Looking good!" he said, looking her up and down with a lascivious grin. She showed off, putting her leg out for him to admire, when she noticed she had beautiful sparkly high heels on. She didn't normally wear high heels because she was too much of a klutz to risk them, but tonight, she seemed to be able to walk just fine in them.

"Aren't they pretty?" she asked him enthusiastically.

And then, he was knocking on the front door again. That was weird. He was already inside of the house. Why was Jaxson knocking on the door again? She was staring at him, confused as could be although he didn't seem to notice anything weird, but before her brain could figure it out, she felt a hand on her arm. "Wake up, sleeping beauty," a man whispered.

Her eyes fluttered open and she stared up at…flowers? There was a huge bouquet of roses right in front of her face. Before her mind could make sense of that either, Jaxson's face appeared as he moved the flowers to the side. "Happy almost-two-month anniversary," he whispered, grinning down at her.

She craned her neck up to look down at her body, sad to see that she definitely wasn't wearing a stunning ball gown and high heels, but rather her super comfy, super old nightshirt that said, "It was me. *I* let the dogs out," across the front of it, with a picture of a Great Dane below. Of course.

At Sugar's movement, Hamlet lifted his head and thumped his tail on the bed, obviously also just waking up for the day. "You make a good guard dog," she told him sarcastically when he put his head down to go right back to sleep. She looked up at Jaxson. "It's our *almost* two-month anniversary? And how did you get in here?"

"I knocked several times, but you didn't answer. You also didn't lock the front door last night. *Again.*"

He'd been trying to get her to start locking her front door, worried for her safety but so far, the lesson just didn't seem to be taking all that well, unless a 40% success rate was what one would call "well."

"I didn't?" She sat up and took the roses from Jaxson, burying her face in their gorgeous buds, drawing in their heavenly scent. "I thought I did, honest…"

She'd been tired the night before, so she wasn't exactly going to swear on a Bible to that idea.

"What time is it?" she asked drowsily, wanting to change topics before Jaxson could launch into the many reasons why a home security system would be a good idea for her to install. She'd been trying to convince him that Hamlet was sufficient, although with his showing this morning, she wasn't sure how believable that argument was going to be in the future, if it ever was.

"One in the afternoon. I thought that since it was after noon, you'd surely be out of bed by now, but…" He tickled her feet that were dangling off the side of the bed and she fell backwards, laughing with delight. "I was *obviously* wrong."

"One is a little late, even for me," she admitted. "It's just so lovely to be able to sleep in on the weekends." She moved the bouquet out of the way and looked up at him. "I was having the *best* dream, about wearing this ball gown that made me look like a million bucks, and you were coming over here to take me out on a date."

"Well, you always look like a million bucks to me, although I wouldn't mind seeing this dress in real life." He shot her a wink. "But I'll take you up on the date offer. Do you have time to do something today to celebrate our almost-two-month anniversary?"

She nibbled on her bottom lip. She probably should do laundry and get caught up on the dishes stacked up in the sink, but really, what was the fun in that?

She sat up cross-legged on the bed, Hamlet inching his way over so he could put his head on her lap. Empty laps were not to be tolerated. "Two questions: Why almost, and two, what did you have in mind?" she asked, stroking Hamlet's soft golden ears as she tried to get her mind to wake up.

"Well, our official two-month anniversary will be next weekend, but I'll have the boys then, so I figured we'd celebrate this weekend instead. And second, Luke Nash – you know him?"

Sugar nodded. "He graduated two years before me from Sawyer High School."

"Well, he's a volunteer with the department and he offered to let us ride his snowmobiles up in the mountains. I guess the snowpack is great right now – not iced over, but plenty there to ride through so we're not hitting dirt as we go. Since it's

March, apparently there's no guarantee that the snowpack will continue to stay ideal like this, so this is a now-or-maybe-not-until-next-winter sort of deal."

"Oh fun!" Sugar said, delighted. "Let me go put on my trip-to-Antarctica outfit and then I'll be ready to go." She bounded out of bed, leaving a disgruntled Hamlet behind who'd started to really get into his pettings, and found a vase to put the roses in. She then shooed Jaxson out of her bedroom so she could get dressed.

"I could help," he said with a leering grin, and she laughed.

"We've only got a few hours of daylight left, and if you tried to 'help' me, I'm pretty sure we wouldn't end up going."

With an exaggerated sigh, Jaxson left her alone to get dressed, taking Hamlet outside for his morning constitution while she struggled into her layers.

Finally done, she waddled into the living room, her arms hardly touching her side. Jaxson let out a snort of laughter behind the cover of an upraised hand, but when she glared at him, he just smiled back innocently. "Hamlet!" he mock-scolded her dog. "I don't know what you're doing over there to make such noises like that." Hamlet looked up, his tail thumping at the sound of his name, and Sugar just laughed.

"Blaming it all on the innocent dog," Sugar said, petting his head. "My poor baby."

"Awfully big baby," Jaxson said dryly.

Sugar chose to ignore that comment. "We'll be back soon, boy. Or, do you think we should take him?" she asked Jaxson, looking up at him.

Jaxson hesitated. "I think he'd have fun, except he'd probably get too cold. He doesn't have much meat on his legs; not much to keep the heat in. I wouldn't want him to be miserable."

"That's true." She sighed, feeling guilty. She really should move somewhere warm, where Hamlet didn't have to worry about dealing with snow drifts up to his chest, or a thermometer that regularly dipped below zero.

They headed out to Jaxson's SUV and then over to Luke's place. Sugar heaved herself out of the passenger seat to chat with Bonnie, Luke's gorgeous wife, while Luke and Jaxson hitched up the snowmobile trailer to Jaxon's Explorer.

"You grew up in Boise, right?" Sugar asked, trying to remember back to what she'd heard about Luke and Bonnie's love story. At the bakery, she heard every gossipy story in town, but since her memory was shitastic, that only did her so much good.

"Yeah. Graduated from Boise State University with my degree in accounting."

"You own the accounting firm in town across from Betty's Diner, right, with Jennifer Miller?"

Bonnie nodded. "Jennifer and I were roommates at BSU for a couple of years. She's actually how I met Luke."

"Ohhh…that makes sense. I always wondered how two Boise chicks ended up in Sawyer to do farmers' bookkeeping for them."

"Well, Jennifer's story is pretty good, but *my* story is even better because it includes a blizzard, a bit of mistletoe, and an old cast-iron tub."

Sugar snorted with laughter. "Okay, that sounds like a fun story," she said with a grin. "You should stop by the bakery sometime – not during the morning rush hour – and tell me all about it."

"Deal."

Luke came over, his dark hair showing beneath the brim of his Stetson. Sugar put her hand out to shake his. "Thanks so much for lending them to us, Luke. I haven't been snowmobiling in ages." She realized how similar and yet how different Luke was from Jaxson. They both had dark brown hair and dark brown eyes, and both were about the same height – maybe six foot or so. But while Luke was a nice-looking guy and all, he wasn't Jaxson. His eyelashes weren't as thick, and his nose didn't have that adorable bump in the bridge of it from being on the losing end of a tackle during a football game.

As if he could sense she was thinking about him, Jaxson wrapped his arm around her waist and pulled her against his side. She was surprised he could find her waist in her get-up, to be honest.

"Ready?" he asked her, smiling down at her. She felt the butterflies in her stomach take up twerking again, and wondered if she would ever not feel this way around him.

"Yup," she said, pulling away to give Bonnie a hug.

"He seems like a good one," Bonnie whispered to her. "Luke's only had good things to say about him so far. I hope he's making you happy."

Sugar pulled back, blushing. "He is," she said softly.

"I am what?" Jaxson asked.

Sugar blushed harder. She hadn't realized he'd be able to hear her – she'd thought he was busy chatting with Luke again. "You're an eavesdropper, that's what. Now, are you going to take a girl out snowmobiling, or are you all talk?"

Waving goodbye to Luke and Bonnie, they set off into the mountains, following the hand-drawn map Luke sent with them. It was a rare bright winter's day, the sunshine bouncing off the snow and almost blinding Sugar as they wound their way up a plowed dirt road. Someone was taking the time to plow it clear after every snowstorm, which meant some local snowmobiler was quite dedicated to the sport. Sugar wondered idly if she knew the person. She probably did. She knew everyone, it seemed.

Jaxson pulled off into a large clearing, packed down from months of people towing snowmobiles in and out. A couple of paths wandered off from the clearing through the pine trees.

Sugar felt a surge of adrenaline as Jaxson helped her unload her snowmobile and then showed her the braking, acceleration, and steering. She took a couple of cautious turns around the parking lot as Jaxson got his warmed up and going.

"Ready?" he asked. At her eager nod, he gunned his engine and they took off. As she followed him down the right-hand trail and through the trees, she noticed something strapped to the back of his machine. With the snow flying and the quick movement of the machines, she wasn't quite sure what it was, and as the trail continued, she forgot about it anyway. It was too beautiful, too fun, too thrilling to be on a powerful machine like this, to think about anything else.

After endless hours, it seemed, Jaxson slowed down and Sugar obediently slowed behind him, an exhilarated grin plastered to her face. She just couldn't get enough. She pulled her borrowed helmet off her head. "That was so much damn fun!" she exclaimed.

"I thought you'd like it," he said. "I brought some food to eat – are you hungry?" He patted what she could now tell was a cooler behind him.

"Oh, yeah!" Her stomach was eating her backbone, but she hadn't wanted to complain and stop all of the fun. But if he was smart enough to bring food with them…she could only hope there was warm soup and coffee packed in there somewhere.

He helped her swing off, her legs stiff and sore as she tried to dismount gracefully. She didn't exactly succeed with that goal, but she did make it off and was standing upright, so she figured it was a win.

He carried the cooler over to a flat rock, warm and dry under the sun's rays, and she settled down with a happy sigh. She was going to be saddle sore tomorrow from trying to cling to the snowmobile with her thighs, but it'd be worth every moment. The freedom of flying over the snow…there was nothing like it.

He pulled out a thermos for each of them and crusty

sourdough rolls that looked suspiciously like the ones that Gage made at the bakery.

"Was Gage in on this?" Sugar asked, reaching for the bread eagerly.

"He told me that this was your favorite bread to eat. I picked up potato and bacon soup from Betty's."

She screwed the thermos lid off, breathing in deeply. "Wow, that smells good enough to eat!" she said with a laugh, and then broke off a piece of the sourdough to dip down into the well and soak up the potato-y goodness.

They ate in silence for a while, listening to the chatter of industrious squirrels too stubborn to flee before the winter storms hit, the sky above almost impossibly blue.

"Thanks for today," Sugar said quietly. "I really loved it."

Jaxson smiled, but his shoulders were stiff, as if he were bracing himself for what was about to happen. Sugar's smile disappeared. *Don't do it, don't ask, we were so happy, just leave it—*

"I need you to tell me the story of how you and Dick met and fell in love."

His words fell like a bombshell in the peaceful winter clearing and she just stared at him, panic welling up, choking her. She shook her head.

"We should go back now," she said dismissively as she stood up, packing her empty thermos into the cooler. "I bet poor Hamlet probably needs to go pee. I haven't been a very good momma to him—"

"I asked Luke to stop by your apartment while we were gone and let him out into the backyard," Jaxson interrupted.

She stared at him, aghast.

"You asked some strange man to come into *my* house while I'm gone and you didn't even ask me?!"

"You're the one who practically graduated with him!" Jaxson tossed back. "He wasn't some 'strange man' when you were borrowing his $15,000 snowmobiling equipment."

She glared at him, anger roiling in her stomach. "You didn't ask. That's the point," she ground out.

"I thought I was being helpful. I was worried that you'd be worried about Hamlet, and wouldn't want to stay out here if you were."

An awful thought rolled over her, steamrolling her into the ground. "You…you dragged me out here, into the middle of nowhere, so you could trap me and force me to talk, didn't you? *Didn't you?*" She was screaming by the end of it, shaking with panic and anger and fear.

Sugar wasn't much of a screamer. She couldn't remember the last time she'd screamed at someone. She wasn't even sure if she'd ever screamed at Dick. Her throat hurt from it, and instead of the satisfaction that she'd always imagined would come from finally letting loose and really laying it out on the world, she instead felt pain. It hurt – all of it.

The manipulation hurt most of all.

"You planned this," she whispered.

"I wanted to be able to talk without being interrupted," he admitted. "But it wasn't with ill intent, Sugar, I promise. I just thought it might be easier if we were out here, away from everyone—"

"—Trapped without any way out!" she cut in. She stormed over to her snowmobile. Yup. The engine stop was gone. There was no starting it without that in place.

"You son of a bitch," she whispered. "You damn son of a bitch."

Jaxson came over, his hands up in the air, pleading with her. "I want to move forward with you, Sugar. That's all. Ever since…" He paused, trying to come up with the right wording. "Ever since our trip to Franklin, things haven't been quite right between us. Like a picture just a little out of focus. We're here, and we're happy, but it's not what it could be. What it should be. We need to talk and move on from there."

"And so you thought trapping me out here with you,

without a choice or a way out, would make me *talk to you*?!" She was screaming the last part again. She was surprised by that. She hadn't expected it. It just came out.

And it felt terrible. Not liberating. Not amazing. Just… awful.

All of this was awful.

"Maybe," he snapped back, "if you'd talked to me the last two times I brought this up, I wouldn't be forced to do it this way."

Her terrible memory was coming back to haunt her. She realized, with a sinking feeling in her gut, that she'd blocked those memories out. Jaxson *had* tried to ask her about Dick and her. Twice. She'd blatantly ignored the question and had started talking about something else.

Both times.

As strange as it seemed, she'd somehow forgotten about that. She really was good at blocking shit out – whatever she didn't want to deal with, she didn't.

He was watching her face closely, and seemed to realize that she remembered what he was talking about. "I didn't want to do it this way, Sugar," he whispered in the still, winter air. "I just think if we're gonna make it and move forward, you've got to tell this story to me. You're holding it inside, sure that if you tell me, I'll hate you forever. I can't prove that's not true, if you won't tell me what it is."

She was sagging underneath the weight of it all, and he reached out to pull her against him, stroking her hair, whispering into it and she realized then that she was crying. She hadn't even known it was happening, but there they were, the tears trickling down her face.

Such a crybaby. She hated crying so much.

Crybaby.

She remembered then that Dick used to call her that. She'd forgotten that too. She'd pushed it down, deep inside of her.

"Aren't you sick of a crying girlfriend?" she asked bitingly, trying to push Jaxson away before he could do it to her. If she withdrew first, then it wouldn't hurt as much. She'd learned that lesson a long time ago.

"I don't think you've cried enough," Jaxson said softly, still stroking her hair, holding her against him as she finally let go and sobbed, releasing – if only a little – of the pain she'd been carrying around for so long.

She pulled back from Jaxson's embrace. If he was going to force her to talk before he let her return to civilization, well then, she would. She knew when she'd been beat, and…

She'd been beat.

It didn't mean she had to be excited about it, though. Or gracious. Instead, she stared off into the pine trees, refusing to meet Jaxson's eye. It would be easier if she didn't.

"I knew it was stupid to date him," she finally said woodenly, incapable of emotions any longer. Maybe they had broken completely and she'd no longer be able to feel joy or pain or happiness.

That was a lovely idea. She would be excited at the thought, but she found she couldn't manage that feeling either.

She was just…empty.

"A couple of friends in high school told me that he was bad news; there were whispers about him, but…I didn't have many boyfriends in high school. I was slow to develop," she gestured towards her breasts, "and until about my senior year, I looked like I was a 12-year-old boy. I was friends with all the guys, but I wasn't desirable."

Dick hadn't asked her out until she'd hit her senior year; until she'd developed her curves, as her mother delicately put it. Which should've been Clue #271 that Dick was focused on all the wrong things, but instead, she'd just been thrilled to finally have someone like her, no matter the reason.

"My parents approved of Dick, and strangely enough for a teenage girl, that made him even more desirable in my eyes. Usually teens only want to rebel and piss their parents off, but...I didn't. I'd never really lived up to their expectations, and had spent the first 17 years of my life trying to make them happy, and failing."

Something that had never really changed. Not for any length of time, anyway. She'd made her parents happy for a little while, so short she had a hard time remembering it now, but she knew intellectually that it'd happened.

"So there's this handsome guy, asking me out, and my parents are happy for once because he's the judge's son – which practically makes him small-town royalty – and so I'm dating him, even though all of my friends were telling me that he liked to push, to see how far he could get girls to go with him. In bed," she clarified, as if that wasn't painfully obvious.

She rolled her eyes at herself.

"He was a perfect gentleman the first couple of months. He was a couple of years older than me so he'd already graduated by this point, which made him even more desirable. I was just about to turn 18 – I hit the big 1-8 just a couple of weeks before graduation – and with the Romeo and Juliet Law in place, we were okay to date, you know? We had fun together; I think I was more enamored with the fact that a guy liked me and wanted to date me, than I was with him in particular. I probably would've dated just about anybody at that point, because finally, *someone wanted me*! It made me feel special."

Here was the bad part. The part everyone in town knew, and yet, no one had told Jaxson.

A part of Sugar found that hard to believe – people *loved* to gossip. Why would no one have taken advantage of the opportunity to tell Jaxson all about how his new girlfriend had once been the town whore? She wondered for a moment if someone *had* told Jaxson and this was some sort of test, to see if she'd tell him the truth. That was something Dick would do, no doubt about it.

She shifted her weight slightly so she could look him in the eye. If this was a test, he'd have a little smirk on his lips, and a sly look in his eyes, already rejoicing in the idea that no matter what she said, he'd figured out a way to make her lose.

But Jaxson's eyes were not sly or rejoicing. He was not smirking. He was simply looking down at her non-judgmentally. Listening. And instead of muddy green eyes that could never seem to settle on a particular shade, Jaxson's eyes were a warm, rich brown, true and straightforward and trustworthy.

So she took a chance. Again. Because his eyes were brown and not green, and in that moment, that was all she had to cling to.

"Graduation night from high school, Dick starts telling me that now that I'm an adult and grown-up, it's time to try my first drink. I really was pretty naïve," she said with a bitter laugh, "and had never tried alcohol. My parents are super strict, and pretty much impressed the idea upon me that one drink meant I'd end up in hell for eternity, or at least addicted to the stuff. I'd always been too scared to try it before, but Dick…he has a way of wheedling you, making you feel stupid and immature if you don't go along with his ideas, and so you end up doing it because who wants to feel stupid and immature?

"So I bowed to peer pressure. I'm like, the damn poster child for the shit that happens when you bow to peer pressure. I should be giving speeches to gymnasiums full of teenagers about what an awful idea it is. I don't know if I can force teens to grow a backbone just by pointing out what shitty shit happens if you don't have one, though." She tried to laugh ironically, but it came out as a choking groan instead.

Close enough.

"Dick and I go to a party being thrown by one of my graduating classmates – this kid I'd never been particularly close to, but with a graduating class of less than a hundred students, I obviously knew him. He was trouble and I knew it, but…peer pressure.

"Dick gets a drink for me, and watches me closely as I drink it, yelling 'Chug, chug, chug!' as I do, and as soon as it hits my system, I'm woozy. So out of it. I don't remember much of this next part; some people there have helped me piece together what happened. Dick got drunk one night, years later, and bragged about how he'd slipped a date rape drug into my drink that night. He'd decided that he'd paid the price, and waited long enough to get 'what was coming to him,' so it was time for me to do my duty as his girlfriend.

"He took me to a bedroom in the back of the house, and was stripping me down and I kinda remember pushing his hands away, but it's cloudy, like it happened in a dream, or maybe to someone else altogether and I'm just imagining that it's me…I'm not even sure if I fought him or not, or if I've just convinced myself that I did.

"Then, there are people there. In the bedroom with us. Laughing and pointing and I'm holding my jeans up over my tits to cover them, because it's all I could find, but it was too late. The kid hosting the party? He'd taken some pics of me. Full frontal nudity. He sent them to everyone at the party, and then they made their way onto Facebook. This was before Snapchat and Instagram, or I'm sure they would've ended up there, too.

"My parents…well, that was the end of their approval of my choices, that's for sure. For a few brief shining moments, they'd been proud of me, but after that night, never again. They told me that if I was old enough to get drunk and old enough to get caught in bed with a guy, then I was old enough to marry him. I'd brought a lot of shame down upon them, and I was going to make this right by marrying Dick. I was 18, by just a few weeks at that point, so I could've fought them, I guess. I was an adult. On paper.

"But I'd never been any further than Boise. I had no car, no place to live, no job, no money of my own. I was completely dependent upon them, and so I did what they wanted me to.

"Two weeks later, I found myself at the courthouse, with just the judge – who was marrying us – Dick, and my parents, and I was getting married. It only took that long to make it happen because we had to get the paperwork through. The really ironic thing was, I was a virgin on my wedding day."

She laughed hysterically, shrill and tight and painful.

"Can you believe it? The town whore, who had nudie pictures spread all over the place, was still a virgin. My classmates busting in on us that night had meant Dick hadn't finished the deed, and my parents sure as hell weren't allowing us to be alone after that, until we were properly married. I didn't even see him again until our wedding day. My parents locked me up in my room for those two weeks. I got married in a dress I had hanging in my closet – *not* white. My parents wouldn't let me wear white."

She felt Dick's hand on her, forcing her to move and she lashed out, punching and hitting, trying to defend herself and keep from being forced back into the bedroom when Jaxson's voice finally penetrated and she came to again.

She was out in the forest. In the snow. With Jaxson. Dick wasn't there. He wasn't going to…

The sobs overtook her, shaking her body as she cried it all out. The shame, the betrayal, the self-hatred…it all washed out of her on a never-ending river of tears.

Finally, exhausted, Sugar leaned back in Jaxson's arms to look him in the face. She was ready for his condemnation now. Ready for him to tell her that she deserved what happened to her, because she hadn't been strong enough to say no to the party, no to the drinking, no to Dick, no to her parents. If she'd been more like Emma – someone who'd knee a guy in the balls and make a run for it – then she wouldn't have had the last eight years of her life happen.

She wasn't sure what would've happened – she might've gone to college. Moved away. *Done* something with her life.

All because of one night. Because of her complete inability

to stand up for herself; to find a backbone somewhere in her body.

But instead of the condemnation that she so richly deserved, he was still looking down at her with…love? It looked like love in his eyes.

It couldn't be love, though. No one could love someone as spineless as her.

"Were things awful from the get-go, or was he nice at first?" Jaxson asked softly. He didn't seem to be upset with her elbowing him in the stomach, and Sugar wondered again at his patience. No one else would put up with her. Not as nutty as she was.

And yet for a moment, just a single moment, she was going to let herself relax against him. Let him carry a little of the weight on her shoulders. She could rest up, and then pick up the weight again. After she was a little stronger.

"He started out okay," Sugar said softly, trying to force her mind to go back to the beginning. It seemed like so long ago, and she'd been trying so hard for so long to push it all out; block it out of her mind. It was hard to force her mind to bring it up now, all these years later. "Not Husband of the Year material, but…normal, I guess.

"His dad paid the security deposit, and first and last month's rent on a little house as our 'wedding gift.' I thought he was being really kind, but as time passed, I realized that he was just doing what he always had to do – Dick rarely had money or a job, and his dad paid for a lot of our expenses. He didn't do it graciously; he made me feel like such a mooch, such a leech, for taking money from him so often. Not Dick – he was the perfect son. *I* was the one falling down on my job of keeping Dick in style, forcing his father to continue to do it. I think the judge had almost been excited about me marrying Dick because he'd thought that this would mean that I'd pick up the slack and let his father off the hook of taking care of his grown son financially.

"But Dick didn't get the memo, and he kept telling me that it 'wasn't fitting' for a judge's daughter-in-law to work like a common person. Which is patently ridiculous, of course. I think Dick just figured his dad would continue to take care of us, and didn't understand that behind the scenes, his dad was pushing me to work. Eventually, Dick relented, and I got a part-time job down at Mr. Petrol's, running the cash register. I had to sign every paycheck over to him, and I wasn't allowed to even have a debit card. If I needed to buy something, he came with me to the store.

"I eventually figured out what he was spending our money on, since we were living pretty much rent- and utility-free. Alcohol. I was raised by parents who'd never so much as had a glass of wine at supper, so I didn't know what alcohol smelled like. I didn't recognize the signs for a long time. I just thought he was tired sometimes, so that's why he was slurring his words, and falling over. I was the most naïve person you would've ever met in your life at that point.

"Our lives were okay – not great, but okay – up until his sister died. Have you met Wyatt Miller yet?"

Startled by the change in topic, Jaxson shook his head, still just staring down at her unblinkingly, watching her every movement, listening to her every word.

Sugar squirmed a little inside. She wasn't sure if any guy had ever listened to her as intently as Jaxson did right now. It felt...weird. It made her feel a bit like a fraud – no one was as interesting as Jaxson was acting like Sugar was right now. What she had to say wasn't worthy of this kind of attention. She was just...Sugar. Nobody of consequence.

"Turn around," she told him sharply, broking no arguments. His eyebrows hit his hairline, but he nodded and turned around, facing into the snowy forest, sunlight glinting off every surface.

Sugar breathed a little easier. That felt better. Now she

could just pretend that she was talking to a tree. A very tall, very good-smelling tree.

He'd think she'd completely lost her mind if she told him that. Thank heavens he wasn't a mind reader.

"Wyatt Miller is the oldest of the Miller brothers here in town. He's an ornery son-of-a-bitch, although I've heard he's become a lot calmer – less prone to punching – after he married his second wife, Abby. She was his jailer after Wyatt got in trouble for beating Dick to a bloody pulp."

"Hold on, Wyatt married his jailer?!" The amusement was plain in Jaxson's voice, and Sugar couldn't help grinning – for just a moment – at it too.

"You start to get desperate in a small town after a while," she told him dryly. "Anyway, Wyatt was Dick's brother-in-law."

"I think I'm gonna need a family tree for this one," Jaxson grumbled.

"Probably!" Sugar said cheerfully. "Dick had an older sister named Shelly. She married Wyatt and they had a little girl together, Sierra. The judge would invite everyone over for a family dinner, and there's this hulking, handsome, rough-around-the-edges farmer at the table, scowling at everyone. Shelly told me that he was a lot nicer and friendlier at home, but the judge never cared for him, and Wyatt never cared to hide the fact that the feeling was mutual, so towards the end, Shelly and Sierra started coming over by themselves. Wyatt would always have some pressing chore to do. Everyone knew what was happening, but since it made dinners less stressful and painful, I will admit I didn't mind too much.

"And then…it happened. Shelly and Sierra died in a car wreck. Hit by a drunk driver going to Franklin to get milk one night. The judge never did forgive Wyatt for killing them."

"Wyatt was drunk and ran into them?" Jaxson asked, incredulously.

"No, but you'd think so, the way the judge reacted. He felt

like it was Wyatt's job to get the milk – he shouldn't have had his precious daughter out on the roads after dark like that."

"But how was Wyatt supposed to know? And what, women are never supposed to drive after dark?!"

"The judge is a sexist pig," Sugar said bluntly. "Start there. And start with the fact that the judge would've been happy to have Wyatt die that night on the road, but to have his Shelly taken away from him – the judge would never forgive Wyatt for letting her die. As if Wyatt had a choice."

Sugar snorted with disbelief. Wyatt may've been standoffish and curt at the suppers they'd shared together, but you couldn't question the love he felt towards his wife and daughter. She wasn't entirely sure Wyatt would live through their deaths, and when he found love again with Abby last year, she'd been glad for it. He deserved love.

"If Wyatt took Shelly and Sierra's death hard, you should've seen the judge and Dick," Sugar said to the tree. She noticed a bit of hair sticking out at an odd angle on the back of his head, and smoothed it down with her hand. He sucked in his breath in surprise and she quickly dropped her hand again.

He was just a tree and she was just talking to it. Trees didn't need their hair fixed.

"Every meal after that was all about how Wyatt had caused them to die, and he deserved to die, and—"

"The judge and Dick were gonna kill Wyatt?" Jaxson broke in with disbelief.

"No, I don't think they'd have ever done it. They just liked to talk about how it should happen. Not plans or anything concrete. Just that it should happen to him someday soon. But in my world, I went from having a sister-in-law and niece who I could talk to and hang out with at family meals, to them dying and leaving me alone with a husband and father-in-law who were quickly descending into lunacy. I'm not trying to make this all about me, of course," she said quickly, before he could point out how selfish she was being. "It just made things more—"

Jaxson turned around and put his hands on her shoulders in one swift move, staring down at her intently. "Sugar, you don't need to apologize," he said. "Of course it would affect you. You're telling me your story, and what happened to you. It's okay to be affected by all of this shit."

"Right. Yeah. Of course." She squirmed a little at the thought, though. It just seemed so selfish. "Turn around," she said, giving him a scowl. With a sigh, he turned back around. "So Dick's drinking…it got way worse after that. *Way* worse. It got to the point that if he was sober, that was unusual. I got better about dodging his fists because he was too drunk to have good aim, so…bonus points for that?" She tried to laugh as if it was no big deal, but the laugh came out choking again.

Dammit. She really needed to work on putting up a better front. *Never show your soft underbelly.* She was practically rolling over and begging Jaxson to stab her. She felt panic well up inside of her at the thought, but she ruthlessly pushed it down. It was okay to talk to a tree. It couldn't hurt her.

"Then, after losing…losing my baby, things got even worse. Hard to believe, I know. Emma, always the practical one, told me to go to Gage and ask for a job.

"You have to know that the Dyer kids didn't grow up here; their grandparents lived here, running the bakery, but as soon as their father, Tim Dyer, graduated from high school, he joined the Marines and started traveling the world. He and his wife, Donelle, have their three kids, and they bring them back to Long Valley during the summers to visit their grandparents, but it wasn't until the dad hit his 20 years in the Marines that he retired. Well, it just so happened that Gage graduated from high school the day before his dad retired, so instead of moving back to Long Valley with the rest of the family, he went off to college.

"So it was weird, because I became besties with Emma and

of course knew Chris, but I didn't really know Gage until he finished his schooling and came back to take over the bakery from his grandparents. They required that he get his degree before they'd let him take over the business, so he'd been pretty focused on getting that done and hadn't been home a whole lot.

"Anyway, Emma kept pushing me to go to Gage – almost a complete stranger to me – and get a job working the front counter at the bakery. Apparently, he needed help and Emma came up with a pretty brilliant plan: Gage could pay me with two paychecks. One I could take home and show Dick, and let him spend, and one I could cash and stuff under the mattress. That way, I could finally save up to leave him. I hated to be a bother to Gage like that, but Emma kept telling me that it'd be okay, and I could trust him. She was right, of course, but I was still terrified at first that Gage would rat me out to Dick. That thought used to keep me up at night. Trusting someone else like that was…hard. But in the end, he saved me. I'll always be grateful to him for that, even if I'm not in love with him."

She laughed a little at the thought of loving Gage – a genuine laugh this time – and Jaxson admitted ruefully, "I apologized to him for that, by the way. I just didn't know back then, how Sawyer worked."

Sugar shrugged, and then realized that Jaxson couldn't see her. "It's okay," she said aloud. "I probably would've thought the same thing in your shoes. Plenty of people have made that mistake."

She took a deep breath. Finally, a conclusion in sight to this godawful story.

"Dick's pride and joy was his Jeep, this horrid hunter-orange color. That's pretty much his saving grace, or at least the town's saving grace. Everyone around here has figured out that if they see this Jeep heading towards them on the road, it's better to just dive into the borrow pit to get out of the way, rather than risk dying in a head-on collision with him. The irony of Dick killing someone in a drunk driving accident would be too rich for words.

"A while back, he went on a three-day bender, which was pretty bad, even for him. He ran out of beer, and went down to Mr. Petrol's to buy more. I guess Wyatt was there and saw how drunk he was, and because of how Shelly died…well, Wyatt lost it on him. Beat the living shit outta him, actually. Dick ended up in the hospital for a couple of weeks – busted ribs, reconstructive surgery on his face…I imagine Wyatt saw red, like you did the night you found Kendra in bed with Ivan, because no sane person would beat someone else up like that. He pert near killed Dick.

"In the ensuing chaos, I realized I had my chance. I had my little stash that I'd put away, and I had a comatose husband in the ER who couldn't stop me. I made a run for it. I mattered so little to Dick or his dad, no one even bothered to wonder where the hell I was at – why I wasn't fawning at my husband's bedside over his injuries – until it was time to come home, and they wanted me to play nursemaid to him. Dick has informed me since then that I was a downright awful wife, for leaving him in a lurch like that. Except maybe not such nice phrasing. He wasn't exactly happy with my run for the border." She chuckled a little.

"I filed for divorce and had my lawyer get the case moved to Ada County, instead of it being heard locally. I knew Judge Schmidt would fight it every step of the way – not because he liked having me as his daughter-in-law or something, but because Dick would want him to, and Dick always got what he wanted. I was divorced from him before the bruises all even faded away. I'm still not sure if he knew exactly what hit him.

"He wouldn't leave me alone, though, so I got Hamlet – the biggest dog I could find. A breeder over in Copperton sold him to me for cheap because apparently his tail isn't the right shape or some such shit, and he wouldn't be able to be shown as a show dog, which is what she raises dogs for. So I got him for a steal, considering he's a purebred. One visit to my house after that, and I haven't seen Dick again. He can't breathe while in my vicinity because of the dog hair, and I figure that's revenge enough."

Jaxson let out a deep laugh as he turned around and pulled Sugar into his arms. She stiffened up for a moment, not sure that she was okay with him hugging her, but after he didn't push or grab or hurt her, she relaxed. He was just holding her in his arms, and it felt…nice.

Better than nice, actually.

"That was a pretty brilliant solution to your problem," Jaxson said admiringly. "I'm proud of you for thinking to do that."

She grinned against his chest. "Thanks. I'm kinda proud of myself for that one, too."

They stood there in the clearing, holding each other and saying nothing, and Sugar realized that she was okay. She'd told Jaxson her worst secrets – losing her baby and being glad for it, being trapped into marrying Dick instead of standing up to people and telling them no…

She'd told him everything, and he didn't tell her that she deserved it all. He'd said he was *proud* of her. She couldn't remember the last time anyone was proud of her. Even Emma was disappointed in Sugar's lack of drive to take on the world like she had. Just accepting her for her was…

Not a thing. Not in Sugar's world.

She felt a little bit of panic creep into the oasis of calm.

"You're not disappointed in me?" she blurted out. She kept her head snuggled against his chest. She couldn't work up the courage to look him in the eye.

"Disappointed?" Jaxson repeated, incredulously. "Damn, woman, I don't know how I could be. You've been handed more piles of shit than a zookeeper, and instead of just letting it all happen to you, you've fought back the best way you knew how, without any family support, and very little money. I couldn't be more impressed with your ingenuity, or your willingness to do the hard work needed to get out of that situation. I don't know that I've ever met someone like you before. This world needs more Sugars in it, that's for damn sure."

Sugar gulped. That sounded way too impressive. He must not have understood everything that she'd said. Later, he'd get angry with her for misleading him, and maybe have to smack her around for being a liar or something. It was better to set the record straight now.

"I could've said no to Dick wanting me to drink at the party, or no to getting married to him, or no to turning over my paychecks at the gas station to him, or—"

"Sugar, you were barely 18," Jaxson interrupted, clearly not believing her view of the world. "You were as naïve as a newborn babe, and he saw you coming from a mile off. He knew that your sweet nature – no pun intended – meant he could manipulate you, and he did, for a while. That's on him, not on you. The fact that he was willing to do that says a lot about him, and none of it's good. You shouldn't have to be a cynical person, questioning every move someone makes, just to protect yourself from a person like him. If you do, he's not someone you want to be around anyway. Which I think you've well proven at this point.

"But you can't keep beating yourself up. You gotta move on; let it go. We can't go back in time and change decisions; we can only make sure not to repeat the same dumb mistakes again and again."

"So don't take Dick back?" Sugar asked dryly. Even as she deflected, using humor to shield herself, Jaxson's words echoed in her mind. *You shouldn't have to be a cynical person, questioning every move someone makes, just to protect yourself from a person like him.*

"Well, I definitely vote no on that idea," Jaxson said with a laugh. "But I might be biased on the topic."

She gave him a small smile, her mind not really focused on what he'd just said. It was stuck, like a needle skipping on a record, playing and replaying that sentence in her mind. *Questioning every move…protect yourself…*

She *had* become a cynic. She hadn't meant to. But she'd become wholeheartedly focused on protecting herself from harm, to the point that she wasn't willing to let anyone else in. It was less scary if she didn't. It was less painful.

She felt a full-blown shiver shake through her body, and she realized that the story had taken so long, the sun was starting to set and the thermometer had started to drop. Realizing that they needed to head back before full darkness hit, Jaxson tipped her head back, gave her a soft kiss on the lips, and then jerked his head towards the snowmobiles. "We better get going," he said softly. "We don't want to be out here after dark."

He put the engine stop into her hand, and she headed to her borrowed machine numbly, her mind swirling as she went. Everything that had happened today…it was painful. Overwhelming. Like cleaning out a closet of bad memories. It was good to get it done, but exhausting all the same.

As she swung her leg onto the snowmobile and put the stop back into its slot, she couldn't help replaying the idea of Jaxson being a tree – a solid tree that she could rely on, and who wouldn't hurt her. Not ever.

It was a terrifyingly wonderful idea, if she was brave enough to truly believe it.

CHAPTER 37

JAXSON

J AXSON LOOKED AROUND at the men, including Angus and Chris. In the past couple of months, after Angus had started really enjoying learning about firefighting, he'd asked Jaxson if he could bring his best friend along. Thinking back to his conversation with Gage, Jaxson had said yes, figuring Chris could only improve in his life choices if he had something to do after school that didn't include mind-altering substances. It'd only been a couple of months since he'd started working with the teens, and already, it seemed to his optimistic eye that they'd changed a little. Smiled a little more, anyway.

Jaxson would take it.

"All right, let's go through donning your personal protective gear. Since this is a volunteer department, we're already behind the eight ball when it comes to response times, so we've got to make up for it by being faster than anyone else when it comes to putting on our gear and getting to the scene of a fire. There's a couple of tricks that make you faster if you think about how you put on your gear. Fast but scattered isn't necessarily *fast*, if you know what I mean. Grab your—"

Everyone's radios squawked at once, the cacophony

echoing in the cavernous fire station. "Calling all emergency personnel, there is a fire down at the Muffin Man; I repeat, calling the Sawyer Fire Department and EMT Department, there is a report of flames down at the bakery." The radio crackled for a moment, and then, "Chief Anderson, Sugar is at work."

Even as panic like Jaxson had never felt before poured through him, he couldn't help smiling a bit at that. Just a twinge of the lips – *only in Sawyer would the dispatcher tack that on* – and then it passed, leaving terror in its wake, freezing his body in place while also setting it on fire, a singularly awful feeling.

The Muffin Man? Why? How?

But he couldn't freeze up. He had shit to do; people to save. *Sugar* to save.

He looked at the men assembled in front of him, all staring at him, mouth agape. Not a sound was heard in the station. Everyone knew why the dispatcher mentioned Sugar. Here it was – his test to see if he was truly worthy to be a fire chief or not. Everyone was watching and waiting to see what he did. He would bomb this test, or pass it with flying colors.

There would be no in-between.

"Let's go, let's go, let's go!" he hollered, and the spell was broken. The men began scrambling into their turnout gear, which had been so conveniently laying out in front of them. Jaxson figured that their response time to this fire would break all records for the Sawyer Fire Department. Which, if they were gonna have a fire that they'd respond to quickly, this was it.

"I want to go with you," Angus said, pulling on his arm as Jaxson was trying to pull his suit over it. Jaxson hesitated, staring at the two teens standing defiantly in front of him. They were still mostly untrained, and would cause more problems than solve, that was for *damn* sure.

"You guys haven't had enough training yet," Jaxson said briskly. "I can't have you in the way—"

"We're going to go down there no matter what," Angus said bluntly. "You can't stop us. But that's Chris' brother in there. We have to know that he's okay. We could get down there faster if we rode with you."

After a moment's hesitation, Jaxson's mind whirling with everything that needed to be done, he jerked his head. "You can ride down with us, but you better stay out of the way. No helping in any way, got it?"

They nodded solemnly as Jaxson finished pulling his gear on. Moose, as the new Sawyer Fire Department Deputy Chief, had been on top of things, getting both trucks started and warming up. They'd pulled them out of the fire station earlier that morning so they would have room inside to train, and stay out of the miserable cold.

Sawyer had hit another cold snap – although it was the middle of April, Jaxson had been told many a-time to not expect good weather to stay and stick until at least June. Staring out into the white wonderland outside, Jaxson could only hope the water in the tanks hadn't frozen in place, since the weather had been too cold to start replacing the fire hydrants around town. Jaxson remembered all too well that the hydrant in front of the Muffin Man was only for looks at this point. Water in the trucks was all they had.

He nodded his thanks to Moose for getting the trucks started and warming up, grateful that he at least had a deputy chief that he could rely on. He didn't even want to think about how JimBob would've responded to this call.

He looked around. "Whoever's ready to go, jump on the new truck and let's get moving. Moose, you drive the tanker and meet us over there with everyone else." Moose nodded, and Jaxson swung up into the cab of the fire engine.

It was time to do his job, but even more importantly, it was time to save the woman he loved. He'd been holding off telling her that, not wanting to scare her away after all that she'd been through, but now, that reasoning seemed ridiculous. What if she died without knowing that he loved her?

What if she died?

As he tore through town, the sirens wailing, he didn't feel that usual rush of adrenaline that accompanied every fire he'd ever been on before. He'd often thought that he was an adrenaline junkie who was just lucky enough to find a well-respected career where he could use that need for danger in a positive way, instead of doing stupid shit like base jumping or skydiving or something.

But today was different. He'd never felt this terror before, trying to overwhelm his senses and shut him down. Black spots flickered at the edges of his vision, and he realized that he'd stopped breathing, quite literally. He forced himself to take a deep breath, and then another.

Although the journey felt like it took years, maybe even decades, they finally arrived at the scene, and everyone began offloading, pulling out hoses, setting up the stabilizer jacks on the truck. Jaxson grabbed his helmet and face mask and jumped out, eyes darting around, looking for Sugar amongst the people milling around on the sidewalk. There was Mr. Stultz and Mrs. Gehring, but no Gage or Sugar.

"Oh thank God you're here," Mrs. Gehring said, swinging her way over with her cane to look up at him, her faded blue eyes pleading with him. "I was eating and then it started to smell smoky and then the young boy who runs the place started yelling for people to get out, and I came out here but I haven't seen Sugar or Gage yet. I don't know where they're at. You gotta get them out."

"That's the idea, ma'am," he said, trying to keep a smile planted firmly on his face and not show the panic building up inside of him. "Please step back – I'd hate to have you get hurt too." He looked up and bellowed, "If you're not a firefighter or EMT, step back!"

The last thing he needed was the giant front windows

shattering from the heat and launching shards into the growing crowd. He spotted Angus and Chris, wearing their Junior Sawyer Fire Department t-shirts, and that gave him an idea. He pushed himself over to them, the weight of his gear and the crowd slowing him down.

"I need you two to keep the crowd back," he told them. "Can you do that?" They both nodded solemnly. "Don't let 'em near those windows. They could shatter and do some real damage." They nodded again, when Jaxson felt someone tapping on his shoulder.

He spun on his heel to find the police chief standing there, his pot belly hanging over the edge of his belt, his thumbs in his belt loops. Jaxson was ready to spit fire of his own – if the police chief was just here to tell Jaxson how to do his job, he could go to hell – when the man said, "It's a chimney fire. A couple of my deputies saw sparks coming out of the smokestack on the back wall, in the kitchen area."

Jaxson sucked in a breath of disappointment, his mind running through his options, remembering the layout of the kitchen as he did so. If Chief Horvath had actually bothered to purchase a fire truck that did more than just look pretty, Jaxson would have a ladder on top of the truck that he could use to drop a chimney bomb down the chute and onto the flames. The powder in them were nothing short of magical, and put out fires easily and quickly. Without a ladder on the truck, though, and the chimney being right up against the back wall, they couldn't trust leaning a ladder against that wall, and risk having it cave in on them. Nor could they walk on top of the roof.

They'd have to put it out the hard way – by going in.

You have to find Sugar. Find her. Find her. Find her.

The panic was almost overwhelming him, but he pushed it down. He could hyperventilate later. "Thanks, Chief," he said gruffly, and then turned to see that Moose had arrived, along with Levi and Luke, and in the back stood Troy, quiet as always. Jaxson looked at them. "Just like we trained for. Let's go."

He wasn't much for giving rousing speeches, not when a building was on fire.

Not when his girlfriend was in the building that was on fire.

He slipped his mask into place and his helmet on his head, and then they began working their way through the smoky building methodically, leaving no part of the dining room untouched. A small child or dog could be cowering in the corner, and they'd never see them in this smoke. They had to be methodical, never letting fear or adrenaline rule their actions. They couldn't just charge into the flames and hope for the best, no matter what his gut was screaming at him to do.

Moose and Levi were laying hose while the other men kept their hands free. Fighting fires was only part of the deal; saving lives was more important.

Sugar's life, especially. Everyone deserved to be saved, but Jaxson couldn't help focusing on Sugar. He wouldn't be human if he didn't focus on her in that moment. Nothing else mattered – it all faded away.

Just Sugar.

The gloom of the smoke-filled bakery made it hard to see anything, but Jaxson could feel the heat of the flames as he moved around the counter and towards the back. He pushed through the swinging doors that separated the kitchen from the front, the charred wood falling uselessly to the ground. He could hardly see his hand in front of his face, so when he felt his boot kick flesh on the floor, he almost jumped in surprise. Instead, he knelt, finding Gage's thick, corded arm muscles leading up to his torso. He stood and spun, looking for someone to help him, and found Moose at his back.

He gestured down at Gage, and he had the ever-so-brief thought that he needed to work on getting in-helmet radios for his men, and then he pushed the thought away. He'd focus on that later. Moose nodded, but instead of leaning down and helping Jaxson heft Gage up, he turned and grabbed Levi, pulling him forward through the smoke so they could lift Gage together.

Jaxson gave a brief nod of understanding, reminding himself to thank Moose later, and turned back into the smoke. He could see the flames clearly now, and a red-hot stove pipe leading up from the ovens along the wall. The brilliance of it was evil, glowing and taunting him through the smoke.

He shook his head. He had to focus. He kept shuffling his way forward, searching with his feet as much as with his hands and eyes, looking for Sugar.

What if she'd gone out the back, and didn't need saving? The fire was growing bigger, the crackling sounds more ominous.

His mind spun with his choices – the worst choices he'd ever faced in his life. He could focus on finding Sugar, or on putting the fire out. One choice meant potentially saving her life, but letting a block of Sawyer burn to the ground, and the other meant saving this part of Sawyer but letting Sugar die.

And then there was the fact that Sugar may've gone out the back door and could be just fine right now. He could let a block of Sawyer burn to the ground for no reason at all.

It didn't matter, though. He couldn't do it. No matter how slim the chance that she was still in there, he had to keep looking.

The terror, which had been scattering his thoughts to the wind, suddenly focused them. Finding Sugar was all that mattered. He pushed the heat, the flames, the smoke, the worry that he was too late, to the side. He would leave that building with Sugar in his arms, or after he'd covered every square inch of the place.

And not a moment before.

He continued to methodically criss-cross the tiled floor, shuffling along, and then it happened. A soft barrier in front of his foot. He dropped to his knees and discovered Sugar's limp body in the smoke. He scooped her up into his arms, ignoring protocol that dictated that two men carry unconscious civilians out of fires. Sugar was so small, she was practically half a person anyway.

In that moment, Jaxson would've taken the arm off anyone who dared to touch her. He held her possessively against his body as he headed back out of the kitchen, nudging a couple of men on the way out to show them that he was holding Sugar. They nodded in understanding, and began spraying the fire. Now that all lives were saved, they could focus on saving property.

Except, *was* she alive? In his mask and helmet, his body covered in full fireproof gear, he couldn't know. He couldn't feel a pulse through his gloves, or spot the slight rise and fall of her chest through his goggles. He just had to carry her outside, and pray that she was all right. He stumbled against some chairs on the way out, Sugar's body and the smoke keeping him from being able to see much of anything, but he didn't care.

He kept going.

He just needed to get her outside.

He just needed to find an EMT to save her.

Nothing else mattered.

He pushed the glass door open, the bell tinkling merrily as he spilled out onto the sidewalk, smoke following him in waves as he searched frantically for an EMT. A shout went up as the crowd spotted him, and a guy whipped his head around and headed their way, leaving Mrs. Gehring behind. He had a navy blue EMTs of Sawyer t-shirt on, and Jaxson almost sagged with relief. They were here. They would help save Sugar.

Another EMT, a woman this time, came up, pushing a stretcher in front of her. They were saying something but over the roar of adrenaline and the fire and everything else, Jaxson didn't know what they were saying, only saw their lips moving. But he knew what to do anyway – lay her down on the gurney. Let them take care of her.

And so he did, as hard as it was to let her go. He didn't want to. He hurt as he laid her down, because some irrational part of him believed that if he just held her, he could make her better. He could heal her through the force of his love for her.

Thankfully, his rational side prevailed, and he stood back, letting the EMTs push her towards a waiting ambulance, the lights flashing as they chattered back and forth about heart rates and smoke inhalation, and then…

The worst part of it all: He had to watch them load her and drive away, and he couldn't go with them because he had a job to do, and he was sure, in that moment, that his heart was being torn in two.

To let them take Sugar away without knowing if she was dead or alive; if she was going to make it or die on the way to the hospital…

He had done nothing harder in his whole life. And for the first time since he'd learned the thrill that came with fighting fires, he hated his lifelong passion for making him choose like this. No one should *ever* be asked to make this choice.

Levi was tapping him on the shoulder, indicating he should take his mask off so they could talk, and Jaxson responded mechanically, doing what he was supposed to do.

As Levi asked about the strategy they'd need to implement to bring the fire under control and not take the adjoining buildings down with it, Jaxson answered, his body knowing what to do, even if his heart hated him for it.

CHAPTER 38
SUGAR

BEEP. BEEP. BEEP.

Sugar swatted at the air. Her alarm clock was going off again, just like it did every morning. Was it really time to get up already? She felt like she'd been run over by a truck. Surely she didn't have to actually get up, right?

The beeping continued, annoying Sugar. She swatted again, trying to reach the clock, and then she remembered that it was across the room, on her nightstand. No wonder she wasn't turning it off. She'd moved it months before.

With a groan, she tried to roll off the bed so she could crawl across the room towards the clock. But instead of hitting the hardwood floors of her bedroom, she was hitting a cold metal barrier.

"Whoa, whoa," a soft voice said, stroking her hair back, pushing her onto her back. "Where do you think you're going?"

That was weird. Sugar couldn't make her brain figure out why someone was in her bedroom, but her eyes hurt too much to open them up. She opened up her mouth to tell this lady that she needed to turn off her alarm clock, but her throat hurt too much to talk, and only a small croak came out instead.

Frustrated and alarmed, Sugar cleared her throat to try it again, and instead, began coughing spasmodically, her whole body tensing up as she realized that something was in her nose and throat and she was choking to death. She began trying to pull at the things trying to smother her, her panic growing by leaps and bounds, and then people were calling out all around her and she felt a whoosh of cold liquid in her arm, which was so weird, and then she was drifting again, her body relaxing against the pillow and she was falling down the well into the darkness...

CHAPTER 39

JAXSON

J AXSON SURVEYED THE KITCHEN, or what was left of it. The chimney that had started it all was black again, instead of that monstrous brilliant red, but then again, the rest of the kitchen was black, too. The smoke damage on this one was going to be tremendous. Jaxson could only hope Gage had excellent insurance on the bakery. He would need every penny of help he could get to rebuild the place.

They'd managed to keep the fire from spreading to the adjoining buildings, though, and for that, Jaxson was incredibly proud of his guys. Even Dylan, on his first real fire that he could fight, had stayed focused throughout it all. Probably more focused than Jaxson had been.

Is Sugar okay? Is she still alive?

For the thousandth time, he cursed himself for not making the EMTs swear that they would call him with updates. He burned to get onto the radios and ask, but knew that they were for official business, not so a guy could check up on the love of his life.

"Why don't you go check on Sugar?" Moose asked, coming up to stand next to Jaxson. "I can take it from here."

Jaxson turned and stared at Moose for a moment, his mind

whirling with everything he *should* be doing, versus what he *wanted* to do. It was The Choice again, the damn choice between Sawyer and Sugar, and this time, he couldn't do what he was "supposed" to be doing any longer.

He jerked his head in appreciation, shoved the clipboard with a checklist of items to complete after a fire into Moose's hands, and headed for the front door.

Finally, his duty as fire chief was done. Now he could be simply Sugar's boyfriend. The relief of it all almost knocked him to his knees, but he hurried to his SUV instead, pulling off his mask and helmet as he moved, wanting to get to the hospital as quickly as his gas pedal would allow him.

For the first time since he moved to Long Valley, Jaxson was happy to be the only person in town driving a brilliant green Ford Explorer. It meant that the cops all knew who he was, and where he was going. He tore around corners, ignoring traffic expectations like stopping at stop signs, or the posted speed limit, or anything else. Nothing else mattered except Sugar.

He got to the small hospital, throwing his SUV in park and sprinting for the door, moving faster than he'd ever managed to move in full gear before. Now that he was allowing himself to wonder how Sugar was doing, he found that breathing fully was hard to do. Thinking clearly was even harder.

A vaguely familiar looking redhead looked up from the desk and, catching sight of him, hitched her thumb over her shoulder. "Second door on the right," she called out to him as he blew past her and down the hallway she'd pointed towards.

He nodded his thanks but didn't break his stride. Nothing mattered now except seeing for himself that Sugar was okay. *If* she was okay.

"Jaxson, stop!" a voice cried, and he spun in a circle, trying to see who was talking to him, when he saw Dr. Torgeson come huffing up, out of breath. "They told me you were on your way over. Listen…Sugar's alive, but…she has a lot of smoke inhalation damage to her lungs. We've sedated her because she kept trying to pull her breathing tube out. If she does that, she'll die. Without the extra-high oxygen content from the air we're shoving in her, her body won't be able to pull enough oxygen out to keep her body alive."

Jaxson nodded his understanding, silently willing the man to talk faster. If he didn't get to his point soon, he'd just toss the doctor over his shoulder and let him continue to blather on while they walked into Sugar's room together. Every moment away from Sugar was a moment of pure pain, the kind of torture Jaxson had never felt before.

"She's delirious from the pain and keeps slapping at the air with her hands. We're not sure what that's all about. Just keep calm, don't startle her or give into her demands to remove her breathing tube, okay?"

Jaxson nodded curtly and then hurried into the room, happy to finally be given permission to go in.

At the sight of Sugar, so small and delicate and dirty against the white hospital sheets, his breath caught. She seemed to be completely asleep at the moment, so he settled down next to her in the visitor's chair, staring at her, willing her to wake up and tell him that she was all right.

He skimmed his fingertips across her face, the ash and soot from the fire darkening her normally pale skin. With everything wrong with her, he wasn't surprised that the nurses hadn't had time to clean her up, especially not with Gage also in the hospital. Two burn victims in one afternoon was probably a pretty big strain on the small staff.

Gage. Jaxson felt a bolt of guilt at the fact that he'd forgotten to even ask after his friend to find out how he was doing.

He tucked Sugar's hand next to her side and stepped out into the hallway, grabbing a harried nurse as she went by. "I'd like to clean Sugar Stonemyer up a bit. Do you have hot water and a washcloth I could borrow, or alcohol wipes or something?"

"The CNA should be along in a minute and she can do it,"

the nurse said curtly, obviously thinking that the task of cleaning a patient would be underneath a man.

Reverse sexism. It's also a thing in Sawyer, Idaho.

He kept his smile plastered on his face. "I'd prefer to do it, if that's all right. I'm sure the CNA has other things she can do."

"All right," the nurse sniffed. "I'll send the CNA in with the supplies."

She hurried off before Jaxson could ask her about Gage.

He walked back into the small hospital room, his gaze never leaving Sugar's. He'd take care of her. Show her how much she meant to him. Make her finally believe that the fact that she'd been manipulated as an 18-year-old girl wasn't reason to be miserable for the rest of her life.

Sugar began thrashing around just as Jaxson got to her side. She was slapping the air, just like the doctor had said, and noises were coming from her throat that he was just sure were supposed to be words, if only she'd been able to form them.

He grabbed her hands and held them in his, trying to keep her from doing any harm to herself, while he looked around the room. If Sugar was constantly doing the same thing again and again, she had to be reacting – even if only subconsciously – to something in the room. She hadn't opened her eyes yet, so not something visual. A smell? A sound?

As she fought half-heartedly against his gentle grip, Jaxson closed his eyes and tried to clear his mind. What could be triggering Sugar? Was it the antiseptic smell of the hospital? Maybe it reminded her of losing her baby.

But the movements were so specific; nothing to do with a baby at all.

His eyes popped open and he felt a huge grin spread across his face. *Duh.*

She'd settled back down for a moment, so Jaxson took a chance and went out into the hallway again, keeping an eye on her as he went. Hanging out in the doorway of the room, he waited until he spotted an RN with *Charge Nurse* pinned to her lapel. "Ma'am," he called out. "I think I know what's going on with Sugar."

Nurse Knutsen, according to her nametag, gave him a questioning glance as she came over. "'Going on'?" she echoed.

"Yeah, with her hands. Hear that beeping? The heart monitor or whatever?"

She gave a quick nod, obviously in a hurry and wanting Jaxson to get to his point so she could move on with her day.

"Sugar thinks it's her alarm clock. She keeps trying to turn it off. Can we unplug it or something?"

"Unplug the heart monitor?" the nurse replied, staring at him in shock. "If she were having a heart attack, we'd never know!"

"If she keeps pulling on her IV and her breathing tubes, she's never going to get better," Jaxson pointed out in his best I'm-being-reasonable voice.

"Let me find the doctor," Nurse Knutsen grumbled, leaving.

Just then, the CNA showed up with a wash basin of warm water and a couple of washcloths. "I heard *you* wanted these?" she asked, scrunching up her young nose in confusion. She could only be all of 16, and the idea of a guy – in a firefighter suit, no less – wanting to wash a girl was obviously hurting her head.

Jaxson grinned. "Perfect," he said. He walked back into the small room and over to the even-smaller sink in the corner to wash his hands, scrubbing off the grime and dirt until even his callouses shone. "Do you know how Gage is doing?" he asked over his shoulder.

"The bakery dude?" the teenager asked.

"Yeah, the owner. I'm assuming he's here? I didn't hear a Life Flight helicopter land, anyway."

"He's just down the hallway. They got him out first so he's a little better off than Sugar. *You* got him out first, I guess," she amended, looking at his turnout gear, still dingy and dirty from the fire. Jaxson made a mental note not to hug Sugar in his current condition. He really needed to go home and change, but the idea of leaving Sugar struck a note of panic in his gut that wrenched it so hard, he felt borderline nauseous from it.

No, he wasn't leaving Sugar. Not yet.

"I found him but two of my guys carried him out," Jaxson clarified, taking the water and cloths from her. "What's your name?"

"Zara," she said cheerfully, following along behind Jaxson as he moved back to Sugar's side. He began by washing her hand – washing, rinsing, and washing again, until the cloth came away clean. "I'm new here."

He moved further up her arm. She was so small. It was a wonder she'd lived at all.

"Well, Zara, how old are you?"

Jaxson wasn't sure if he really cared or not, but he wanted something to do – something to think about – other than the woman lying in front of him, and whether she'd ever wake up or talk again or tell him that she loved him.

Yeah, it was easier to focus on Zara.

"Sixteen. The candy striper program here doesn't allow you to start until you're 16; otherwise, I would've started last year."

"You like helping people?"

She nodded eagerly. "I'm gonna be a doctor someday. I'll come back here and run this hospital."

Jaxson grinned at her as he moved up to Sugar's shoulder. Someone had changed her into a hospital gown before he got there, for which he was eternally grateful. He needed to reach all of her, but didn't want to have to fess up to her later that he'd been the one to strip her down in public, even if it was in a hospital. As touchy as she was about some things, he just wasn't sure how she'd react to that news.

"I think that's a mighty fine achievement to shoot for,"

Jaxson said. "I think this community could use someone like you." *Young, with ambition?* Yeah, she was just what this community needed.

"You don't think I should pick something else better suited for a *girl*?" she asked. The question, if not the tone in her voice, said it all. She'd already been told that line of reasoning by a person or two.

"I think a girl can do anything she sets her mind to," Jaxson told her seriously. "And if you ever get sick of nursing, you should come on down to the fire station. I'll put you to work laying out hoses in a fire."

"Did Angus help you put the fire out?" Zara asked, her tone studiously neutral.

"No, he just started training a couple of months ago." Jaxson began working his way across Sugar's collarbone and upper chest, carefully staying far away from any private parts. "He needs a lot more training before I let him into a fire, especially like the one we had today."

"Is it true that he's in trouble for burning down the mill, so that's why he has to be a firefighter?"

Jaxson wasn't about to touch that with a ten-foot pole. Sharing gossip with a teenage girl about the mayor's son seemed like a mighty fine way to lose his job lickety-split. "He's actually part of a pilot program – him and Chris. We're starting up a new program here in Sawyer where you can start training as a teen to become a firefighter. Like you and nursing."

"Oh." The teen scrunched up her nose, obviously not happy with the lack of punishment in Jaxson's answer. "Because Angus is a dick to me," she said baldly, making Jaxson partially choke as he tried to contain his laughter. "I was hoping it was a punishment or something."

"A dick, huh?"

"Yeah. He's the cutest guy in school, but all of the girls hate him because he isn't nice to any of us. Or anyone at all, except his friends. All he does is talk about how he's the mayor's son and can do whatever he wants to, anytime he wants to."

"Sometimes guys need a little more time to grow up," Jaxson said diplomatically.

"Zara!" Nurse Knutsen hollered from the doorway of the room. Sugar began thrashing around but the nurse ignored her. "There are bedpans in 8 and 9 that need to be changed out."

Zara wrinkled her nose. "I better get going," she said forlornly.

"Bedpans not your favorite?" Jaxson asked with a grin.

She tossed him an as-if look and headed for the door.

"Can you tell the doctor I really need to see him?" Jaxson called out after her. Nurse Knutsen had came and gone so quickly, Jaxson hadn't had a chance to remind her.

"Sure!" the teen called out, and disappeared around the corner.

Jaxson turned back to Sugar. "Ready for me to wash your other arm?" he asked her. "Good. Here goes." He switched sides of the bed and began carefully working his way down her thin, pale arm.

He would make Sugar better, if only through force of will. If he wanted something bad enough, he'd always made it happen.

He wouldn't fail now.

CHAPTER 40

SUGAR

S HE HURT, but she didn't know why or where or how, just that she did, and she was drifting, hearing but not understanding, as people moved on the other side of a roll of cotton, talking but not in words she knew.

Her lungs. It hurt to breathe. She tried to pull in air and there was something in her way and she didn't know what. She tried to tug on it and get it out but her hands were pulled away.

"Shhhhh…it's okay," Jaxson crooned. "You're okay. Just sleep and get better."

Why was Jaxson there? Nothing was right, but before she could question him or get her eyes to open, she was drifting again.

Then he was there again. "You're all right, Sugar. You're okay. You can just rest."

But this time, she didn't want to. She wanted to wake up. With a monumental effort, she pried her right eyelid open, and then her left. The world swam around, bright and painful in front of her, and she shut them quickly against the pain.

"Where…" she tried to say, but it came out all croaky.

"She probably wants a drink of water," a lady's voice said,

and then a straw was between her lips. "Here, suck on this slowly."

Sugar obediently sucked down water, feeling better as she could practically feel the water flow through her body, revitalizing her. "Where am I?" she rasped, drained by the effort it took.

"The Sawyer hospital," Jaxson said, squeezing her hand. "You were in a fire. Do you remember?"

She shook her head and then paused, flashes coming back to her. Bits and pieces of flames and smoke. Screaming. Was she screaming, or was it someone else?

She nodded slowly.

"You were lucky," Jaxson said softly. "Lots of smoke inhalation but no serious burns. On the ground like you were, across the room from the oven, the smoke wasn't as thick. Passing out was probably the best thing that could've happened, short of you getting out before the fire got bad, of course."

"Ga…" she got out, but Jaxson knew what she was asking.

"He's doing good. Asking about you, and the restaurant. You two are the luckiest people I've ever met." She squeezed his hand. She didn't feel real lucky at the moment – she rather felt like she'd been beat up by Mike Tyson before being dragged along a dirt road behind a pickup truck – but she didn't feel up to arguing with him, so she didn't say anything at all.

"Sleep is what you need to do. It's the best thing you can do right now."

Sugar nodded her understanding, or maybe she just meant to nod, and then she was drifting in the world of white again, where there were voices but no words.

CHAPTER 41

JAXSON

T WAS QUITE POSSIBLY the longest week of his life, but finally, the day came when they'd let Sugar go home.

Her parents never showed up to the hospital, although Jaxson knew they had to have known what happened. Something like this didn't happen in a small town without everyone in a 50-mile radius hearing every juicy detail of it. Even Jaxson knew that by now.

The fact that her parents couldn't be bothered to come check on their daughter spoke volumes about them, and none of it was good.

Dick, on the other hand, *had* tried to come by, a bouquet of flowers in his hands, but Nurse Knutsen took one look at him and told him to leave. "Doesn't she have a restraining order against you?" were her exact words. When Dick tried to argue, the nurse picked up the phone. "Why don't I call the sheriff and have him come on down and discuss this with you?" she'd asked bluntly. Dick skedaddled after that.

Jaxson was quite sad that he'd missed it all. The guy had stopped by during one of the few times that his firefighters had insisted that he leave while they watched over Sugar for him.

He'd been at home, showering and shaving, when Dick had come by.

Better luck next time. Maybe Dick could try again, and Jaxson could do a citizen's arrest on him, too. He'd enjoy that.

Maybe a little too much.

He carried Sugar into her apartment, despite her protests to the contrary. "I can walk," she insisted in her new sexy, smoky (all puns intended) country singer voice. He'd told her that she could start a new career as a crooner at all of the local bars with her new voice. She'd rolled her eyes at him.

But they were even, because he was ignoring her protests about being able to walk. He figured they were even in most respects; just one of the many reasons that he loved her.

Hamlet came bounding out of Sugar's bedroom from his spot on the bed, whining with joy and wagging his tail so hard, Jaxson figured he was in imminent danger of dislocating his spine from the force of it.

"Hi, baby," Sugar said in her new scratchy voice and Hamlet paused for just a moment, clearly confused as to why she sounded so strange. But he quickly forgot about his confusion as he continued to dance around them in joy.

"Bedroom or couch?" Jaxson asked, holding her in his arms as easily as he'd hold a newborn babe. As tiny as she was, he figured she weighed just about as much.

"Couch," she croaked and he grinned as he laid her down.

"Maybe not so much a country singer after all," he said mock-seriously. "Maybe more like an amphibian. A frog, perhaps. You can talk Gage into changing the name of the bakery from the Muffin Man to the Lily Pad."

She stuck her tongue out at him.

He laughed.

"Want some tea with honey?" he asked, already moving into the adjoining kitchen to start it.

She nodded wearily. Coming home, even if it had just meant being carried, had exhausted her.

Jaxson cursed again at the fact that he'd been forced to move her back into her apartment. He'd wanted to move her into his, but he was in a walk-up apartment, and as worn-out as she was, adding a couple of sets of stairs to the process of getting outside would only mean she'd be even slower to make it out the door.

He put the kettle onto the stove as Hamlet faithfully stood guard over her on the couch, his head resting on the couch cushions next to her hand. Jaxson wondered for a moment what would've happened if Hamlet would've been there at the bakery when the fire broke out. Would he have dragged Sugar to safety?

Jaxson rather thought so, although he could only hope that he'd never have a chance to test that theory.

Friends popped in and out over the next couple of days to wish Sugar well, and bring her soup. As Jaxson studied the contents of the fridge, he figured Sugar had enough varieties to choose from to last her a good year at this rate.

She was gaining in strength too, and color was starting to come back to her cheeks.

Still, Jaxson treated her like spun sugar – on the edge of breaking if he breathed wrong. He'd almost lost her, and looking back on how close it'd been, how he'd almost convinced himself that she wasn't in the bakery anymore…

It made it hard to breathe sometimes. When the panic would overwhelm him, he'd cover it by running to her side and asking her if there was anything he could get for her. He'd take care of her, and then she'd be all right, and then he could stop worrying.

On the fourth day, Sugar finally looked him straight in the eye, and said, "Jaxson, stop."

He was busy trying to spoon-feed her some chicken chowder the neighbor had brought over. He paused, the spoon halfway to her mouth. "Stop what?" he asked, confused. He blew on the soup. Maybe it was too hot. He'd tried to cool it down enough for her, but if he was burning her mouth, he'd just feel awful. It was already tough enough that he'd almost let her burn to death. Burning her mouth wouldn't do.

She put her hand on his arm, pulling the spoon away from his mouth where he'd been blowing on it with all of his might. "Stop hovering. I'm okay. Look at me." She took the bowl and spoon out of his hands and set them down on the side table, then took his hands into hers. "Really look at me. *I'm okay.*" She whispered those words as she stared at him, and he stared back, the first time he'd let himself just *be* since the fire.

"I thought you'd died," he blurted out. "Or were going to die. And I was going to let it happen. And then I had to choose between staying at the fire or going to the hospital with you. I chose to stay at the fire. I shouldn't have. I should've chosen you."

"Why, so you could've hovered over me even longer?" Sugar grinned at him. "Babe, there was nothing you could've done for me when I first got to the hospital. The doctor and nurses had to take care of me at that point. Your job is to take care of this whole town, not just me. You were right to make that choice."

He broke down then, and he cried. Which was the most horrifyingly awful thing he'd ever done in his life, but he couldn't seem to stop. "I love you, Sugar," he finally got out.

Which was *not* the way it was supposed to happen. He was supposed to have flowers and a grand gesture and shit that girls loved, not tears. Tears were weak. Tears were for babies.

She pulled him against her chest and held him. "I love you, too," she whispered against the crown of his head. "I shouldn't, you know. You're a guy. Guys are bad. I don't know if anyone's told you that or not, but it's true. But somehow, I love you anyway, and it's a little scary, I'll admit. Jaxson, we've got each other. And in the end, that's what matters."

And as she stroked her fingers through his hair, cradling

him against her, Jaxson realized the wisdom of her words, and he let go. They could share this pain together, and it'd be okay.

Which was the most amazing gift of all, in his mind.

EPILOGUE

SUGAR

AUGUST, 2018

T HEY WALKED OUT of the Ada County courthouse in
Boise, and into the bright sunshine, Aiden and
Frankie flanking them, chattering excitedly. After
countless trips in front of the judge, letters from the mayor and
city council regarding his work as the city fire chief, and finally
being able to prove that he had someone stable to watch the
kids if he got called out to fight a fire – his wife, Sugar – Jaxson
had convinced the courts to give them a more equal custody
agreement. The time Ivan, Kendra's boyfriend, showed up at
court unexpectedly, drunk and ranting about her "brats,"
surely didn't help her case.

Sugar was damn proud of her husband, and she grinned up
at him, just as thrilled as the boys over the news. They were
finally going to be a real family.

Even more of a family than even Jaxson realized, actually.

She bit the inside of her cheek, the excitement shooting
through her at the thought. "Let's head back to Sawyer – I
think Gage made a special cake to celebrate our victory," Sugar
told her boys. All of them. Hamlet was in the car, his giant

head hanging out the window, tongue lolling happily. Anywhere that the boys were was Hamlet's happy place. Sugar was his momma, but Aiden and Frankie were his *friends*, and bound to do things that they weren't supposed to do, like feed him human food.

Yeah, he loved them a whole lot.

The boys scrambled into the backseat of the SUV, Hamlet happily sandwiched between them, and the five of them drove through the winding mountain passes back to Sawyer, singing and laughing and teasing each other every mile of the journey.

They pulled up in front of the restored Muffin Man, put back together after the spring's fire, none worse for the wear. It was amazing how much the Sawyer community could pull together to help each other out when need be. After spending most of her life wishing she lived anywhere but there, Sugar had finally come home…to the one place she'd never left.

The boys went running ahead, bursting into the bakery with shouts of greetings to their other best friend, Gage, who tended to do things like slip them cake pops or donuts when no one was looking. Hamlet lay down on the sunshine-warmed sidewalk outside to take a snooze, happy to accept the pettings and love of anyone who walked by. Sugar figured Hamlet was about as well loved in town as Jaxson, and that was really saying something. After he'd been able to save Gage and Sugar and the Muffin Man from that damn chimney fire, the town had abruptly reversed course, deciding that he knew what he was doing after all.

Gage looked up and caught Sugar's eye. She nodded just slightly, and he hurried into the kitchen.

"C'mon you guys, let's sit down," Sugar urged, herding Jaxson, Aiden, and Frankie away from the display case, where they had all been drooling over Gage's newest cupcakes. "He made something special just for us."

With a promise like that, it wasn't hard to get them to sit

down, and within moments, Gage put the cake squarely in front of Jaxson.

A giant, stork-shaped cake.

Jaxson's eyes flicked over the cake and then up to Sugar. "Really?" he breathed.

Her chest hurt and her eyes filled with happy tears as she nodded, no words left inside of her. This moment was much too wonderful for words.

Jaxson sprung up, throwing his chair to the floor with a crash as he threw his arms around Sugar, squeezing her tight. As he swung her around and around, kissing and laughing, the boys fell to arguing. Frankie thought it meant they were going to have a pet bird at home, although he couldn't figure out why the cake was in the shape of a stork, not a parrot, while Aiden, older and wiser, began trying to give the birds and the bees talk to him.

Sugar pulled back with a burst of laughter when Aiden told Frankie that storks only delivered babies to *old* people.

"When?" Jaxson breathed, ignoring his sons for a moment, his eyes feasting on hers.

"March," Sugar whispered, her eyes happily refilling with endless tears of joy. Jaxson wiped them away with the calloused pad of his thumb.

"You're all I need, but a baby – a *wanted* baby – I've never been happier."

And then he kissed her, to the groans and heckling of their audience.

Sugar ignored them and kissed him back. Someday, they'd understand.

🔥 🔥 🔥

Quick Author's Note

Hey y'all! 

First off, THANK YOU for making it all the way through *Flames of Love*. Gosh, I hope you loved it.

If you did, you'll be thrilled to know that you don't have to say goodbye to Jaxson, Sugar, or Long Valley! The drama, the love, and the fires continue in Book 2 where you get to learn Moose's backstory (and what a backstory it is! I promise y'all – you did *not* see this coming).

It all begins when Moose has to walk through flames to save the one woman he absolutely should not love, but does anyway…

You'll just have to read *Inferno of Love* to see what I'm blathering on about! It is available at your favorite book retailer or local library, so be sure to find it there and enjoy.

Here's to many more years of loving Long Valley together,

Erin Wright

Be sure to find my books at your favorite bookstore, retailer, or library

Or, buy them directly from me at
https://ErinWright.net/My-Books

If you prefer, you can also scan this QR code with your phone:

ALSO BY ERIN WRIGHT

~ COWBOYS OF LONG VALLEY ROMANCE ~

Accounting for Love

Blizzard of Love

Arrested by Love

Returning for Love

Christmas of Love

Overdue for Love

Bundle of Love

Lessons in Love

Baked with Love

Bloom of Love

Broken by Love (TBA)

Holly and Love (TBA)

Banking on Love (TBA)

Sheltered by Love (TBA)

~ FIREFIGHTERS OF LONG VALLEY ROMANCE ~

Flames of Love

Inferno of Love

Fire and Love

Burned by Love

~ MUSICIANS OF LONG VALLEY ROMANCE ~

Strummin' Up Love

Melody of Love (TBA)

Rock 'N Love (TBA)

Rhapsody of Love (TBA)

~ SERVICEMEN OF LONG VALLEY ROMANCE ~

Thankful for Love (TBA)

Commanded to Love (TBA)

Salute to Love (TBA)

Harbored by Love (TBA)

ABOUT ERIN WRIGHT

USA TODAY BESTSELLING AUTHOR ERIN WRIGHT has worked every job under the sun, including library director, barista, teacher, website designer, and ranch hand helping brand cattle, before settling into the career she's always dreamed about: Author.

She still loves coffee, doesn't love the smell of cow flesh burning, and is currently living out her own love story in a tiny town in rural Idaho.

Wanna get in touch?
https://erinwright.net
erin@erinwright.net

Or reach out to Erin on your favorite social media platform:

facebook.com/AuthorErinWright

x.com/ErinWrightLV

youtube.com/@ErinWrightLV

pinterest.com/ErinWrightBooks

goodreads.com/ErinWright

bookbub.com/profile/Erin-Wright

instagram.com/AuthorErinWright